— First Edition —

Forty Candles

on a cowboy cake

Other Books by Rick Steber

Rendezvous
Traces
Union Centennial
Where Rolls the Oregon
Heartwood
Oregon Trail – Last of the Pioneers
Roundup
New York to Nome
Wild Horse Rider
Buckaroo Heart
No End in Sight
Buy the Chief a Cadillac
Legacy

Tales of the Wild West Series
Oregon Trail
Pacific Coast
Indians
Cowboys
Women of the West
Children's stories
Loggers
Mountain Men
Miners
Grandpa's Stories
Pioneers
Campfire Stories
Tall Tales
Gunfighters
Grandma's Stories
Western Heroes

RICK STEBER

– A NOVEL –

– TWO STAR –

Published by – *TWO STAR* –
An imprint of Bonanza Publishing
PO Box 204
Prineville, OR 97754

This book is a work of fiction. Names, characters, businesses, organizations, places, events, and incidents either are the product of the author's imagination or are used fictitiously. Any resemblance to actual persons, living or dead, events, or locales is entirely coincidental.

Book design by Jody Conners
Cover photograph by Robert Agli
robertagliphotography.com
Cake decoration by Amber Maxwell
Cover design by Gary Asher

ISBN 10: 0-945134-35-5
ISBN 13: 978-0-945134-35-0

PRINTED IN THE UNITED STATES OF AMERICA
FIRST EDITION

"This is the worst trip I ever been on."

(*Sloop John B.* – The Beach Boys)

A TRAIL SONG

Oh, for me a horse and saddle
Every day without a change;
With the desert sun a-blazin
On a hundred miles o' range,

Just a-ridin, just a-ridin,
Desert ripplin in the sun,
Mountains blue along the skyline,
I don't envy anyone.

I don't need no art exhibits
When the sunset does his best,
Paintin everlastin glories
On the mountains o' the West.

And your operas they sound foolish
When the night birds starts his tune
And the desert's silver-mounted
By the kisses of the moon.

Just a-ridin, just a-ridin –
I don't envy kings or czars
When the coyotes down the valley
Are a-singin to the stars.

(From *A Trail Song* by Elwood Adams, circa. 1908)

Chapter 1

Son, let me tell you something: an expensive horse, and an expensive woman, are usually way more trouble than they're worth. (Kelsey Wilder)

Sitting in that dude bar watching the ancient beer sign cycle—waterfall, river, lake, "It's the Water"—it hit me if I was gonna drop dead sudden-like, I sure as hell wasn't gonna die young. I was bracing myself to turn forty and the bitter taste of whiskey was reminding me of all the dusty trails I've traveled down and two-bit jackpot towns I've barrel-assed through. Not that I wanna live in the past, I just don't wanna let completely loose of it neither.

A quick glance in the mirror was proof I wasn't getting any younger. Over the past few years my hair had gradually changed from a youthful rusty brown to a little salt sprinkled at my temples and a light flicker of gray now dusted my scalp. Before long my head was gonna look like a television screen after the test pattern ends. I'm talking black and white here.

That positively shows my age. Hell, they haven't made a black and white in what, like twenty years?

Another thing I recognize, I probably ain't as athletic as I used to be but partner, let me tell you, I can still handle myself way better than some twenty-year-old city boy with shrapnel in his face, sagging low-rider pants and a headset blaring ghetto music—if you can even call that shit music.

Around me at the bar a hip young crowd—down from Portland and up from California—were smoking, drinking and struggling to western dance to a weird Texas Jewboys, Kinky Friedman tune. The subdued lighting was focused on a spot strobe glancing off a revolving mirrored ball. It set off skittery flashes of light that flitted around the room like hot sparks kicked from a lively campfire. For the town of Sisters, Oregon this was the kickoff to the social function of the year, the rodeo that bills itself as the "*Biggest Little Show In The World.*"

Right off the bat, let's get one thing straight—pure and simple—I ain't nothing but a buckaroo. Live life like a tumbleweed, go anywhere I haven't been, try anything I haven't tried. Figure I can deal with whatever comes along—me against a bronc, against a bunch of range cattle, against another man. Like most buckaroos I bump around some. Pretty much always thought I wanted land, to own a spread of my own. Here lately I've come to grips with the fact you own land, but it owns you back. Trade my freedom for a mortgage? Every month write a check to the bank and some bozo who doesn't know jack shit about the difference between a bull and a steer is riding shotgun and telling me what I ought to be doing. I don't think so.

I have the reputation as a cowboy rounder, a skirt-chasing fool. But on the night I turned forty, the girls in Bronco Bob's didn't much appeal to me, not with their high-priced duds, lacquered lips and haughty attitudes. For me getting one of these self-important princesses in the sack would be about as difficult as meat hunting in a cow pasture. I prefer a little more challenge, unless I'm real horny, then I might hump a bush if I thought there was a rabbit in it.

In spite of the fact I was sitting alone, minding my own business, an occasional nervy gal who I guess liked my tall ranginess and ruggedly handsome good looks—no brag, just fact—would saunter over and ask me to dance. I turned them down flat. "No thank ya, ma'am."

I concentrated on my drinking, was bouncing ice cubes off my front teeth and recalling a time at Winner's Inn, there in Winnemucca, Nevada, when I saw this high-toned gal, had skin the color of milk toast and long legs that stretched all the way to heaven. Her body was wrapped in a brown fur coat, tight as a Christmas package. Her eyes were on me and I responded by sliding off my stool, moving onto the dance floor, cutting in. She stepped away from the fellow she was with and slid onto me. Instantly I was suffocating in mink. We danced every dance and her body carried on quite a conversation with mine. Then she whispered in my ear, "Under this coat I'm not wearing anything." I took her down the hall to her room.

Good story but hell, none of that actually happened—anyway, not to me. I read something similar in *Penthouse* Forum, changed a few things around, and dreamed it happened to me. On more than one occasion I've been accused of embellishing a story but sometimes a story needs a little dressing up. I smiled at my reflection. It smiled back. I recognized the fact that on that particular night, my life needed a good swift kick in the seat of the pants to jolt it out of its rut of dullness. I called for another drink and vowed when it was gone—if my world was still the same—I'd call in the dogs, piss on the fire and head for the ranch.

Sitting on the stool beside me was a big woman, from California she said. She had a body like a 300-pound potato, spiked hair the color of a purple fuchsia, and wore a sleeveless shirt. On her hefty right bicep was tattooed "Baby Doll."

She had a girlfriend sitting beside her who could have been a cover model for *Cosmo,* or one of those other women's magazines. The potato finished her drink, pushed it away, took hold of the model by the arm and escorted her onto the dance floor. I was relieved they were gone, was starting to lift my new drink and take a sip, when I caught a series of reflected images in the mirror—heads turning, eyes widening and the double doors at the entryway swinging inward with a swirl of erotic motion.

She stepped into the room. My first view of her was really nothing more than an impression of dazzling golden hair. It hung clear down to her waist. The kind of hair a cowboy rounder like me just loves to see fanned across his pillow in the morning light. I mumbled to myself, "God bless America."

When it comes to women, most men go for flash—bleached blond hair, long legs, nice ass, big tits. I tell myself I generally prefer understated qualities, wanting my woman to be like a lovely rose that just keeps opening and unfolding and never fades and never dies. I imagine I'm attracted to a gal because of an accumulation of a lot of little things: her gracefulness, confidence, maybe she arches her back like a cat stretching in the sun, licks her lips suggestively, thoughtfully twists a loose strand of hair, has a shy smile, a good sense of humor, or she has striking cheekbones, a sparkle in her eye, a carefree attitude. But don't get me wrong—I won't up and cull a gal just because she has a set of huge knockers.

The blond in the bar turned toward my side of the room and I saw her full on. There was no way for me, at that point, to foretell that she was on the prowl seeking a vengeful affair. What I saw was a young gal built just right, as loose-limbed as a Doc Bar quarter horse filly. I took the liberty of scanning my way up her frame: from the red cowgirl boots that emphasized exceedingly long and well-proportioned legs, to a western skirt pulled taut across inviting hips, a silver belt cinched around her slender waist and a white blouse, the clingy kind you can see right through if you've got any sort of imagination. Topping off this fantasy was a flat-brimmed straw hat, pushed way back on her head, away from a face that could have been stolen from a wet dream.

She stood there, legs spread slightly apart, arms hanging loose, taking in the entire room in one long, lingering look. And then her stare seemed to fix on target and she came flowing across the room as if on a string drawn straight... to me. I had never heard a crowded bar suddenly become so strangely quiet. I forced myself to concentrate on my drink, scrutinizing the way beads of condensation had formed and were slowly trickling down the sides of the glass.

She slid up and onto the empty stool beside me, leisurely extending one shapely leg and crossing it over the other. Bare skin made a faint swishing sound. She said, "You look like you're the only real cowboy in here. You a real cowboy?"

Her voice was like McKay Creek, bubbling softly as it tumbles from the upper reaches of the Ochoco Mountains. I waited her out. It's been my experience that, especially in the beginning, the less you say to a beautiful gal, the better off you are.

Finally I answered. "Bet your sweet ass I am."

"Know how I knew?"

It seemed as though a tropical breeze was suddenly blowing away the stagnant air in the room and I fussed with the back of my collar, allowing a little waft of air to slide down my back and touch my spine.

"You're the only one in here with cow shit on his boots."

I looked at her then, gave her a toothy grin, touched the brim of my Stetson, marbled with sweat and High Desert alkali dust, and asked, "Wanna see my horse?"

She smiled coyly, said, "Maybe we should get to know each other a little better," and lowered her eyes. When she looked up she winked at me and that wink got me. The irises of her eyes were so blue if I fell in I'd need a rowboat to keep from drowning.

"Cheyenne Miller," she said.

"Cheyenne, named after the town in Wyoming or Frontier Days, world's largest rodeo, started in 18 and 97, granddaddy of 'em all?" I said. Apparently she didn't feel compelled to answer and instead offered me her hand. I took it. Her grip was shockingly firm. I noticed the hairs on the back of my arm standing at attention like a bunch of raw recruits in front of a drill sergeant.

"Clint Wilder. Friends call me Waddy."

"That's a strange one," she commented.

"Yes ma'am, it is," I told her.

"What's it mean, a Waddy?"

"A buckaroo, someone who drifts from ranch to ranch, never settles down."

She raised a precisely shaped eyebrow and said nothing. I gathered she wanted me to continue and so I did, rambling words along a dusty trail without any purpose or destination in mind. "Suppose it suits me. Sure as hell never asked to get tagged with it. I'd preferred to have a good nickname, something like Rooster, after Rooster Cogburn, the character John Wayne played in *True Grit*. Now that was some movie. He won an Oscar for it, only Oscar he ever won. I was a kid when it came out. Saw it like five or six times."

"What made that such a good movie?"

"John Wayne is this one-eyed, quick-triggered lawman. Gets hired by Mattie Ross, cute teenage gal, to hunt down her father's killer. I still remember the words on the poster, claimed, 'Rooster is a hard man in a dangerous world.'"

"Is that how you see yourself?"

"Hell no."

"How are you different?"

It felt as though I was being grilled in a job interview, didn't particularly like the drift of the conversation and the way this young gal seemed to be hogging the questions, but all the same, I answered. "Rooster had respect for women, a good sense of humor and a soft spot for Mattie. He called her

Little Sister. But he had a mean streak in him, too. I don't have a mean streak. I'm a go-along, get-along sort of guy."

Rather than shutting up, I just kept talking. "My favorite part of the movie was the ending, when Rooster takes the reins in his teeth and charges the outlaw gang, gunning down the bad guys with a revolver in one hand and a rifle in the other."

After saying that I attempted to give the conversation a quick spin. "So, what was your favorite John Wayne movie?"

"Never saw any."

I was shocked. "You never saw Duke on the silver screen? Why not?"

She just shook her head. "Is he still alive?"

"Died in '79."

"Yeah, well, that was before I was born."

Her comment sent me in a tailspin. I was feeling like a goddamn cradle robber when the bartender came to take her order. She wanted Chivas Regal, a double, and 7-Up. The way I figure things is, a bartender is nothing more than a pharmacist with a limited inventory. He brought her medicine and I nodded, letting him know to put it on my tab. The band switched to a new song, something to the effect that women were made to love, money to spend and life you never get to do again. Yeah, but if you live right, once is plenty.

She took a sip of her drink and I was mesmerized with the way her pink tongue darted out to lick away moisture from her top lip. She leaned toward me, so I could hear over the music and noise. "What are you doing tonight?" Her breath was hot and smelled minty, as though she might have popped an Altoid before coming into the bar.

I bestowed a little Black Velvet wisdom. "Thought I'd drink 'til I got putrified."

"Do that and miss all the fun," she purred. "Let's play."

I placed a wrist on her shoulder, allowing my open hand to dangle dangerously close to one of her breasts and gave her a line that's been in my repertoire since Mt. Hood was nothing but a hole in the ground. "Ma'am, I've been from Spain to Maine and everywhere between. Been rolled over, bowled over, been to a dog show, a goat ropin' and three county fairs. I swear to God you're the prettiest thing I ever did see. What sorta game you wanna play?"

"Dance with me."

I like a direct, take-charge type of woman, up to a point—as long as she doesn't always insist on being on top. We stood and it was a strange thing, as she moved into my arms and her body touched mine, there was still enough wayward static roaming around the joint that I felt tiny shocks of electricity jump from her nipples to tingle against my chest. We danced and did such a stylish job others stepped out of our way. The two of us owned that dance floor.

As the number was winding down I took the liberty of using one finger to tilt her chin up. She looked at me. I squeezed in behind those blue eyes. She gave an animated shudder, caught her breath and I spun her away, twirling this ultimate Friday night honky-tonk sweetheart at the end of my arm—long blond hair and cute little rump bouncing—and then brought her dancing back to me on tiptoes.

With my belly full of booze and the beautiful blond clinging to my bicep, I was full of myself and feeling pretty damn cocky. I pushed through the doorway and came face-to-face with a dude wearing a Bailey straw hat, cowboy-cut shirt snapped all the way to the collar and a silver cow skull bolo tie. He stepped backward out of my way. It was either that or I'd have run him over. In passing I nonchalantly flipped up the strings of his bolo and, in my best John Wayne imitation, told him, "Hey, Pilgrim, you can wear the hat, walk in the boots, but if you don't have the balls, stay away from the chute." As soon as I said it I felt stupid. It was the booze doing the talking. Beside me Cheyenne giggled like a high school girl on a hit of helium.

We made our way across the muddy parking lot. Cheyenne, one hand firmly gripping the back of my belt, was hugging up against me as though she feared I might get away. Fat chance. Getting away was the furthest thing from my mind. I wanted this cute, young blond as bad as I'd ever wanted anything.

At that time of year, the snow is long gone, but it can still get cold enough at night to freeze. In the mornings, when you ride a horse or drive a truck across the puddles, the ruffled edges break like shards of fragile glass. In the cold, clear sky a gorgeous slice of moon, bright as chrome, looked down on us and stars sparkled.

Cheyenne exclaimed, "Look at all the stars."

You can always tell a city gal, they're astonished that the country sky, with no light pollution or smog to smear the view, contains so many stars. She pointed upward and wanted to know, "Is that the big dipper?"

"No Babe," I kidded, "big dipper's in my pants."

Apparently that was a signal to her because she stepped in front of me, wrapped both arms around my middle and raised her tempting face to me the way a California poppy will turn as the sun slides across the sky. She smelled of a bottled fragrance, something with a sexy name: *Pleasure, Lust, Obsession* or *Desire*. On the other hand, I smelled of horse sweat and cow shit but apparently my bouquet of aromas in no way diminished my sex appeal. Her eyes closed. Red lips puckered. I leaned down and kissed her. Her mouth was soft and the kiss delicious. A wind started with a gasp and the pine trees shuddered. Hands worked their way under the back of my shirt and fingernails dug into the meat on either side of my spine. As she squirmed against me it was rather obvious she had a specific need which would be difficult for me to satisfy in a vertical position, and especially in a bar parking lot. I pulled away and she stood there panting like a dog that had run ten miles on a hot August day. I planted a dainty smooch on her warm, damp forehead and moved in the general direction of my pickup and horse trailer.

My horse was tied to the outside of the trailer, standing with one rear foot tipped, sleeping. His lower lip trembled. Good ol' Charley was probably dreaming of a golden summer day and rolling fields of sweet green pasture. I touched his flank and he came awake with a loud snort through flared nostrils.

"You weren't kidding. You do have a horse."

"I don't kid, Darlin'." I smiled.

Charley was a dandy saddle horse, quarter and thoroughbred, hell of a runner and damn fine at working cattle. He tossed a fleeting look over his rump, stamped a foot to draw attention, and when that failed he lifted his tail and plopped a string of aromatic road apples on the ground.

I walked Cheyenne to her car. Back in the bar we had reached an agreement. She was coming to the ranch, driving herself. I presumed her thinking was that such an arrangement allowed her to stay as long as she wanted and, if the mood struck, she had the means to escape.

She slid the key in the ignition, started the silver Honda Accord, flipped on the headlights and waited for me. I stepped around to the shady side of the horse trailer and as I relieved myself I informed Charley, "Well, ol' boy, I may have to turn forty but when I do at least I'll have a deep seat in the saddle." I laughed. Charley snorted and when he loaded it was with a rush of flying hooves.

A boiling cloud of white volcanic ash, phosphorescent in the darkness, billowed behind my pickup and horse trailer. In the rearview mirror the headlights from the Honda fell back and were strained through the dust. I was nearly alone. Pine trees crowded the narrow, washboard road and along the ridge top trees stood like black sentinels against the star-studded sky.

Away from her I could think more clearly. I had seen the diamond engagement ring and the wedding band on her left hand. She was married. I knew that. Of course I had enough good sense not to broach the subject. She might mention it, after the act, while we were lying in bed. I've had gals be both remorseful and joyous. With a female you never know how cheatin' is gonna hit her.

In my mind, stepping out with a married gal has never posed a question of right or wrong. My only concern has been to simply avoid a potential confrontation with a jealous husband. I don't wanna piss some fellow off and end up with a bullet in my gut. Most generally I pick and choose, try to be selective and avoid dodgy situations. The way I see things—forget gold rings—it's typically a matter of two consenting adults and a bucketful of hormones.

After thumping across the cattle guard marking the boundary of the 25 Ranch—I managed it for a rich California real estate developer and most of the time I called it the Two-Bit Ranch—I stopped, waiting for Cheyenne to catch up. And when she did I walked back to her car and gave her a taste of Black Velvet. I always have a bottle under the seat. It comes in handy for any situation from love bit to snake bit. For my trouble I stole a kiss.

"How much farther?" she wanted to know.

"Gettin' close," I lied, not wanting to confess it was several more miles to headquarters. I know it isn't for everyone but I like living in the bush. That way I can take as much of the real world as I want and then step away from all the bullshit.

To the south, the city of Bend lit the sky like a radioactive cloud. Redmond was off to the east. And to think, neither town had even been invented until after the 1900s. Look at them now. Bend had transformed itself from a jerk-water logging town to an upscale resort community inhabited by an elite class of privileged retirees who bragged incessantly about their roundabouts and public art. One time I made a suggestion that the public art at the newest roundabout be a goddamn golden retriever chasing his tail around, and around, and around. My comment never got so much as a laugh. The city of Redmond had become a glorified bedroom community to Bend. And farther to the east I saw the lights of Prineville, no longer the "Cowboy Capital of Oregon," but a town bursting at the seams, trying to play catch-up to its unattractive Central Oregon stepsisters.

I wanted my world to be like it used to be. No lights. No houses. No roads, power lines, fields. Back when the country was nothing it was good, like Alaska and Australia probably still are. I took a hard swallow of whiskey and felt its soothing effect relax my body, shredded on the outer edges by the fatigue of a day spent working cattle and an evening in the bar. On the way to my rig I fished a piece of beef jerky from the pocket of my Levi jacket, tore off a generous chunk with my teeth and chewed. I climbed in, dumped old Molly in gear and kicked her in the seat of the pants.

I don't know why I call my pickup Molly, don't even know why she is a she, except sometimes she can be a bit temperamental, especially on a cold morning or if I've worked her too hard the day before. Molly is a Ford, three-quarter ton diesel. Never could understand a man who drove a Chevy. They just don't hold together off-pavement. I ain't sportsman enough for a Jimmy or farmer enough for a Dodge. My money says Ford is tough and dependable, just like the advertisement says. Few times something does go wrong they're easy to work on, anyway the older models like mine are. The new ones, full of computers, catalytic converters, and federally-mandated, environmentally-friendly crap, ain't worth diddly-squat. That's my personal opinion.

If I took inventory under the seat, I suppose Molly would yield a hot-shot, a handful of dead flashlight batteries, a chunk of log chain, baling wire, twine, a horseshoe or two, bolts, nuts, washers, some screws, a socket set but no ratchet, fence tools, mismatched gloves, empty whiskey bottles and some Coors cans thrown in for spare change. Just a typical buckaroo Cadillac—nothing much out of the ordinary.

I chewed the jerky and knew in my heart I would have this spicy blond, but to be perfectly honest I was feeling a smidgen of embarrassment because I had, ah, sort of, kind of—this is a little hard for me to come right out and admit—but I might have come fairly close to promising this one gal, Sam, short for Samantha, that maybe if things worked out, she and I, might, get, get, get hitched. Not right away, mind you, but somewhere down the road a good far piece. She had two kids. Travis was five. A real cute little guy who desperately wanted me to be his daddy. And Joleen, eleven, trapped somewhere between Legos and Legs. She was sorta stand-offish.

Sam was near my age, couple years younger but well preserved. I remember her when she used to barrel race, back in the olden days when I was still following the rodeo circuit. And then she got married, didn't barrel race no more, dropped out of sight until last year. I caught up with her in a bar. She was having a night out with some of her girlfriends, celebrating her divorce. I asked her to dance. One thing led to another. What can I say?

If a cowboy could pick a wife like he picks a cow, based strictly on breeding, size, conformation, milk capacity and the type of calf she throws, then it would be a whole lot easier. The way it works is a man chooses what he considers to be the best of the breed and settles down to the responsibilities of raising a family. In the real world a fellow is supposed to marry for no other reason than love, banking on the abstract hope his intensity, and her intensity, will be there in three months, six months, five years, thirty years. It never has been for me. I've changed women about as often as I've changed Levi's.

Hell, I ought to just admit it. Truth is I ain't the marrying type. I live free and easy, would much rather have forty good years of long-lining fillies than spend eighty years in a pasture of sweet clover wearing husband hobbles. "*Sugar-pie, please take out the trash.*" "*The sink's leaking, would you mind fixing it, Sweetie?" "Can you give me a hand carrying in the groceries, Honeybunch?"* Forget it. Who needs it? I sure as hell don't.

I asked myself, if that really was the way I felt, why in hell did I ever make such a semi-promise to Sam? My only rationalization was to say that maybe, staring down the double barrel of forty years, I had momentarily lost my nerve for living alone. It was possible I might live long enough to become a broken-down, lonely old man.

When I finally did reach the ranch I forgot what I was thinking and stepped out of the truck so quickly I was swallowed in the dust I had made. Cheyenne eased up behind, swung her rig around and squeezed in the narrow space between the horse trailer and the barn. It was as if she was trying to hide, or something. She hurried to me, wrapped her arms around me in a tight embrace, nibbled my earlobe and breathed, "Let's go in."

"Keep your britches on, Honey," I told her. "I gotta tend my horse."

I turned Charley loose into the alleyway leading to the corral. He whirled and raced away, fire spitting from contact between horseshoes and gravel. With my free hand I flipped on the barn light, stowed my saddle and blanket in the tack room and went directly to the grain bin. I could hear the fat mice inside swimming to get away as I dipped a pair of buckets into the pile of rolled oats. Outside in the corral the young horses moved in disarray toward the feed bunk. The older horses, in single file, pushed them aside, snaking out to nip with their teeth or taking well-measured aim and kicking. After pouring the oats into the wooden trough I broke a bale of hay, spreading the flakes around so there wouldn't be any excuse for fighting, folding baling wire back and forth in my left hand while mindlessly watching the shifting shapes of the horses: vague shadows moving through the shafts of shade and light.

I found Cheyenne where I had left her. She was being serenaded by a pack of coyotes and I put an arm around her waist and directed her toward the house. I knew the house would be clean as a whistle because I employed a woman to come out from town once a week to wash dishes, run through a load or two of clothes and tidy up a bit. She had been there the day before.

I opened the door and stepped past the recent history of the place, reflected in a line of worn out cowboy boots and overshoes with missing buckles and splotches of manure from cattle long since hauled to town and passed through the drive-up window at Burger King. I flipped on a floor lamp and tossed my Stetson on the deer-horn hat rack. Cheyenne followed my lead and while her hat was joining mine I went to the firebox, crumbled up some of last Sunday's newspaper, grabbed a handful of kindling and started a fire in the big stone fireplace. Once it was going good I tossed on chunks of tamarack and asked Cheyenne if I could fix her a drink. She asked for Chivas Regal but I poured Black Velvet and she sipped it without complaint.

In the fireplace the wood began to take and flames shot around the big wedges, giving a noisy, orange glow to the room. I gathered Cheyenne in my arms, said, "You're shivering."

In a harsh, needy whisper she instructed, "Take me to bed." She sure as hell was plain-spoken. Something like that, I don't have to be told twice. I tilted my glass until the amber liquid was gone, set it aside, took her arm and directed her down the hallway. When we passed the open door to the bathroom she said, "One minute," and ducked inside. I continued on, popping the pearl snaps and stripping off my western shirt as I went. I sat on the edge of the bed and, regretting I had not used the bootjack by the door, began prying off my boots.

Light was seeping down the hallway from the fireplace in the living room as Cheyenne made her way to me. I watched her approach, her reflected image in the oval mirror above the bureau, and told myself that old mirror had never seen a more lovely sight. Even before Cheyenne reached me she was busy unbuttoning her blouse and there was more to see than the obvious, like one of those paintings where you think it is a simple landscape but if you look closely there'll be figures hidden in the lines: a rock becomes an Indian chief, a cloud a sleeping bear, trees a line of cavalry soldiers. The moment was like that, full of hidden sights and liberated meanings.

It has been my experience that most gals, when they go to undress for a fellow, will usually do something provocative. One moment their ripe flesh is pounding against material and then, with very little movement, clothes fall away and the visual sight of them naked flows into the viewer's eyes and mind, the same way water follows the gentle contours of the earth and seeps into the soil.

It was no exception with Cheyenne. She shrugged out of her blouse and her breasts were flawless, round and ripe with proudly erect nipples. In one quick motion she unbuckled her belt, the skirt fell to the floor, she stepped from the circle of willowy fabric, bent to retrieve the skirt, tossed it over the back of a chair and stood in front of me wearing only red cowgirl boots and black frilly panties. Her hands were on her hips, elbows cocked, legs daringly apart. She casually tossed back a few strands of long blond hair and, knowing the effect her near nakedness was having on me, she prolonged the moment for my gratification, or maybe for her own.

Flaunting a mischievous leer she kicked off her cowgirl boots and pulled off short nylon stockings. And then, in one agile movement, she tucked both thumbs inside the elastic band and tugged down her panties, flexing one knee and then the other, leaving me in the perfect position to attest to the obvious fact she was a natural blond, with a body made just for sin.

I pried off one stubborn boot, stood and reached for her. She threw back her head. I grabbed her roughly and kissed her neck. She laughed and I felt the vibrations down low in her throat. And then she came into my arms with a rush, burying her face against my bare chest. I felt the incredible heat of her nakedness. I kissed her eyelids and I kissed her lips. She met my kiss with equal passion and her mouth opened wonderfully wide. Her lips yielded and made it seem they would yield forever, when she suddenly became assertive and pushed into me with such force she caused me to take a quick step backwards and onto the foot that still had a boot on it. As we kissed, my hands roamed her flesh and wherever my fingertips touched, the muscles below the surface quivered and shivered.

"Where do men like you come from," she gasped. She went limp, her breathing became labored and I laid her on the bed. I used brute force to pull off my remaining boot, slipped out of my pants, and like a period at the end of a long, rambling, incoherent sentence, my trophy belt buckle made a hard metallic clank as it came in contact against the hardwood floor.

Lie in the arms of a woman and take your chances. She could give you a dose of the clap or something far worse. She gets knocked up and you're facing child support payments for the next couple decades. Funny, when it comes right down to the moment, none of that really matters. I went to bed with Cheyenne for the same reason bull elk fight with their horns, or Dall rams crack skulls. For no other reason than unadulterated, basic animal instinct.

If I had been thinking with the head on my shoulders, instead of the one between my legs, I might have considered the various possibilities and odds, both long and short. What was the likelihood Cheyenne's husband had followed us? What if Sam paid me a surprise visit? Even though she was supposed to be working, waitressing at the 86 Club in Redmond, she had done that very thing once before, trading shifts with a girlfriend and driving to the ranch on a whim. As luck had it, that time I had been alone.

Cheyenne and I were deep in the throes of lovemaking and I don't rightly know what it was, but something sidetracked me: perhaps a sixth sense that clued me into the fact we were no longer alone, the hollow sound shoe leather makes sliding on a wood floor, the sudden ungodly quietness that seemed to have settled over the bedroom. Cheyenne sensed it too and froze beneath me.

There was certainly no mistaking the lethal grind of metal against metal. In less than a heartbeat I recognized the sound of a live shell being jacked into the chamber of my Remington Wingmaster, model 870. I always kept the 12-gauge leaned against the wall by the front door. Of course it was loaded. What's the use of keeping an unloaded weapon? Might as well have a stick propped up there.

Panic goosed me. Instinct took over. I rolled off Cheyenne, felt the coolness of the sheets against my skin and the weird way my body seemed to want to dissipate in an awkward rush of papery wings, trying but failing to fly away and out the window. And I was aware of Cheyenne. Her movements jiggled the mattress as she scurried to the far side and slid off the bed. There was a dull thump as her body dropped onto the floor.

There came a blinding flash, and it seemed as though an electric current swept through my body jumping gaps between each individual molecule. A scorching blue flame burned across my retina and I was buffeted by an ass-kicking whomp of sound and an angry wave of concussion. Chunks of ceiling plaster rained down. I gasped for breath and tasted sheetrock dust, burned gunpowder and the metallic residue of fear. And if all this was not assaulting enough to my senses, there came a pent-up squeal of tormented rage, the likes of which I had never before heard from a human being. The closest I can come to describing that sound is to say it was a cross between the way a stuck pig will squeal and something even more feral, maybe the shriek of a mountain lion chased off his kill. It caused the hair on the nape of my neck to twitch, muscles in my ass to spasm, and blood to solidify in my arteries. Under such numbing circumstances I would never have thought myself capable of speech, and yet I found myself talking, my voice so calm and rational it jolted me. "Put it down. Sam, put the shotgun down."

I could clearly see Sam in the diffused light leaking down the hallway. She was standing at the foot of the bed, holding the shotgun. Her facial expressions slowly began to change: the hard defined lines softened and her jaw began to relax. Finally, she simply pitched the shotgun onto the bed, turned away and stormed out of the room. I did not, could not, move. I lay listening to her angry footfalls recede down the hallway. But the door to outside never opened, never slammed shut. She was still in the house. I was afraid she might go for a knife, come slit my cheating throat. Jesus H. Christ!

I pried myself off the bed, kicked my legs over the side and somehow managed to struggle into my pants. Without benefit of shirt, socks or boots, I made my way down the hallway and found Sam sitting in a chair pulled tight to the kitchen table. Her head was tucked in the crook of an elbow. She was crying.

I knew, at a time like this, there was no sense in wasting words. Besides, what could I possibly say? But the longer I stood there, the more my stomach jiggled with sympathy, empathy, or compassion. I never have quite figured out the precise difference between the three, but I knew I had screwed up, let down Sam, let down little Travis and Joleen, too.

Eventually, Sam turned and faced me. Her cheeks were splotchy, wet and shiny. She wanted to know, "Why? Just tell me why?"

I was being asked to justify my fling with the beautiful blond. I shrugged. I was helpless, or maybe I was just hopeless. I did manage to tell her, "It ain't exactly black and white." To her credit Sam never reacted, never so much as flinched. I figured something more needed to be added to the mix and told her, "I don't know. Just don't know." And I didn't know.

Sam, as mean as six mink in a cage, snarled at me, "Don't give me that crap."

I attempted to explain, "I never set out to hurt you." My gut took another twist and I gritted my teeth against the sting. Jesus, could I ever use a shot of whiskey to settle my stomach.

"You have lipstick...." She pointed at my cheek and then, once again, burst into tears.

I wiped at the offending smudge with the heel of my hand, wondering why it is that lipstick comes off a woman so easily and off a man so damn hard. I tried to console her, "Had nothing to do with you, Sam." As if that was supposed to explain it all away. She cried harder. I felt even more uncomfortable, glanced around the room, and noticed a bottle of champagne and a birthday cake on the coffee table near the fireplace. The cake was unique, with colorful candles encircling the frosted likeness of a cowboy riding a bucking bronc, a classic pose that could have been stolen from the Pendleton Round-Up, or maybe from the Wyoming license plate. I made a quick count and figured there had to be forty candles, one candle for each year of my existence. Light those sons-of-bitches and it'd be a conflagration comparable to a forest fire ripping through a stand of beetle-killed lodgepole pine.

I thought, "Forty candles on a cowboy cake," and slowly began putting it together, knowing Sam had gone to the trouble of having the cake made special for me, had driven to the ranch, failed to see Cheyenne's car parked behind my pickup and horse trailer, and assumed I was alone. She was planning on giving me a birthday surprise but the table got turned. Boy-oh-boy, did it ever. Must have been quite a shocker for poor Sam, stepping into the house and hearing the goings-on in the bedroom. She must have gone straight for the shotgun. Was her first inclination to shoot me? If so, when it came down to it, why did she have a change of heart?

I went to Sam. She was sobbing violently and, when I placed my hands on her shoulders, her muscles jumped like a hound dog straddling an electric fence. Eventually she wound down enough that I asked, "Wanna cup of coffee?" I did not really expect a response, was not surprised when none came my way, and used the opportunity as a diversion to move to the sink and counter, where I poured water and several heaping tablespoons of Folgers into the coffee machine and flipped the switch. While it brewed I slipped down the hallway to the bedroom.

I flicked on the light and paused to stare at the gaping hole in the ceiling above the bed. Locating Cheyenne proved a little more elusive. I found her in the closet on the floor, knees pulled to her chest, arms wrapped tightly around her bare legs. I had this unsettling image of her as a baby, cooing and drooling. I lifted her to a standing position and waited for her to come alive. She was covered in fine white dust and her blue eyes were blue-black, blank and skittish. Her mouth moved helplessly, searching for syllables and words. She tried to touch me but her hands had lost their sureness and her fingers crawled over my bare chest.

I urgently whispered, "You gotta get the hell out of here," and began gathering her clothes and helping her dress. She was trembling but she never cried, never whimpered. I guessed she was shocky but she did manage to help me some, and even sat on the bed and pulled on her boots by herself. I asked, "Want me to run you to town?" She shook her head no.

I smelled coffee and knew I better get back. Before leaving the room I wanted to know, "You gonna be okay?" Cheyenne never responded. I leaned to kiss her but she turned away from me, leaving me to wonder if I'd gotten that kiss, would her lips have been as cold as a cadaver?

On the way, I ducked into the bathroom and used a towel to brush away some of the incriminating sheetrock dust from my hair and face. Upon reaching the kitchen, I poured a cup of coffee and set it in front of Sam. She pressed a wad of Kleenex to her eyes and her body was racked by spasms and shudders. I turned my head and caught sight of Cheyenne crossing the living room, moving as silently as a shadow passing through water. She started to reach for the horseshoe door latch, stopped and used both hands to smooth down her skirt. That image of her, the way she paused at the very brink of danger, hands sliding over, almost caressing that cute butt, was sexy as hell to me.

The door opened and closed. I noticed Cheyenne's straw hat hanging from the deer horns, knew I should get rid of it, but doubted I ever would. A car engine turned over, started, and I heard the ping of tires spinning loose gravel. I watched through the black window as red taillights winked at me between trees. She was gone.

The evening could have played itself out with Sam choosing to forgive my indiscretion and us eating birthday cake, drinking champagne and going to bed. That never happened. Sam finished her cry and simply announced, "I'm out of here."

I brushed off my bed as best I could and lay down, but sleep was hard to come by. For the longest time I stared through the window glass at the cold, white, ancient stars knowing for a damn solid fact I wasn't the only one losing sleep. I was acquainted with Sam's bedroom and pictured her there, wide awake and mad. I wondered where Cheyenne might have bunked, figured that young gal probably had had enough excitement for one evening and had found her way home.

As I lay there, I thought how much my life was like that Robert Frost poem, the one about the road less traveled, where two roads diverge in a yellow wood. For me the twist was ninety-nine roads diverged in the desert and I was in the process of taking all ninety-nine. Where had it gotten me? Forty years old, half my life lived and what did I have to show? Sure as hell none of the tangible possessions most people surround themselves with—wife, kids, house, land, money in the bank.

What I had managed to accumulate was a good horse, a pickup truck that still got me around, a drawer full of trophy buckles, and an All-Around championship saddle from Miles City, Montana. Not the type of wealth most folks brag about, but I've always prided myself on traveling light. Accumulate things and things tie you down. Just give me my saddle, the buckles, the horse and the pickup truck. And my hat, I need my Stetson. Better add my Tony Lama boots and my chinks. I wouldn't wanna have to try to get along without boots and chinks. Give me those few things and I'm as happy as a fat hog in a garbage pit.

What I'm most thankful for is my Ph.D. in Cowboyography. My main teachers were Grandpa Barton and my Old Man. Others taught me, too. They were the men I've had the pleasure of riding alongside. Cowboys—the real deal. The first three letters of cowboy, C-O-W, pretty well spells it out. A cowboy has to be able to look at a cow and know instinctively if she is in good physical condition. How do you know? You learn from experience: look at her hide and if the hair is slick and the hide tight she is on good feed and eating fine. Her eyes tell if she has any pain or discomfort. If her bag is not too full, or too small, and if her calf is playful and happy, the calf has suckled recently and the cow is not dried up. Those are obvious signs but there are many more subtle clues to communicate to a cowboy how his cattle are faring.

Enough said about that, getting back to my slight case of melancholy about turning forty and having nothing material to show for it. I'm of the opinion there are intervals in a man's life when he needs to put the brakes on and take inventory. For me this particular moment must have been one of those. It took a while to realize what was eating me, besides getting caught in the act with Cheyenne, was that my life—so far—was pretty average, anyway average for a buckaroo. Oh sure, plenty of stories circulated about my nefarious escapades: bar fights, bucking broncs I had ridden, women I poked, things like that, but those stories would never endure. They would die with the passing of my generation.

I lay in bed listening to the coyotes cry in the hills. That slice of moon, setting now and so golden it seemed to be dripping yellow, was poised above the hard edge of the ridge and as it slowly sank it impaled itself on a stubby, gnarled pine snag.

The time it took the moon to set. The time it took to live a life. Time? What was time? Just seconds, minutes, hours, days, lifetimes. I must have dozed, because I dreamed I was riding Charley across the desert. It was late in the afternoon and storm clouds were marching away. Beams of pale light played across clumps of sage turning silver leaves slick and shiny from the hard shower that had passed through and sweetened the air. The little washes ran rivulets of muddy water. A damp breeze heaved a sigh. Stars began to emerge and a strange calmness came to the High Desert. Someone once told me the naked eye is capable of seeing only a few thousand stars in the billions of stars scattered across the galaxies. But I saw millions and the Milky Way filled my mind. I was content.

When I awoke, the east-facing window was swelling with flat, gray light and the top row of pine trees on the hill was standing out in a jagged black line across the blush of the emerging sky. A rooster flapped its wings and crowed a warning to the hens to get a move on. "There's eggs to lay!" he cried, "Production! Production!"

My Old Man used to open the door to my room, holler, "*Daylight in the swamps!*" Hell—growing up like I did on the ranch—we were nowhere near a swamp.

I sat up, stretched and swung my legs over the edge of the mattress. When the soles of my bare feet came in contact with the cold floor, I felt the chips and chunks of plaster. I groaned. If I needed further confirmation all I had to do was look up. I never did. Instead I got up, slipped on my clothes and went down the hall to the bathroom. I had my day lined out—there were cattle to move and in the afternoon I needed to go over things with my hired men, line them out for the work that needed to be accomplished in the coming week.

I went to the kitchen to fix breakfast but, seeing my birthday cake just sitting there, I elected to cut myself a piece, taking most of the frosted cowboy, saving the horse for later. The cake, moist chocolate, didn't go down particularly easy and I don't suppose it should have. In fact, it would be my guess that a substantial percentage of the population would call me a total asshole on several counts: for two-timing Sam, horsing with a married gal, and then having the audacity to sit there and fork birthday cake into my mouth. Some might even jump to the conclusion I lack respect for women. That's horseshit. I love women—every chance I get I love women.

To be perfectly honest, most any problem I've encountered in life, in one way or another, involved a woman. I'm the first to admit I don't understand what makes a gal tick. All the same—and I certainly didn't know this at the time or I might have tried to prepare myself like a man will do, tightening up his stomach muscles just before he gets hit in the gut—but I was about to get my comeuppance. Two women were heading straight at me from opposite directions. One was hell-bent on domesticating me while the other was about to make my life more rowdy and interesting than it had ever been, even in the wildest of times.

Chapter 2

If you can't make the ride at least have the decency to hang up and give the crowd a thrill. (Harley Hutchinson)

Some mornings on the High Desert are so perfect they make a fellow forget any misery that might be riding his coattails. It was just such a morning and Charley was feeling his oats, acting a little snorty as we made our way across Long Meadow to move cattle from one range to the next. Like a young man off to rendezvous with a pretty girl, I pushed Charley into an eager lope and then an easy gallop.

It had been a wet spring and the earth was spongy with moisture and vivid splashes of wildflowers were in bloom here and there. We cut a trail through sleek grass, shaking loose dewdrops that fell, reflecting the sun's fire like broken glass. A meadowlark, with its feathered yellow vest and tweed coat, sat on a boulder, puffed up its chest and twirled a lighthearted melody. I grinned at the bird's tune and assured myself that life sure as hell don't end at forty.

We reached the edge of the meadow, penetrated a fringe of timber and as we began to climb, I slowed Charley to a comfortable walk. The pine trees stood close, their green tops hanging thick under the sun, protecting the forest floor from the weather. Here the soil was dry. Charley stepped lightly, long slender legs wary of rattlesnakes, metal horseshoes crunching brown pine needles and kicking up duff and a powdery dust that became suspended in the air behind us, creating a visible trail to mark our passing. The forest of cinnamon colored, straight-grained ponderosa pine became even denser and the temperature dropped a few degrees. We followed a creek that gurgled like the voices of children at play, growing steadily louder the higher we climbed. Indian paintbrush and lupine decorated the sides of the trail. Occasionally, through breaks in the trees, the peaks of the snow-capped Three Sisters appeared, towering above the ridgeline. Once, when we crossed the creek, I gave Charley rein and he leaned his long neck and slurped cold water, runoff from the mountains.

We clambered up a long embankment and the timber began to thin some and slanting rays of sunlight warmed the back of my neck. I shivered. The air remained cool. Everywhere I looked translucent ribbons of wispy vapor drifted and swirled like ghosts dancing through the trees. Sounds were recognizable—tree frogs, song birds, saddle leather squeaking rhythmically under my weight, the jingle of spurs, the rasping of the horse's tongue on the bit-roller. A ruffed grouse flushed with a whir of beating wings. Charley snorted in surprise and shook his head.

I thought to myself I must be the luckiest son-of-a-buck in the world because at that very moment millions of people were driving to work, clogging the freeways, hurrying to jobs they hated and bosses they despised. While they drove they worried about wars, inflation, taxes and the high price of gas. They tolerated traffic congestion, smog and noise: got up, went to work, punched in, worked, took a break, worked, ate lunch, worked, took a break, worked, punched out, went home. They planned for, and made the most of, each weekend. It never lasted long enough before the monotonous cycle of work began all over again.

But the life of a buckaroo involves hard work, too. We invest sweat equity to make sure we bring in a good calf crop. I know because four generations of my family have been involved with ranching, starting with Great-Grandpa Alvie. He came to Central Oregon, kicked out the Indians and basically stole the land. All the early day cattlemen did the same thing. That was the way the West got won. The screenwriters and book writers can romanticize all they want, but the bottom line is the stockmen took what they wanted and fought like hell to hold it.

On the home place, where I grew up, it was easy to see where the Indians had been. Evidence was everywhere, several thousand years of carvings on rocks and indentations on the meadow where wigwams had once stood. Occasionally, we found mortars tipped on their sides, pestles lying nearby and there were piles of obsidian flakes where warriors had chipped points. Not that I hold the modern Indian in especially high regard. Sure they got the short end of the stick, but the same thing has happened throughout history to any conquered people. Most Indians I know are content to lie around and feel sorry for themselves, bitch about the mistreatment of their ancestors and at the same time make sure they keep their hand out and grab every last dime they can steal from the public pot. I've been around too many Indians when they've been drinking, and let me tell you it ain't a pretty picture. It's my personal belief that most Indians spend their lives about two drinks shy of hitting the warpath.

After the Indians had been put on reservations, Great-Grandpa Alvie had to fight the sodbusters. Homesteading was a scam perpetrated by the federal government to encourage the population of the West. People, on the outside chance of plowing up prosperity, fell for it hook, line, and sinker. Early day land developers touted Central Oregon, promising, *"The temperate climate of the High Desert makes this a wheat-grower's paradise."* And land agents assured the homesteaders the 320 acres the government was bestowing on them was plenty of ground for a good farm. For a finder's fee they offered to show the interested parties the parcels of available land.

Eastern dreamers and schemers flooded into the country, using their savings to build houses, barns, sheds, chicken coops, schools and churches. They broke the land out of sagebrush, burned the timber and planted crops. *"Stay put five years and it's all yours, free and clear. Sign here. Sign your life away."*

The homesteaders found the first few winters to be mild, rains came on schedule and the virgin soil grew thick stands of grain. Along came the dry years and jackrabbits, grasshoppers and Mormon crickets took over. The sodbusters tried to stick it out, even when by all rights they should have given up and moved on to something with a shred of promise.

They stayed and struggled for one reason—because the land possessed them. No other motive. That's what happened to them and it was the same with Great-Grandpa Alvie, Grandpa Barton and my Old Man. They stayed so long in one place their souls merged with the land. And in the end the soil reclaimed them.

I used to be able to go back to the home place, look around and remember Grandpa Barton and my Old Man working on some piece of equipment, dropping a snag, bringing in a herd of cattle, cutting a colt. Everything out there reminded me of them and things we had done together.

Then Grandpa Barton died and a few years later my Old Man followed suit. Even though my Old Man had promised me the ranch, Mother was first in line. She promptly sold out to a fast-talking, deep-pocketed land developer. The ink hadn't dried on that deal when she became involved with a damn real estate broker who thought himself a big shot. He wore turquoise jewelry, flashy shirts and an expensive, ten-X beaver cowboy hat with a buckaroo telescope crease. He tried to impress me by telling me he picked the hat up on Rodeo Drive in Beverly Hills. He might have looked the part of a gentleman rancher but I never saw him on a horse. And another thing about that interloper, he maintained a perfect tan, even in winter. Within a year, the two of them were married. They high-tailed it to Salt Lake City where Mother used part of her windfall to buy a pricey house. I've seen her exactly three times since and I don't rightly care if I see her again. She stole my heritage. That's all I have to say about that subject.

Let me tell you, our old ranch was plumb beautiful: timbered ridges and a big open meadow where deer grazed and every spring and fall the honkers dropped from the sky and landed on our lake, where they fed and rested up for the remainder of their journey. Besides the geese, we had an array of other migrating waterfowl. And no matter where you were on the place, the snow-capped Three Sisters seemed near enough to tuck into your hip pocket. In my mind the home place, the way it used to be, is what heaven ought to look like.

The developer spoiled our meadow, made it into a goddamn golf course. The hills where we hunted and cut timber and firewood became a subdivision sliced by paved lanes, avenues and cul-de-sacs that were given Indian names. The old log house, built by Great-Grandpa Alvie, where Grandpa Barton and my Old Man were born, was deemed unfit for the Tiger Woods crowd. The bastards burned it to the ground. And the bone yard, where we kept an accumulation of old machinery we reused for parts, was sold for scrap metal. The only hint that remains of our ranch is the mortise-and-tenon barn. They converted that into a recreation center.

Bunch of goddamn crap is what it is. Pitiful. In a nutshell, the developer took a productive cattle ranch and turned it into a people zoo devoted to the grand game of golf. I can't stand to drive by the place no more and see rich folks in bright colored clothes knocking little white balls around. By my way of thinking, a golf course is a horrible waste of a good cow pasture.

My nostalgic ramblings ran their course and, as I reined Charley along the game and cattle trail, I began to appreciate all the obvious signs that spring was busting out around me. The dappled leaves of the aspen had emerged and were blushing shades of pastel green. Pine pollen was so thick I could taste it on my tongue. The volcanic soil and the growing grasses were giving off a sweet, pungent fragrance. The sounds of birds and the drone of insects provided harmony to my ears.

Witnessing the changing season, the continuing cycle of life made a deep impression on me and helped me appreciate the fact that the whole world is held together in a delicate balance. Any one little thing can upset the apple cart. I know folks who believe you're born, die, get buried and the worms take over. That's it. But you look around at Mother Nature and figure She has got more to the plan than that. What if birth and death are not the beginning or end but only another spiral in a tightly coiled lariat?

The canyon pinched off and I forced Charley to climb. He lunged upward to a high saddle between two ridges where I laid the reins over the horn and allowed him a blow. Here the pines were old, small, crowded and the shallow soil gave off the appearance of being worn-down by the relentless west winds. Overhead a rumbling jet dragged a hefty contrail down the freshly scrubbed sky while a bald eagle rode a thermal updraft, circling, soaring and becoming so small it was little more than a speck in the distance. The eagle leveled off and began a lazy glide that curved toward an unseen body of water. I knew the remote lake was there and imagined that big bird: gunmetal gray wings tucked tightly, coming in fast and low, white-tipped feathers sweeping. Talons unclenching: flashing, dipping, splashing and making a thin streak on the mirrored surface. Wings flapping with brutal force, pulling the eagle up with a plump Kokanee trout clutched in its talons, droplets of water falling from the struggling fish like tiny diamonds tumbling from the deadly blue sky.

I had the unsettling feeling I was seeing too much and made a concerted effort to draw myself back to level-headedness. In the distance I saw the cluster of buildings that comprised the headquarters of the 25 Ranch, my ranch, but owned by a man who used it as a tax write-off and who didn't give a good-goddamn about cattle or land except how it effected his bottom line. His accountants notified me what to buy and when to buy it, proving to me that ranching was fast becoming a business controlled by heartless out-of-state dickwads. They owned land strictly for economic gain, and in order to brag to socialites they met at fancy cocktail parties that they possessed twenty-thousand acres, or fifty-thousand acres of prime real estate in sun-drenched Central Oregon, or along the backbone of the continent in Colorado, or in the wilds of rugged Montana.

Seeing the ranch buildings made me remember the night before and I wondered if Sam, ever again, would have anything to do with me. Eventually I worked my way around to Cheyenne. I considered the fact that so many changes in life come about as result of happenstance. The slightest nudge in a particular direction can cause a girl to become imbedded in a fellow's mind and if that occurs the scar is likely to follow him all the way to his grave. I laughed. That certainly wasn't going to be the case with Cheyenne. How long had I known her? Like three or four hours, tops. I hoped she made it back to town, figured she had and detested my bad luck because that gal was like a jigger of Tabasco. I would never know exactly how hot she could have been. But then again, sometimes life has a funny way of doubling back on itself.

—✶—✶—✶—

I lightly touched my spurs to Charley and we dropped off the divide and went about the business of ranching. Moving cattle has always been my recreation. A cowboy knows, according to the pasture, time of day and their need for feed and water, where the cattle will be congregated. There are always exceptions to the rule, a few knuckleheaded cows that have to be pushed from thickets or river bottoms.

I opened the gate into South Fork pasture, made a big circle and drove a small herd toward the opening. The calves kicked up their heels in play while the mother cows raised their heads, sniffed the air and started moving. A coyote angled away, stopping every few steps to look back over his shoulder.

After moving all the cattle into South Fork pasture, even the reluctant ones, I peeled off the hill and started back across Long Meadow. The day had turned unusually hot and humid and I was sweating freely by the time I arrived at the barn. I slid down, stretched, unsnapped my shirt to allow the air to cool me and stamped my feet on the ground to circulate the blood in my saddle-cramped legs. I pulled the saddle and bridle and turned Charley out with a pat on his rump.

I carried my gear inside and on the door to the tack room, pinned with a pocketknife, was a note. I recognized the discolored ivory handle of the old Buck knife as belonging to Jake Holt. Jake worked for me. The note was scribbled on a weigh slip from a load of cattle already taken to market. Right off I knew something serious had happened.

Jake's note read: "Bones—hart attak. Tuk him ta twn."

Bones was my other hired hand. He was an old-timey buckaroo, had even worked for the stock-contracting outfit when my Old Man first put it together. When I took over the 25 Ranch I made a few inquiries and found Bones working at a sale yard in Twin Falls, Idaho. I hired him over the phone to come work for me because, even though he was well past his prime, he was still a damn fine cowboy and an especially good hand with cattle. I let out a huff of air and cursed, "Christ on a crutch!" because it would have been a whole hell of a lot better if Bones had died straddling his horse instead of being carted off to spend his last few hours in a hospital.

I drove Molly hard and fast: following Deschutes Market Road into Bend, turning on 27th Street, taking a right on Neff Road and pulling to a stop in front of St. Charles Medical Center. I walked into the lobby and found Jake waiting for me. He was a rawboned man who wore a gray-black mask of a beard and his eyebrows were so long and scruffy they made him look rather disagreeable. He held his hat in his hands and was absently fingering the brim. When I walked up and laid a hand on his shoulder he looked at me with somber eyes, said, "Sorry, Boss. It don't look none ta good."

He told me what little he knew—that Bones had suffered a massive heart attack and was living on borrowed time. I gave him back his pocketknife and went upstairs. When I pushed open the door to Bones' room I was greeted by a cavalcade of competing smells: medications, a near toxic level of disinfectant, and the stench of hopelessness. Bones, what was left of him anyway, was lying on a bed. His eyelids were open, but his coffee-brown irises stared off into the jaws of eternity. An IV dripped fluid into one arm and a heart monitor pinged, displaying each feeble beat with a blaze of orange light on a charcoal-gray screen. I picked up a chair, swung it around and sat down with my chin resting on the back. I watched the way Bones' shallow breathing barely moved the lightweight yellow sheet. His hands were folded, almost piously, one over the other and laid on his belly. His forearms were tan and the muscles tight as braided sinew, but his upper arms, marked by a shirt line where the sun never touched, were white and the muscles slack.

It was difficult for me to see his frail body in such a defenseless position. I looked down at my own right hand and noticed an angry black-and-blue mark, just above the knuckles, a souvenir from where a wild spring calf managed to kick me during branding. My Levi's were spattered with cow shit and my boots were dusty. I spoke without looking up, "Bones, if this is the end of the line, you shouldn't have no complaint coming."

But maybe he did. As far as I knew he never married, never had kids. He was a tramp buckaroo and that's all he ever was. Just a man who never owned more worldly possessions than fit comfortably in a set of saddlebags. To be honest, I felt a stab of uneasiness, maybe even fear, because I thought I might be seeing myself in the same position Bones was in, thirty or forty years down the road.

Last Christmas I gave Bones a bonus. The hundred bucks came out of my own pocket and I thought he'd buy himself something extra: binoculars, a new bridle, a shirt, coat, a pair of pants. I heard, after the fact, that he went to town, gave it to the volunteer firemen's fund, said to buy presents for kids Santa couldn't afford to visit. That was the type of man he was, a giver.

In his day Bones could do it all: work cattle, ride roundup, break colts, shoe a horse, beat a knife from a railroad spike, fix a windmill with baling wire and spit, throw a diamond hitch on a pack mule. But the thing I admired most about him was the way he told a story. From time to time, if he had a few drinks under his belt and was cranked up and in a talkative mood, he recited stories and maybe threw in a cowboy poem every once in a while. I'm sure he took an occasional liberty and embellished a story, as any good storyteller will, but most generally his words rang true as a bell. I could listen to him for hours, and often had.

Bones was never shy about offering advice on the way he thought life ought to be lived. Some of his remarks were clear-cut, some made you ponder a spell. I remember sitting with him on a hay bale, him trying to massage some life back into his arthritic legs, and him telling me, "Worked cows from Oregon ta Montana, from Old Mexico ta Canada. Always one ta fidget 'round like a hot-blooded horse on an ant bed. One ranch after 'nother. Never did stay long 'nough to wear out my welcome. That way they're always eager ta have ya back. Kept a movin'. That's the secret ta life. I left a lotta tracks, seen some mighty fine country. In a way I own it all. Most folks don't understand that line of thinkin' but ya do, don't ya, Waddy?" I had nodded because I sure as hell did.

I wanted to remember Bones around the branding fire, using two sticks to lift a can of pork and beans from the coals, setting it aside to cool and then using his fingers to gingerly hold the can up near the rim, where the heat was not enough to burn him. I see him on his haunches spooning pork and beans in his mouth with the blade of his pocketknife.

And I wanted to remember Bones at roundup time sitting his old brown horse in a prehistoric, high-backed Hamley saddle. Watch him patiently wait as a half-dozen cows and calves amble from a bull pine thicket. The lead cow sees or smells Bones, stops abruptly, throws her head and curls her tail in alarm, ready to run at the drop of a hat. Bones talks the uneasiness right out of her. "Don't be scared, momma. Come 'long with me. I promise ta take ya where there's a big ol' pile of sweet alfalfa hay, an' water so cold it'll tickle your teeth. Easy does it, girl. Come with me. Bring your friends. Mosey along. Ain't no reason fer ya ta be in no hurry. Ya can't never hurry, hurry."

There was time for everything. Just as now, there was time for his dying. I took one of his hands, held it and his fingers resisted, wrestling sluggishly, as if trying to pull away. My tear-filled eyes focused on his face, a face that seemed to be made of some material harder and more durable than flesh, maybe stone. I knew the arteries in Bones' temples were beginning to leak and the thin envelope around his brain was bulging like a plastic dam holding back a full head of ditch water. Behind this thin veneer of life stood a black-hooded figure busily erasing the past, all those days he buckarooed, all the way back through the events of his childhood. When death slipped up on him, Bones squeezed my hand hard and then let go. Almost immediately his eyes glazed over, and his lifeless skin began to take on a bluish tinge that would, in time, turn as dark as saddle leather.

I have seen turkey vultures in flight and they are the image of pure elegance and grace, carving perfect circles in the sky. But on the ground they move awkwardly. Their world is the sky. And I remembered Bones, the way he was toward the end, when he limped to his horse and, using every ounce of strength he could muster, pulled himself up and onto the saddle. Once he had his seat he was like that vulture, the picture of composure and dignity as his horse flew over the land. The wild bird and the buckaroo—their lives alike in so many ways—simple, clear, concise, certain, true.

One of the machines was squealing and several nurses invaded the room. With a swirl of pointless activity they scurried around on a futile mission to revive the motionless body. I told them, “It’s over. Leave him be.” They ignored me.

I stepped away, went to the window and stood there in my sweat-soaked shirt looking at town and the rounded hump of Pilot Butte glittering under the heat of the noonday sun. A soft hum vibrated around me and it seemed as though my feet did not quite touch the floor. I watched a flock of crows pass and thought about what I had heard survivors on television say when they came face-to-face with death. They claimed to have experienced a bright light at the end of a long tunnel and said how tough it was to turn around and return to this life. I figured that by now Bones must have seen the light. I wondered what happened when he reached it.

I found Bones’ clothes in the closet. They were neatly folded, even his chinks. On top of the pile was his brown Resistol cowboy hat, brim rolled tight on either side. The crown adorned with a thick mixture of gumbo mud and honest sweat, so thick it looked as though it could have been applied with a putty knife. I checked his pockets: a couple of dollars in a money clip, some change, a bone-handled Case pocket knife, a sack of Bull Durham smoking tobacco, brown cigarette papers and a book of matches from the Horseshoe Tavern in Prineville. That was it. A pair of scuffed cowboy boots stood apart from the clothes and they were graced with a set of fancy, gal-legged spurs. The silver shanks were shaped like a woman's leg, bent slightly at the knee, adorned with ornate Victorian whore's stockings and high-buttoned shoes. I took the spurs for remembrance's sake, and because I always had fancied them.

I muttered, "One less saddle tramp." And I knew the West was a poorer place for the loss.

Bones had told me he wanted to be cremated and his ashes scattered over "Big Nasty." That's what the old timers call the High Desert. To the untrained eye, in all directions and everywhere, the country east of Bend appears uniformly the same and unworthy of mention, a place of sagebrush flats, rocky outcroppings and juniper-studded hills. But scratch the porcelain plane of sameness, expose it, and the underbelly of Big Nasty is anything but uniform, monotonous and constant. I ought to know, I've buckarooed there most all my life.

After making arrangements at the funeral home I headed for the ranch. By then the thunderheads had boiled over and were clogging the sky with thick clouds, fluffy white on top and an ominous dark hue below. I went directly to the corral because, sometimes when you're feeling low, it really helps spending time with a friend. I don't have a better friend in this world than Charley. I stroked his muscled neck to sooth myself. He raised his head and sniffed the fresh scent of the coming rain.

The army of clouds marched on us and there were quick sparks of lightning and corresponding rumbles of thunder. I counted aloud, figured roughly a half-mile per second and determined the storm was still four or five miles away but drawing steadily nearer. Charley trembled. "You'll be alright," I assured him and petted his neck.

Thunder boomed and echoed off the foothills. The moody sky became even more sullen, purple-black, and a few tentative raindrops fell, thudding in the corral. The intensity increased and the ground was peppered with fat drops. A swirling wind sprang to life. The sharp smell of damp manure rose in the air but was flattened by a blaze of lightning and the jagged crack of thunder. Rain raked the air, drummed the tin barn roof and ran in rivulets off the corrugated eaves. Charley moved away to stand under the protective overhang of the barn. I stayed rooted to the spot, removed my hat, tilted my head upward and allowed the rain to spank my cheeks and drip into the open collar of my shirt. My clothes hung heavy, but I was oblivious to the rain and to the danger.

The fast-moving storm passed swiftly. I came to my senses and the sun was sliding off the rim of a cloud and shining down. A taxi was parked in the driveway, near the main house—there were three houses on the property: the main house, my house and the bunkhouse. At first I reasoned Jake might have taken a taxi, that maybe he was too drunk to drive, yet I knew when Jake went on a toot he might be too drunk to walk, but he was never too drunk to drive.

A man wearing a suit and an ill-fitting straw cowboy hat emerged from the back seat of the taxi and I knew immediately there was only one person it could be—my boss and owner of the 25 Ranch—Mr. Walter Meyer. He stood motionless while the cabby hustled a pair of leather bags to the main house. After the driver had been paid, the taxi lurched away, flying down the long drive.

"We need to talk," called Meyer as he walked in my direction. The tone of his voice was like a father calling a son who had done something wrong.

I don't much care for rich folks but I make an effort to try and tolerate them, to a point. Managing ranches, I've seen more than my share of men who have money and are scared to death of losing it. They surround themselves with attorneys, accountants and financial advisers. Honest to God, and you can take my word for this, rich folks are different from you and me. They are self-centered to a fault and take advantage of every loophole they uncover. If you boil it down to one thing, I suppose I'd have to say rich folks don't have proper character, or enough common sense to tell them the difference between right and wrong. Hell, I don't know what I'm talking about.

I took a couple steps forward, leaned both forearms on the top rail of the corral and waited for the big shot to come to me. While I was killing time I sucked in a breath and tasted conflicting smells: the fragrance of barn-stored hay against the stench of wet manure and the acrid reek of urine. Behind me horses shuffled their feet restlessly. A barn cat ran light-footed, a mouse held crosswise in its cruel mouth. My wet clothes dripped rainwater. I told myself I wasn't in any mood for a scolding, or a lecture.

Meyer snapped, "Why didn't you come get me?"

I lifted one foot and placed it on the bottom rail, glad to have the corral physically separating the two of us. Not for my protection but for his. "Didn't know you were coming."

"I called last night, left a message on the answering machine."

"It was my birthday. I was celebrating."

"I buzzed the ranch."

That was his usual way, buzzing the ranch with his Aero-Space Commander and I was supposed to drop whatever I was doing and race to pick him up at the airport. He didn't want to be inconvenienced.

I'm not the type to take much more than an ounce of shit off anybody, even the boss. I groused, "You pay me to run your ranch. You don't pay me to run a fucking taxi service."

He made a slicing motion, throat high. "I'm fed up to here with you. You need to learn to take orders."

I didn't say one damn word.

"My accountant thinks I should fire you. He says the ranch has shown a profit each of the last three months. That's totally unacceptable."

While Meyer talked I tried to imagine what kind of an animal he reminded me of, concluded it was most probably a weasel. He had told me when he hired me the 25 Ranch was not to be a paying proposition. Think about it. Ranching so you can beat the government out of a few bucks on taxes. It pissed me off and I guess I momentarily lost a little of my cool, because I found myself saying, "If you wanna lose money why don't you buy four or five Caterpillars. Park 'em at the main gate. They'd make real dandy flower planters."

"Don't mock me." He jabbed a finger dead-center at my chest. "Remember who signs your paycheck!"

Rather than do something foolish, like vault the fence and beat the sorry bastard to death with his own finger, I removed a can of Copenhagen from my shirt pocket, tapped the lid to settle the snuff and leisurely packed a dip under my lower lip. The brown flakes lay there festering for a few long seconds while I thought how money is no yardstick of a man's worth, and how much I despise the fact that a man with money assumes he has authority over a man with less money.

Without warning I went off, giving him both barrels at once. I said, "Run a ranch to lose money. Goddamn dirty rotten shame is what it is. I'm embarrassed for you. You ain't worth the powder it'd take to blow your clueless ass into Grant County."

"Just because you talk big doesn't make you a big man. You're through!"

"Fine. But you ain't gonna fire me. I quit!"

"Get off my land."

I crawled over the railing and strode away, never gave him the time of day or the satisfaction of a backward glance. I gathered my belongings, stuffed most of my personal gear in my big war bag, took Grandpa's rocking chair, and piled it all into the back of Molly. I threw a canvas tarp over the top and tied it down with a lariat. Then I hooked onto my horse trailer, loaded my saddle, tack and Charley, and got the hell out of Dodge.

I thought about Mr. High-Pockets walking into my bedroom. The way his jaw would most certainly drop, his look of utter consternation when he saw the gaping hole in the ceiling and probably the roof, too. I had to laugh.

I caught up with Jake at the Pastime tavern, a working-man's joint where a buckaroo or a logger could sit elbow-to-elbow and feel comfortable. Large photographs, dulled and discolored by light, smoke and age, decorated the walls. They depicted a different era: back when High Desert cowboys dressed in woolly chaps and rode desert mustangs, and Cascade loggers dressed in snagged tin pants and posed on giant logs. The simple bar rules were prominently posted, "*Men, No Shirt, No Service—Women, No Shirt, Free Drinks.*" A reversible plastic sign dangled in the window of the Pastime, beside the door, proclaiming, "*Open,*" but from the customers' view it declared, "*Sorry We're Closed.*" The interior was an indistinctly lit shotgun arrangement of various colored tables and mismatched chairs.

The Pastime was the last of the old time establishments in the town of Sisters. The others had gone "western" and catered exclusively to the tourist trade. In fact, just about the whole damn town had gone western once the merchants discovered they could slap up a false front, a hitching rail, decorate with fancy lights and glitter and charge prices that would make a frog's ass pucker.

The only female customer in the joint was a lumpy gal sitting alone at a table. She was hunched over a beer, spooning French fries with gravy ladled over the top into her red slash of a mouth. A group of regulars—useless old men drinking their way toward assisted living, or the grave—were seated at the bar. That's where I found Jake. I slid onto a stool beside him.

Jake was a mulish drinker and rarely drank for pleasure. He continued to work on his beer while I filled him in on the fact I was no longer his boss, going so far as to try and justify what had happened by saying, "Meyer, that son-of-a-bitch, has his head so far up his ass he can't wiggle his ears."

Jake made a clicking sound with his false teeth and followed that with a long, serious gulp of beer. The barmaid walked past and I asked, "Sweetheart, can we get a couple here, please?"

A familiar voice called, "Come on, Waddy, ain't ya gonna buy your ol' pard a drink? Make it three, Sugar."

I turned and stared at my traveling partner from the distant days of my rodeo past. It was almost comical to see how he had aged: no cowboy hat could hide the fact he was bald, his mustache was more white than black and a liberal dose of wax made the ends curl unnaturally. A swarm of lines around his eyes, and across his forehead, made his face appear like a topographical map of the Wallowa Mountains. But sure as the sun comes up in the east, it was Harley Hutchinson; all rough edges and no soft middle.

We exchanged an awkward hug and, having overcome my surprise, I took a step back and exclaimed, "I haven't laid eyes on your sorry ass since Christ was in kindergarten."

I introduced Harley to Jake. They shook hands and Jake returned to his drinking. I asked Harley, "What brings you to town?"

"Rodeo."

"You ain't still ridin'?"

"Not likely. That's fer them young bucks. I team rope."

The barmaid brought our drinks. I laid a twenty on the bar and she turned to make change. Harley nodded in her direction, grunted, "Wouldn't ya love ta plug that matched-set into your ears and listen ta her heart beat?"

We drank and shot the breeze: talked about the weather, the price of feeders, alcohol, mosquitoes, gals we had known and adultery. We talked some about what a tough bastard my Old Man had been and recalled the names and bucking habits of some of his string. We agreed that the best stock came off the Warm Springs Indian reservation because, up to the point when they were rounded up, nobody had ever screwed with those horses.

After we got done talking horses Harley mentioned he had been married five times. "None of 'em took," he claimed, as he pulled at the corners of his mustache. "They was all buckle bunnies. Only one I regret marryin'. She was a gal with kids, three of 'em. Knew it was wrong the minute I tied the knot. Walked straight from the church ta the nearest bar, told the bartender ta give me whatever it was that kilt Hank Williams... only a finger or two less."

The conversation meandered around like the Crooked River crossing the Ochoco Valley and I found myself talking about my confrontation at the 25 Ranch and quitting my job. Harley one-upped me with his own boss-man story. He was famous for that, one-upping a guy.

"This here one time I was feedin' out fer this outfit outta Elko and ever' Sunday the boss man'd come 'round, tell me everythin' I was doin' wrong. When I couldn't stomach it no more I took a butcher knife ta 'im, cut his throat, not 'nough ta kill the dirty prick mind ya, just 'nough ta draw blood."

I believed him because when we had traveled together he was never predictable. He was tethered with two-pound test leader and could break loose at any point. I once saw him walk out of a store with a case of beer slung over his shoulder. The clerk didn't have guts enough to stop him and make him pay. Another time, pulling into John Day, we had to stop for the only stop light in a couple hundred miles. Harley kicked the rig out of gear, unlimbered his rifle and shot out the light. I heard through the grapevine he did a stretch of hard time in a federal penitentiary for all but beating a Mexican kid to death. But that subject never came up.

I asked Harley, "You remember Bones? Used to ride pick-up for my Old Man."

"Good hand. Hard worker. Take a wild bronc an turn him inta a lamb in nothin' flat. Hell yeah, I 'member ol' Bones," he said.

"Well, he was working for me. Today, out of the blue, his heart blew up on him. Sure hate to see a good man go down."

"Don't worry 'bout it, Waddy. Death, she ain't nothin' but a speckled pony." He cackled at that and then was quiet for a moment before adding, "Ya know, I wouldn't mind gettin' in a little trouble." He swung off his stool, sauntered across the room and out the door. The next I saw of him he was propping the door open with a pool cue and coaxing a horse inside. The horse was halfway through the doorway when Harley bellowed, "Hey, Tits, set up a round on the house or I'll 'ave my horse dance on this here pool table."

"Okay! Okay," the barmaid yelled. "Just get him outta here."

When Harley returned, sliding onto the stool beside me, I inquired, "So that's a little bit of trouble. What would you've done to get in a lot of trouble?"

"I wouldn't 'ave asked. I'd just 'a' made 'im dance. Did that once at Molalla. Judge give me 30 days. I was supposed ta buy a new pool table. Never did. An' they ain't never caught up with me."

"Not yet." I grinned.

He grinned, too, but it was short-lived. He punched my arm, "I gotta hell of a good idea. Fer ol' time sakes what say—I'll ride a saddlebronc if you do. Ya game?"

I thought for a moment. What did I have to lose? Besides, the drinks helped to make it seem like a good idea at the time. I told him, "Turn me loose."

"All right! Tits, where's our beer," barked Harley. He turned to me. "What was that you used to say… something 'bout I ain't a bareback rider...?"

I hadn't thought of that saying in forever but remembered it word-for-word. "I ain't a bareback rider, I'm a barebelly rider. Grab a handful of hair and yell, 'Inside.'"

The two of us were off and running. It was just like old times except, twenty years back, when we were still kids, we were probably cuter, funnier and way more loveable.

Way I have it figured—I want my life to be hot or cold but sure as hell not lukewarm. The risks a person assumes are simply the price you're willing to pay for living. Anyway, the kind of living where you squeeze out every last drop before they tighten the screws on your coffin lid. In my estimation, riding a saddlebronc at age forty can't be much more risky than driving rush-hour traffic on the Banfield Freeway.

Harley and I drove several miles out of town to the rodeo grounds, signed up and drew our horses. Mine was named Gravity, which I thought was appropriate since a bronc rider is always fighting the inevitability of gravity. It's never the going up that's the problem, it's the pull of gravity coming down.

We climbed a set of metal stairs over an alleyway and dropped down to where cowboys were already congregating. Most were in various states of undress: busy taping up a bad knee, wrapping an Ace bandage around sore ribs, adding padding to protect a hip pointer. Cowboys were gathered together in a tight group and when I passed I realized they were praying. Harley must have heard them too, because he offered, "Hell, God probably don't even know there's a rodeo goin' on."

There came a clatter of noise—snorting, banging and cussing—and I knew without looking that rough stock was being squeezed down the alley and into the chutes. I leaned against a metal support post, moistened my lips with my tongue and found my mouth as dry as sand. My stomach rattled with hunger, or nervousness, or both. "Ought to grab a hot dog," I said to no one in particular.

Harley stepped forward, leaned over, reached into his boot top, produced a pint bottle and announced, "I done brung dinner." He unscrewed the lid and lifted the bottle to his lips.

Harley still followed the rough stock events, and if anyone knew the idiosyncrasy of a particular bronc it would be Harley. I asked him, "Tell me about Gravity."

Before he said anything, Harley tucked the bottle in the crook of his arm, took a pouch of tobacco from his shirt pocket and began building a cigarette. He plopped the cigarette in his mouth, produced a wooden match from behind his ear, popped the match head with his thumbnail and lit the cigarette. He blew out blue smoke, turned to me and, with his best imitation of seriousness, said, "It'll knock ya down when ya least expect it."

Harley chuckled at what he thought was his wry sense of humor, took another drink and handed me the pint. I wiped the mouth of the bottle on my sleeve. I don't mind following somebody, but in addition to smoking Harley also chewed tobacco and he was sloppy as hell. Second hand tobacco takes a more liberal stomach than I happen to own.

I knocked down a mouthful, handed back the bottle and savored the warmth as the whiskey worked its way toward my toes. I bit off the words, "Naw, come on, what's he do?"

Harley had another drink and once again offered me the bottle, saying, "It'll make the country look greener." I declined. He said, "Gravity? Well now, he's a hammerhead roan. Been 'round the horn a time or two. Got a reputation fer bein' a tad western. Was ta Nationals four in a row. That was a while back. Might just 'ave a good one left in 'im. Big, strong, ain't none too fast. Don't never do nothin' predictable. Bucks consistent. Dandy draw. Wish I had 'im. Ya should finish in the money—if he has a good day and ya happen ta stick."

Harley was up first. He always had to psych himself before he rode and I gave him his space. I went for a short walk and watched a dog leave his signature on the tires of a horse trailer and then on the pickup pulling it. He was followed at a respectful distance by a second dog that sniffed each imprint, lifted his hind leg and deposited his own endorsement.

I got back in time for Harley's ride. No sense wasting a lot of words. He did everything wrong, failed to mark on the way out, lasted one jump and was unceremoniously dumped on his backside. Anyone who saw the wreck knew it had to hurt, but while he was in the arena Harley never limped or changed expression. A round of polite applause rose from the stands. Harley reached the chute, climbed up and over the railing, dropped down and immediately went to one knee. His face contorted in pain and the corners of his mustache drooped like a hound dog's ears. I was concerned enough to ask, "You okay, partner?"

He blew out a humph of air, shook his head to clear the cobwebs, stood and said, "Swear ta God, sometimes it seems like I'm left-handed on both sides." He dug the bottle from his boot and drained it.

Before he walked away, Harley slapped me on the back and told me, "Give 'em hell, Waddy. Show 'em what yur made of."

I felt for Harley. Out west, when you travel with a man and drink with a man, there are going to be times when the going gets tough and you have no choice but to share your partner's pain. I tried to put that behind me and get my head screwed on straight. If there is one thing I know how to do, it is how to handle a bronc. I'd been riding wild stock since I was twelve and I told myself I could sure as hell handle this dick-bender. The bite of adrenaline seeped into my blood stream and brought with it a great revelation—lately I'd been about as restless for a change as a stud horse in a box stall. It was pretty damn obvious I needed a fix: something big to happen, to get me up and going, headed in the right direction. Maybe I thought Cheyenne would provide whatever it was I yearned for. Then, I might have thought that telling the boss to shove his job sideways up his ass would do the trick. Truth was, neither had been the jolt I needed. Maybe a kick-ass bronc would punch my ticket.

It's my opinion that any man who rides strictly for the payday is as worthless as tits on a boar. I've always ridden for the fun. When I did catch a payday it only meant I could afford to go a few more miles, hit a few more rodeos. Sure, I did it some for the glory and some for the girls, but mostly for the challenge of pitting myself against the strengths of an animal. Climb aboard and you never know what's gonna happen: horse or bull could fall in the chute, go down in the arena, roll on you, hook you, might be a hundred other things. The fun part has always been the ride and being able to compress a bunch of living into the span of eight seconds.

There aren't a lot of men who ride all three rough-stock events. Takes a special breed and I felt privileged to have, for a few short years, been one of them. Saddlebronc always has been a technique event. If you ride right it makes the rankest horse look easy. Bareback winners are determined by the man with the most gas, the one willing to let it all hang out—take chances—make the ride or get throwed. If you're gonna ride bulls you've got to be a little bit, a whole lot, crazy. On top of that, you need nerves of steel and the ability to think ahead, react fast, not hang up, get off clean and dodge danger without getting stepped on, or hooked in the back.

Ain't easy competing in three rough-stock events. Lots of times, after getting slammed in saddlebronc or bareback, it was hard as hell for me to come back and crawl on a bull. Bottom line, you gotta love it. Love it all. I never wanted to be just a bronc rider or just a bull rider—I wanted to be an all-around hand.

I found my feet on the metal chute railing, standing spraddle-legged above the big roan horse still shedding his coarse winter hair. I measured my bronc rein—not enough rein and a horse will pull you over his head. Too much and you flop around like a carp tossed on the riverbank. I ripped loose a few strands of mane hair and, after using my hand and thumb to determine the correct hold, I slipped the hair into the weave of my bronc rein. I've always done that. A little trick I picked up along the way.

The cowboy in the chute behind me went out with a bang of steel, sharp grunts and shouts of encouragement. I eased my weight onto the saddle. The big horse flinched and tried to shy but there was nowhere for him to go. The announcer, his galvanized voice rattling the speakers, was introducing me, saying I was a local cowboy, coming out of retirement after a ten-year break. I tried to get comfortable, but Gravity came alive, lunging and fighting. He struggled and tried to come out over the top. It was a dangerous situation because if he went down, or I slipped off, I could be killed in the chute. Hands reached down and pulled me to safety.

Retirement. I remember when I quit. I was still winning, but the road was getting harder to handle. It had come to the point where the juice just wasn't worth the squeeze. I was tired of too much month and not enough money, all-night red-eye drives, eating road dust, midnight motels and trying to catch forty winks on the shoulder of the road. My mind wanted to keep going, but my body was saying whoa. I wasn't healing like I used to. I was hurting all the time and didn't want to be like a racehorse that crosses the finish line and doesn't have enough sense to quit running. So, I bunched it.

For a few months I drank way too much and chased the ladies way too hard. Then I took a job calving out 500 head of heifers. The ranch was way back in the hills, real remote. There was a big pen for working cattle and a round corral for breaking horses. There was plenty of good hay and enough work to keep three men busy. I lived in a cough drop shaped travel trailer. It had old tires on the roof to hold down the black plastic. No electricity. Packed water. Ate straight out of the frying pan. Pissed off the porch. Shit in an outhouse.

Shot tin cans out the trailer house door. Wasn't a living soul within thirty miles. All the burdens of civilization I had been carrying on my back while following the rodeo circuit fell away like feathers off a molting hen. Hell, it was just what the doctor ordered. I dried out on fresh air and wide-open range.

Gravity settled down. Once again I crawled over the chute railing and began to ease my weight onto the saddle. I found my mark on the bronc rein, took a deep breath and reassured myself, "Everything is gonna work out fine, just like it always has." I was as ready as I was ever gonna be.

"Take a deep seat and screw down your hat, cowboy," someone hollered.

The announcer was saying something about my Old Man having been a prominent rodeo contractor, but I missed most of it. I nodded to the man on the gate. The gate didn't open. I barked, "Outside." The gate swung wide on hinges in need of a squirt of WD-40.

Gravity lunged into the opening and I kept the rowels of Bones' gal-legged spurs firmly planted in thick shoulder muscles. It was strange how serene it all appeared at that moment and, even though images came flying at me rapid fire like an explosion of grainy black and white photographs, I was acutely aware of everything: the jolting power between my knees, the horse's brusque grunts, the biting snap of leather against leather. Dust stung my nostrils. I smelled horse sweat and tasted grit between my teeth. I was conscious of the sun about to set behind the Three Sisters, the stark silhouette of Black Butte and the chocolate brown dirt of the arena. A collective roar filled my ego.

Gravity got right with the program, was flashy as hell and just to show I wasn't some front-row Joe, I turned my toes east-west and raked him from shoulders to cinch strap. My muscles responded to the horse's movements with speed, rhythm, execution, timing. The horn sounded but I never eased off the throttle and as I made a showboat pass in front of the high-priced seats, the crowd leaped to their feet and cheered.

Back in the old days my signature to a great saddlebronc ride was to hear the horn and allow the final buck to launch me into a spectacular dismount. I was famous for it long before Monty "Hawkeye" Henson came on the scene with his flying dismount and stole the show at the PRCA Finals in Las Vegas.

I had to stop myself from giving it a go. Hell, I was forty years old and it would be plumb loco for me to try such a stupid stunt. Off even a hair, I'd get launched into the stratosphere and they'd clean me up with a fork and spoon. But God, I had made such an impressive ride I had to do something. I whipped off my Stetson and waved it.

The Dodge pickup men were there, one on either side, squeezing in. One man unsnapped the flank strap. I swung off onto the rump of the other horse and dropped to the ground as neatly as you please. In a theatrical display I bowed to the crowd like a grandstanding fool, and drank in their applause. What the hell, I had it coming. I was at the top of my game. I felt bigger than life.

I dropped down behind the chutes. Harley pounded my chest with an open hand as the voice of the announcer was rattling off my score. Harley bellowed, "Guess ya can still cut the mustard, ya ol' fart. Eighty-six! Hell of a ride! Ya done won it."

It had been a long time since I had felt the adoration of so many and I reveled in the compliments and well wishes of the cowboys around me. Hell, I milked it for all it was worth. By then the bulls were being run down the alleyway. The bull riders, a bunch of young bucks with bright clothes, long hair and puffed up egos, were busy rosining their ropes, trying to pump up their courage to face a ton of nastiness that just might kill them. I was old news and knew it.

Even before the rodeo was over I was saying good-by to Harley. He was headed to the next show in Reno, Nevada. I hated like hell to see him go because I didn't know when, or if, I'd ever see him again. As I watched him amble toward his pickup, Sam's boy, Travis, came running up, jumped into my arms and told me, "You sure done good. You made Mamma cry."

I held Travis in one arm, tousled his blond hair with my free hand and looked around for Sam, figuring it was likely I was still number one on her shit list. And then she was there, hugging Travis and me at the same time, whispering in my ear how proud she was of me and what a great ride I had made. Even Joleen managed, "Way to go," which was as lofty a compliment as she could muster.

I returned Travis to the ground. Sam came close, hooked her fingers inside my belt and pulled herself close to me. I was half-expecting her to punch me, payback for my misbehavior, but apparently that little incident was nothing more than a tiny black mark, all but forgotten. She cooed, "Come home with me."

Maybe if it had been just the two of us I'd have dragged her off for a beer and a celebratory blanket party. But kids change things. You can't do what you want to do. Spontaneity flies out the window. So, my first inclination was to blow Sam off. "I don't know."

It's never been easy for me to tell a gal how I feel about her, to say too much and tip my hand. I like to play my tender side pretty close to my vest. I suppose the best way to describe my feelings for Sam at that precise moment, is to tell a story. Once, written with drippy white paint on a rock wall out of Mitchell, I saw this romantic missive, "Glena, a little more than most." That's exactly how I felt about Sam. To me she was a little more than most.

She tried to entice me. "I've been saving a couple T-bone steaks for a special occasion. Let me fix dinner for you."

Still, I hesitated, although my stomach was definitely beginning to weaken. A good steak, passed over the fire a time or two, is hard to beat. Besides, Sam could definitely cook and I knew she would fix that steak with all the trimmings.

She lowered her voice and leaned close. "I heard what happened at the ranch. You can't keep everything you own in the back of your pickup. Why not store things at my place. You can turn Charley loose. I've got plenty of pasture that's just going to waste."

I rolled recent events over in my mind and figured I must have set a world record—going from asshole to hero in the shortest amount of time. Hand it to Sam, she was able to step away from something and not carry a barrel of bitterness forward. She was unlike any woman I had ever known. But to be honest, for me, the clincher was free pasture. I had to do something with Charley. I told her, "Alright, I'll be there after a little while."

She brushed her moist lips across my cheek. Travis gave me another hug. Joleen pouted, acting as if her life had become an incredibly boring movie that she was being required to watch. And then they were gone.

I collected my money, which was a bigger payday than winning an All-Around in my prime, moseyed over to the beer garden, not so much because I needed a drink but hey, face it, the sun doesn't shine on every dog every day. After milking the 'atta boys' for an hour or so I departed, swinging by the Country Store at the junction for a half-rack to go. By then I was easing my way toward a beer-drinking mood.

Sam had a five-acre ranchette near enough to the expanding city limits of Redmond to see the glow of streetlights. It was impossible to miss the turnoff because, up tight to the fence, her neighbor had a stack of hay with a red, white and blue tarp stretched over it. It had to be the most patriotic haystack in the U. S. of A.

I pulled into Sam's driveway and noticed groceries on the steps to the house, an eight-pack of toilet paper peeking out the top of the brown paper sack. I grabbed the sack. Sam met me at the screen door. She was drying her hands on an apron adorned with cute little pigs. I shot her a perfunctory, "Howdy, Babe," and she eyed me with a look she might typically reserve for a new car parked in her driveway, with a certain amount of pride in ownership. She opened the screen door enough to reach through and take the sack, saying, "Thanks, Hon."

In my heart I knew this woman was everything a fellow could ask for. She could be as soft, sweet, and as enjoyable as a July shower. On the other hand, as she had proven the night before, she could be as sharp-edged and dangerous as a chunk of obsidian. All the same, she was a catch, a keeper. I told myself that.

In a physical sense Sam was well put together. Her most striking attribute was the red highlights and streaks of bottled blond swirling like rogue waves through her ocean of hair. Despite having had two kids, her body was relatively firm, waist tapered above her hips and her breasts had not begun to sag, or if they had, it wasn't noticeable, not yet. She had high cheekbones and a dusky complexion that could have come from Indian blood, back several generations. Her eyes were almond colored, nose as straight as a plowshare, and she had perfect teeth. I never got tired of her looks. Whenever she was around, she made my world seem a little sunnier. Enough said.

With her arms wrapped around the sack of groceries she leaned toward me and planted a quick peck on my lips. "Good timing. Potatoes are almost ready. I'll start the steaks." As she turned to go inside, I patted her familiar behind with an open hand.

In her wake, and before the screen door even had a chance to slam shut, Travis, a bundle of pure energy, shot through the opening, hollering as he came, "Can I ride? Can I?"

"You bet," I assured him.

I swung the trailer gate open, warning Travis, "Step back." Charley, anxious to unload, came out in a dangerous commotion of flying legs and excited nickers. I told him, "Calm down, boy," waited a moment and tossed Travis onto his back. Travis wrapped his fingers into the coarse mane and sat there beaming while Charley, wanting to be on the move, impatiently shifted his weight from foot to foot.

"Ready to go?"

Travis shook his head no. "Not yet. Let me get used to him. Boy, he's a lot different than Nibbles."

Nibbles was Sam's barrel horse. Years ago he had been a solid mount, fast and sure-footed, but he had gotten old and died around the first of the year. Sam, in tears and not knowing what to do, called me. I brought the backhoe from the ranch, dug a hole in the pasture and buried the horse there. I looked in that direction, to where a circle of sheep wire protected a mound of red dirt planted to wildflowers. The fence kept out the two pet goats, Gus and Joyce, a Suffolk ewe, Mandy, and a rooster named Socrates. Why is it that women and kids feel duty-bound to name every living creature?

"Okay, I'm ready. Giddy-up," Travis told me. I led Charley through the open gate, gave Travis a hand down and turned Charley lose. He shook his head and galloped around the pastures until he found a dust bed and rolled. He stood and shivered like a big dog shaking water.

Socrates, commanding the top of the manure pile, crowed. I told him, "Don't be waking me at daylight. Tomorrow you sleep in."

"He don't lay eggs," Travis commented.

"He's a rooster. Hens lay eggs, roosters don't."

"Why's that?"

"Ask your momma," I said. "Say, how about I give you a ride to the house?"

"Oh boy!"

I tossed Travis onto my back, played like I was a bronc, bucking and then trying to rub him off on the door jam. Once inside I sent him down the hall, telling him, "Go wash up."

The house was filled with delicious smells. I realized how hungry I was as I angled past the mounted head of the 9th largest mule deer ever killed in Oregon. It adorned the wall, not as a trophy of a skillful hunter, but because Sam won it in court. Her ex-husband had killed the old mossyback. However, he had been forced to use her tag because his had already been filled on a lesser buck. Sam told this story in court and the judge awarded her possession of the trophy head. She kept it, but claimed she planned to give it back to her ex-husband someday. Someday hadn't come.

Sam met me, handed me a whiskey and water, just the way I like it. A pair of T-bone steaks sizzled on her Jenn-Air grill. The fan was not able to keep up and the smoke alarm squealed. I waved my hat over the annoying device and the noise stopped. In addition to the steaks I smelled onions, mushrooms, potatoes and corn. The dinner salad, in a bowl on the countertop, was already made. There was a candle on the table and plates waiting for food.

"Anything I can do?"

"You can light the candle."

I had been to the house a few dozen times. Usually when Sam and I were together we went to a movie, or a bar, and ended the evening at the ranch or a motel. I had stayed at her house only when her children were gone. I had eaten at her place on Thanksgiving and again at Christmas. I didn't know where to begin looking for matches. Sam read my mind, told me, "Top drawer on the left. Right there." Her hands were full. She pointed with a nod.

As I lit the candle I noticed there were only three plates on the table and called into the other room, "Where's Joleen?"

"Spending the night with a friend. She's had it planned for a week. I was going to have her come home but...."

"Not on my account," I said, returning to the kitchen.

"I knew that's what you'd say." She shot me a smile that said I was an open book.

I removed my hat, tossed it on old mossyback and pulled one of the straight-backed chairs around so I could look into the kitchen. I took a seat and squinted at Sam as she made efficient movements, ladling food from pans into bowls and onto serving plates.

"I know you better than you think I do," Sam said and teased me with her brown eyes. I leaned back on two legs of the straight-backed chair, nursed the whiskey and frowned because one thing I pride myself on is being predictably unpredictable. As I studied her I thought how different the two of us were. I still had the bark on. She was a peeled pole. She could play the piano and the guitar. I always wished I was musically inclined but the closest I came to it was turning on a radio. I liked to travel. She was rooted to one spot, never went much of anywhere. Her bedroom was persuasively feminine with a canopy bed, ruffles and a furry rug. I was content to bunk wherever I ended up at the end of the day. She was blissfully domesticated. I was brush-wise and mountain-smart, had a taste for the rough country and the wide-open spaces. No doubt a lot of what I did, and what I liked, were things I had brought forward from my mustanging days.

Travis burst into the room drying his hands on his shirt, announcing, "I want to sit next to Waddy. Can I, Mom, please?"

"Sure," I told him, pulling him onto my lap and ruffling his hair. I have to admit, with the smells of cooking in the warm air, the glow of the candlelight, a good-looking gal moving with a graceful swish of her hips and a little partner on my lap, the moment was as sweet as a freshly cooked batch of wild strawberry jam. If I could stay put in time and nothing ever changed, I might be willing to shed my skin. But the thought of wearing someone's brand made me cringe. Trade in freedom for a set of left-hand rings and the next thing I knew there'd be "*his*" and "*her*" towels in the bathroom, "*honey-dos*" in a jar and I'd be standing over a backyard barbecue flipping burgers and wearing an apron that read, "*Chief Cook and Bottle Washer.*" Thoughts like that tend to sober a fella quicker than most anything else.

Chapter 3

Play the cards you're dealt. Remember, life ain't nothin' but a penny ante game. Bully and bluff when you're short. Bet like a dirty bastard when you're long. (Barton Wilder)

A deer with hind legs caught in a fence must, at some point, contemplate its own mortality. And like that deer, I found myself sitting on a stool at the counter of the Gallery restaurant in Sisters, hung up in the barbed wire of my lackadaisical existence. A week had gone by without me making a move. I blew a slew of wrinkles across the surface of my hot coffee and mulled over the rather obvious fact that I needed to get on with my life—catch on at some remote ranch or settle down, make an honest woman of Sam and take whatever job came my way.

I was lifting my cup, fixing to take a sip, when Jay, the postmaster, plopped down on the stool beside me. He said, "Got something for you."

I took that sip, returned the coffee cup to the table and held it with both hands. "What is it?"

"General delivery letter."

"IRS or some damn worthless attorney? I don't want it. Throw it away."

"Can't do that. Anyway, this one looks interesting. Pretty handwriting and smells like a goddamn French whorehouse. Come get it before it stinks up the joint and my wife starts accusing me of having an affair."

I tried to think who the sender might be and quickly boiled it down to maybe a dozen gals who might have sent me the letter. For something to do, and being curious, I followed Jay to the post office. He handed me the letter. I thanked him, went outside, leaned against a big ponderosa pine and rather than look at the sender's address or the handwriting, I simply smelled the envelope. It was Cheyenne's perfume. I caught myself smirking as I slit the envelope tab with my pocketknife and dug out the letter.

Waddy,

Don't know where to begin except to let you know I'm living in Alaska. My husband, I figured you knew I was married, works on the pipeline. He stays out six weeks at a time.

I met a man (just an acquaintance) who owns a big ranch on an island off the coast of Alaska. He's looking for a cowboy to run it and I told him about you. He's in the oil business and loaded. It might be worth your while to talk to him.

Call me and I'll give you his number. I hope you do come up. Please call even if you're not interested in the job.

Love ya, Cheyenne

She had written her phone number at the bottom of the page and I memorized it. The flowery scrawl of her handwriting, the fragrance of her perfume and vivid memories from the night of my birthday, made me want to rush to the nearest pay phone. But I resisted the temptation.

I figured to wait a day or two: let morality and immorality fight it out. See which one came out on top. Besides, there was something that needed my immediate attention. It had to get done.

The following morning I kicked back the covers long before daylight and started pulling on my clothes. Sam rolled over and tried to coax me back to bed. "It's the middle of the night, Sweetie. Snuggle with me."

"Gotta get a move on," I told her, and then added a line that my Old Man was fond of saying, "There's cats to kill and fish to fry, trees to chop and ground to scratch."

"You're killing cats?" She wasn't quite awake.

"Go back to sleep. I'll catch you later."

"Want breakfast?"

"Naw." I planted a kiss on her forehead to keep her in bed and hastily departed. At the front door I paused, listening to the squeak of bedsprings as Travis rolled over, gathering strength for another day of mayhem. Why is it that kids always seem to take up so much space when they are awake, but when asleep they seem so very small and insignificant?

Under the perpetual glow of the nightlight I loaded Charley while the neighborhood dogs, aroused from their slumbers, carried on with rapid-fire barking. As I pulled away and my pickup's headlights began to tunnel into the darkness, I felt a sense of relief at actually tackling this disconcerting task. Once it was over, I could move on to more important matters.

The stars were out and busy as butterflies, making the night seem even bigger, thicker, blacker. On the seat next to me was Bones, or at least the urn containing his ashes. We traveled in passive silence, a pair of sixty-mile-per-hour cowboys riding side-by-side one last time.

I twisted the knob on the radio, dialed in a talk show out of San Francisco and allowed the voices to ramble with the clatter of my old pickup. Ahead, the aluminum foil highway unrolled and off to either side my headlights picked up the scruffy dandruff of billboards and advertising signs announcing the burgeoning city of Bend. I thought about the way the beautiful ponderosa pine forest that once surrounded town had been shaved close for studs and rafters, decking and toilet paper. Natural gas, electric, water and sewer lines now laced the soil and houses-with-a-view were creeping up the sloping face of Aubrey Butte. The glut of subdivisions surrounding Bend had encroached on ancient elk and deer migration corridors. The animals were being forced to timidly thread their way through a maze of backyards, fences and roads to reach their traditional ranges.

In summer, the mountains and high lakes above Bend along Century Drive, were clogged with adolescents of every age engrossed in vacation play. Active folks hiked, biked, boated and rode around on ATVs: Kawasakis, Yamahas, Suzukis, Hondas, Arctic Cats—green, red, blue, black, tan, all churning up dust, kicking up gravel—rider's hands locked on handlebars, cold beers in coolers strapped snugly down with black rubber cargo straps, bouncing over loggerheads, running off birds and game animals.

Couples in their retirement years, deeply tanned and enjoying fat pensions, sipped alcoholic drinks and force-fed each other fun because they had used up their productive years. And, by God, didn't they deserve it?

Young couples paraded around with fat-legged babies in Pampers strapped on their backs like papooses in cradleboards. They slept or bawled. Kids played. Mosquitoes bit. Camp robbers flew away with scraps from picnic tables. Chipmunks gorged themselves on nutrition-less snacks. The warm summer playground spun in repetitive circles of sameness.

In winter, the merry-go-round of fun continued: skiers taking over, downhill and cross-country. And those same recreational opportunists who rode ATVs switched to snowmobiles and jetted up slopes on screaming machines, kicking up rooster-tails, leaving in their wake packed contrails across snowfields of virgin white.

In truth, Bend and the surrounding area was no different from Boise, Elko, Ogden, Bozeman or Great Falls. All the great little cities of the West were on the fast track to becoming big cities, and the sleepy insignificant towns were awakening and working on becoming little cities. It has been going on, this westward shift in population, ever since Ma and Pa loaded the kids in the covered wagon and pointed the oxen toward the setting sun. Pick any western city, tune in the local radio or television stations and be distressed by the same depressing news—murders, rapes, drug deals gone sour, police killings, pileups on freeways, jackknifed trucks, train derailments and poisonous clouds of smog blowing across the landscape.

Out in the rural area this wonderful evolution called progress has brought us western forests in designated wilderness areas. Drawings for big game hunting tags—you're lucky to get to hunt a bull elk once every five years—and the last salmon swam into the Columbia River at high tide and smacked its nose into yet another dam.

In the heart of Bend, I made a sharp left turn and headed east. My Old Man used to say that back fifty or sixty years ago, this highway stretching across the High Desert to Burns and beyond, was so seldom traveled if you did happen to meet someone you always stopped and visited. It wasn't like that anymore. Even in the early morning hours I was confronted by a steady stream of traffic: mostly trucks, an occasional car and now and then a sporadic motor home, whistling the air as they passed, drivers in a hurry to be anywhere but on this lonely road. It occurred to me that every highway is like an artery. Traffic represents the blood cells coursing along the narrow passageway. All I had to do was ease up, pull onto the shoulder, park and watch the bloodstream roll.

I found a new radio station playing golden oldies. I knew most of the songs. A jackrabbit crossed the road and just before it reached safety it glanced into my headlights and its eyes glowed like iridescent jade. Later, I saw a burrowing owl eating roadkill, a mouse most likely. Upon my approach, the owl bobbed its teeny body up and down and swayed side-to-side. It never did fly.

The eastern sky must have made a deal with the sun to launch a new day, because a thin rim of sky behind the Ochoco Mountains slowly began to come alive, glowing faintly with defused light. The first color I could identify was teal, ebbing through a pastel pallet of blues, yellows and greens, finally seeping into an appealing red, the color of wild plum meat. The radio station faltered and spit static. I turned it off, rode along listening to the customary rattles of my pickup and the steady hum of tires spinning across the ribbon of asphalt. I was tired and I yawned a time or two, contemplating that at any given time roughly half the world was light and the other dark. At that moment I was a 'tweener sliding between the extremes, flanked by brilliance and blackness. That notion could not sustain itself. I yawned again. My eyelids were as heavy as if bricks were attached to them. My thinking became random, hit and miss—give me a strong V-8 and not some little four-banger rice-burner. Piss on gas mileage. Let the next generation worry about how they're gonna get around. A country dog can identify sounds and if someone is coming, it will either bark or wag its tail while the owner is still straining his eyes to see who the hell it might be. Every buckaroo I know can vouch for the fact it's a hell of a lot easier to break a bronc, pound in a string of fence posts, or stretch barbed wire to the top of the hill and tie it off, than it is to sit down and write a letter....

I caught a wink of movement and wasn't sure if it was a coyote slinking away, a wily ghost, or a hunk of wind-blown hair. Blond hair. Cheyenne. I chuckled, reined in my roving imagination and forced myself to think about Sam. Sam was a damn fine cook. My mouth salivated at the memory of that T-bone steak. Suddenly I was hungry and wished I'd stopped for breakfast—too late. I had passed the last sign of civilization a long way back.

I'll give Sam her due—she was about as broadminded as any woman I've ever known. On the night I won the saddlebronc event at the Sisters Rodeo, after Travis was asleep, she and I had sat on the sofa and had a long-winded conversation. The subjects varied: what I planned to do about employment, where I saw myself living, how I felt about her and her kids, that sort of thing. Finally she got around to the topic of my infidelity. She was levelheaded about it, never cried. It would have been easier if she had. Then I could have given up and gone to bed.

I had to tell her, "Well, it ain't like we're married." It was a good point.

"Maybe not, but I thought you had more respect for me than that."

She had me there. Even my college learning, two years at Blue Mountain Community College and two additional terms at Oregon State University, wasn't going to be of benefit in my effort to piece together an explanation. I knew whatever I might chance to offer was only going to put me deeper in the shit pile. I simply shrugged my shoulders. "What do you want me to say?"

"Tell me you're sorry."

"I am sorry, but...." She put a finger to my lips and told me "Shhh." She got up, pulled me to my feet and hugged me in a clumsy, one-armed embrace. I felt the upturned tilt of her hip, the way she used it as leverage, and the distinct pressure of a breast pushed against me. She broke off the hug, took my hand and tugged me down the hall to her bedroom. I was forgiven.

Memories dimmed as I drove full-blast toward the emerging sun, now infusing nearby clouds with dazzling splashes of yellows and reds. When the sun broke the plane of the horizon I was momentarily blinded and had to tug down the brim of my Stetson in order to see the highway.

Glancing to the left I caught the reflected image in the rear-view mirror of the snow-capped Cascades lined up north-south like jagged teeth on a pearly white saw. I slowed, veered away from the pavement and onto a dirt road. A band of grazing antelope threw up their heads, wheeled into flight and curled off to the west and away from me. To the east, shimmering rays of sunlight danced across the ground and lightly fingered silvery necklaces strung by spiders in branches of the slick, gray-green sage. This road I traveled would bump and twist for better than a hundred miles, terminating at the town of Wagontire, population 2.

I rode on, giving thanks to the Man Upstairs that Bones had been allowed to live out his days doing pretty much what he had wanted. I told myself that the best we can hope for in this life is to work at what we love best, stay healthy, eat, drink with friends, enjoy ourselves in the sack and if we're lucky, real lucky, get out of this world without a whole lot of pain. If a man like Bones, or really any of us, can't exist on those terms, then why go through the motions? What the hell's the use?

When I was young, I thought life would go on forever. One day leading to another, and another, and another. Lately, I've learned to place a value on basic survival. My view of life may be somewhat naive. I believe experience is the best teacher. A person lives and gathers up experiences, puts them together like pieces of a jigsaw puzzle and pretty soon you start to see the big picture. It's like this: bang your head against a wall and you learn it hurts to bang your head against a wall. You don't bang your head against a wall any more. That's what I'm talking about.

Another thing, I think it's important for a fellow to keep doing what he enjoys for as long as he can. I hate it when someone tells me he only has ten years, or two years, before he can retire. A man retires and he loses direction. When the only thing a fellow has to look forward to is checking his lucky number at Bi-Mart every Tuesday, to see if he has won a can of cherries or a package of coconut cookies, something is definitely wrong. In my book, you retire and you might as well fall backwards into the grave, pull dirt over yourself and have it done with.

Bones was never the type to retire. How many times had the two of us enjoyed the simple pleasures: taking turns packing snuff under our stained lips, leaning against a fender of a pickup truck and shooting the breeze with a friend we met along the road, watching the flight of wild geese, a sage grouse dancing, a big buck sauntering over the hill trailing a herd of does. We never gave a second thought to the time we squandered.

I pulled off the dirt road and parked in front of the crude outline of a homesteader's shack. The paintless boards, washed by the rain and wind and blistered by the sharp, keen sun were giving off a thin veil of silver steam that ascended into the chilly air. I cranked the window down, drew a breath and imagined I could smell the rot of decaying wood and sense the hopelessness of the homesteader who wasted years trying to make a go of this place. If I were to kill the engine, I would likely hear the rustle of the pack rat family living under the floor and the woodpecker when he came to hammer the wood. I watched mud swallows make dizzy sashays in the sky, working to rebuild their nest under the eves, and I caught a slight whiff of the sweet fragrance from the yellow rosebush planted beside the back door, kept alive in infancy by tubs of rinse water dumped there by the homesteader's wife.

I dropped Molly in gear, let out the clutch and a couple miles later we thumped over the cattle guard dividing two grazing allotments. Here the soil, thinned by ten thousand years of wind pulling loose dirt and sand and blowing it eastward toward the Rocky Mountains, showed chunks of bedrock. A few old cows and their yearling calves rested around a salt lick and I looked at them with a practiced eye for diphtheria, pink eye, cancer, bag problems, hoof troubles....

The calves weren't even branded. Run them through a squeeze chute. Catch the head. Flip out the bar so the calf can be branded—left hip. Hair smoking. Iron burning. Neck stretching. Eyes rolling. Gray tongue lolling. Bawling. Pain driving slimy green shit down the calf's back legs. There are waddles to cut in the throat, a nick to take out of an ear—marks and identifications. Shots. Castrations. Dehornings. Powder to keep the flies away.

For me there has always been a certain satisfaction associated with working cattle. At the end of a long day you look at a pen and know all the cattle there are as healthy as you can make them. I get the same feeling working the ratchet on a fence stretcher. It's almost a religious experience to take wire to the crown of a hill and stretch it tight. The wind blows, the barbed wire sings and to me it's like a harp being played by an angel. I know this seems a contradiction in my character, because I really do hate fences. But if I'm the one who built the fence, and I know the work that has gone into it, then I love it. It's not that I fail to recognize the necessity of a fence, I do, but it's hard to accept the reality that fences limit the free-roaming spirit—an obstacle that either keeps you in, or shuts you out.

The names of the High Desert landmarks tell of the country's history and topography: Bakeoven, Rawhide, Crooked River, Poison Creek, Stinkingwater, Dead Indian Butte, Wild Horse Ridge, Happy Valley... every one is a story. I pulled off at Crazy Creek, named back in the 1880s when a hunter by the name of Tuffy Crawford came upon a sheepherder running in circles and leaping wildly in the air. At first, Tuffy thought the herder had slipped a cog, but it turned out he had not seen another human being in three long months. At the sight of Tuffy he was so overcome with joy he momentarily went crazy. Tuffy named the long, narrow, waterless draw, that every hundred years or so saw a trickle of water, Crazy Creek.

One time Bones and I were riding and he told me his most favorite place of all was Crazy Creek. I remember him saying, "Ain't nobody gonna fuck up this place 'cause there ain't nothin' out here the world wants."

After he made that proclamation he went into one of his coughing jags, where it almost seemed he was trying to turn himself inside-out. About the time I thought he had succeeded, he got it under control and, while the last few spasms were running their course, he dug in his shirt pocket, produced a cigarette paper and a sack of Bull Durham and proceeded to roll, then light and smoke a cigarette. Hell, it wasn't the tobacco that triggered Bones' heart attack. Nope, I figure the world just finally succeeded in squeezing all the life out of him.

I reached and touched the urn. The glass was cool and smooth against my fingertips. I spoke to Bones, telling him, "I'm gonna miss you, you old bow-legged bastard." I left him there on the seat, climbed out of my rig, dropped Charley from the trailer, took the slack out of the cinch, tied it off and swung onto the saddle. I reined Charley close to my rig, opened the door, leaned in and retrieved the urn. I stuffed the bulky object inside my coat.

We traveled the dry bed of Crazy Creek and Charley rhythmically jingled his bit as he chewed on something he found in his back teeth. I thought about Bones and him telling me how he got tagged with his nickname. It came from a windy, a tall tale, he once told at buckaroo camp. The story was about a cowboy, out in the hills, with his horse and cow dog. The horse stepped in a badger hole and went down, throwing the cowboy and breaking his leg and pelvis. The horse ran off. The cowboy tried to walk but was too buggered-up to do anything but crawl. Finally, in order to stay alive, he was forced to kill and eat his dog. As he was finishing his last meal he shook his head and muttered, "Ah, Blackie, ya was a mighty fine dog. Wish ya was still around 'cause ya would've really enjoyed these bones."

The story hit the buckaroos as offensive and in such bad taste that they immediately bestowed the nickname Bones on the man with the God-given name of Martin Mobley. The reason I knew his name was because I saw it on a check my Old Man had written. I asked him who the hell was Martin Mobley and he told me.

I levered open my coat, pried the urn free, eased the cork from the narrow neck and, remembering a few lines from Ian Tyson's song, *Fifty Years Ago*, I sang and hummed them to the desert: the jackrabbits and deer, songbirds and sand, sagebrush and juniper.

"If I could roll back the years, back when I was young and limber, loose as ashes in the wind, I had no irons in the fire. I could ride them wild young broncos, the adrenalin came quickly, and Juanita down at Mona's was my only hearts desire... hum-hum-hum-hum-hum-hum-hum... *And the sighing of the pines, up here near the timberline, makes me wish I'd done things different. Ah, but wishin' don't make it so. The time has passed so quick, the years all run together now. Did I hold Juanita yesterday? Was it fifty years ago...?"*

Bones had buckarooed in the days of the wide-open range. Now a man was lucky to travel twenty or thirty miles before he had to either look for a gate, or pull staples from the posts, let down wires and cross over. I heard a noise, looked in that direction and saw a range cow emerge from a brushy thicket. She saw us, wheeled and ran. I suspected she was a barren old hide and it had been a fair number of years since she had used her horns to keep the coyotes away from a newborn calf as it awkwardly attempted to rise from its puddle of afterbirth. The cow was well nourished, but not fat because she had to walk so far to fill her belly. At least the grasses she found were rich with nutrients, not like on the west side of the mountains where I've seen cows all but starve on weak grass tall enough to tickle their underbellies.

Using teeth and tongue to make a quick "click-click" I moved Charley into a trot and, with a tickle of my spurs, into a hard gallop. He leaped the wash that was Crazy Creek and, using this as the starting point, I poured the dry remains from the urn. Charcoal chunks and fine gray powder dusted the wind. Even after the urn was empty we kept traveling fast. Finally I chucked the empty vessel against an imposing boulder. The dark glass exploded in a shower of brittle fragments.

I hauled back on the reins. Charley slid to a stop. My breathing was forceful, like a piston slapping up and down in a cylinder. I made a conscious effort to take in a breath and hold it. When I exhaled, the air came out as a raspy groan, an acknowledgement I supposed, of my heartache, my loss. A raven, from somewhere on a hidden perch, imitated me with a low, mournful cry. A thin flight of Canada geese traipsed silently down the turquoise sky, appearing like a school of fish swimming across a tidal pool. Chunks of sagebrush, as sharp and brittle as chicken bones, stuck straight up through the sandy skin of the earth. A herd of mustangs, having been spooked, were long gone but a thin cloud of dust lingered like a golden haze along the top of the ridge. I laid the reins across Charley's neck, leaned a forearm on the saddle horn and just sat there, missing my friend.

Chapter 4

Son, this ol' world has very few good women—ones who can cook and are always hot for sex—make sure you get a good one. (Kelsey Wilder)

After my demanding morning I could have gone directly to Sam's place, probably should have gone directly to Sam's place, but instead drove forty miles to the nearest bar. After three or four shots the devil won out and I grabbed a fistful of change from the barmaid, stepped to the pay phone and dialed the number Cheyenne had written at the bottom of the letter she sent me. The operator connected me to Alaska. The phone rang once. Cheyenne picked up and across twenty-five hundred miles of wilderness she breathed a torrid, "Hello."

"Howdy, Babe. Got your letter. Thought I'd just give a call."

"Waddy! I was beginning to wonder if you were ever going to get back to me. It's so great to hear your voice."

I was flattered, and it only got better because Cheyenne seemed so excited and apparently was so genuinely happy to hear from me. We exchanged pleasantries and small talk and she made a special point of revealing the fact her husband was away from home, working on the pipeline, and would be gone for the next five weeks.

"Any chance of you coming up?" she purred.

Before I could answer the operator butted in, wanting more cash for the next three minutes. I fed coins into the money-gobbling machine, and waited until the operator was off the line before getting down to brass tacks, telling Cheyenne, "Don't know if I'm coming up or not. Tell me about this fellow, the one looking for a ranch boss. What breed of cattle does he run?"

"I don't know. But he owns an island and he's rich. Want me to give you his number? He said for you to call him collect."

"Just a second," I said and searched my pockets for something to write with, ending up using the lead from a .22 shell to jot down the man's name, Phil Rosenbach, and his number in the margin of the phone book. I tore off the page and prepared to say my goodbyes, telling Cheyenne I'd get back to her and let her know if the job was anything I might be interested in.

The operator interrupted again. "Please deposit three dollars and seventy-five cents for the next three minutes."

"I really hope you make it up here," said Cheyenne. "We have some unfinished business to take care of."

The way she said 'unfinished business' sent a hot tingle of desire racing through my groin. The last thing she said before the line went dead was, "See you soon, Loverboy."

No need reading between the lines. I knew, in her mind, she thought it was a done deal. I pictured her clutching the phone to her breasts, her face flushed with sexual anticipation. I returned to my drink, motioned to the barmaid, a chunky non-descript gal, to let her know I could use a fresh one. As I sipped the new drink, I rolled over in my mind all the compelling reasons for me to make another call: Alaska had always been a place I wanted to visit, to see if it really was the last frontier like they said it was. And I did need a job. But of course I knew the obvious inducement was the possibility, hell, the certainty I'd be hopping in the sack with Cheyenne. Hadn't she called me Loverboy?

My ace in the hole, the times I've gone looking for a job, has always been my reputation. Ranchers recognize me as a good buckaroo and a knowledgeable cattleman who delivers a full day's work for a day's pay. I've never been out of a job for long. I told myself the possibility of working in Alaska was intriguing and then laughed because I knew, in all honesty, I was a moth being drawn to Cheyenne's flame. I returned to the pay phone and dialed the operator.

Rosenbach's secretary accepted my collect call and was quick to the point, wanting to know the gist of my business. I told her. She put me straight through and when Mr. Rosenbach came on the line he had a professionally polished voice, the type of modulation usually reserved for FM radio. He said, "So you are the cowpoke I heard so much about." As he talked, I formed a mental picture of him, figuring him to be a suit-and-tie guy, brown wingtips, on the plump side, with hands as soft as a used car salesman.

I said to the voice, "Understand you're in the market for a ranch manager. Tell me a little about the spread. Cheyenne said it was an entire island. So, how many acres? What breed do you run? How many head? Irrigated pasture or range?"

He was laughing, "Hold on, Mr. Wilder. First, let me say you sure have an awful pretty admirer. She speaks so highly of you. Says you are currently managing a ranch in Oregon. What is your experience with livestock?"

"Sir, my whole background is livestock. Was born and raised on a ranch, cut my eyeteeth riding broncs and bulls. My Old Man was a rodeo stock contractor. I rode NPRA and PRCA—ten years. At one time or another I've worked for the ZX, MC, Big Muddy, Hay Creek, Alvord.... I've wrangled, mustanged, rode rough string, calved out, fed out. You name it, I done it."

"You do sound authentic." I could tell he was grinning. "If I were to hire you when could you come to work?"

"No hooks in my ass. Jump on a plane, be there in a flash. But I wanna know what's involved. Tell me about the ranch."

"The ranch encompasses the entirety of Chirikof Island, located in the Bering Sea west of Anchorage. I own it lock, stock, and barrel. You will live at ranch headquarters. Every week a plane will supply you with whatever you need."

"How about pay?"

"As far as salary goes—I furnish the house, food and whatever you need in the way of supplies. You start at, say, two grand a month, and if everything works out like I think it will, we can talk about bumping that up in six months. Interested?"

What I thought was—room, board, two grand a month—this man is either richer than hell or a complete idiot. But I told him, "Don't sound bad. Hell yes I'm interested."

"Well, do we have a deal?"

"Like I said, I'm interested but I won't commit myself without seeing the spread. How many cattle you running on Chirikof?"

He completely ignored my question. "Tell you what—I am so convinced you will fall in love with my island ranch that I would be willing to buy you a round-trip ticket. I'll take care of the hotel, meals, everything. Come on up, look it over, and if you like what you see, stay, otherwise go back to Oregon with a paid holiday under your belt, and the opportunity to spend some time with your pretty blond friend. What's the nearest airport to you?"

"That'd be Redmond."

"Fine. A ticket with your name will be waiting for you. Bring your gear and be ready to go to work. Fair enough?"

"Plenty fair," I told him. When the line cleared I dialed Cheyenne and told her I was headed north. I charged that call to the 25 Ranch.

On the way to my stool, I found myself whistling a happy little tune. I was on a roll and the barmaid picked up on it. She said, "You must have gotten some good news."

"Sure enough did. Fellow wants me to take a look at a ranch in Alaska, wants me to take over as manager."

"You get to go to Alaska?"

I smiled, "Reckon so."

"I've always wanted to go. Take me."

Tapping my watch I told her, "Be ready in an hour."

She laughed and returned to work, taking beers to a couple of pool-shooting bikers. When I finished my drink I went to my rig and, since I wasn't in the mood to face Sam and tell her my news, not just yet, I decided to drive to the mountains, go for a short ride and allow Charley to stretch his legs.

I fought the traffic in Bend, where Audis, Mercedes, Lexus, Infinities and even macho Hummers weaved around me like I was a post man and they were cutters in a strange game of street basketball. Upon reaching Century Drive, navigating its confusing roundabouts, avoiding delivery trucks in the industrial section, passing subdivisions with million dollar houses stacked one on top of the next, I finally hit the open road and put the confusion of upscale sophistication behind me. I climbed into the wooded foothills of the Cascades, pulled down a dirt road and got Charley ready to ride.

I assumed all this backcountry was public land but was brought up short when I heard the clatter of heavy equipment at work and rode upon a huge sign with a prominent logo of a mountain bursting through a circle. It advertised, "*Resort at the Mountain*," and claimed this soon-to-be-born development would feature, "*Every amenity from an equestrian center to a golf course*," bragging, "*awash in sunshine 300 days a year*." In smaller print were key words: *"360 degree view—gated community—an Arnold Palmer designed championship golf course—green building practices.*" The final pitch was, "*...come experience every elegant nuance of the Resort at the Mountain.*"

Behind the sign, a Caterpillar was crawling on steel treads, screeching and squealing, sinking into pumice soil, pushing dirt around, black smoke seething from the exhaust stack. I saw the dozer man working levers. He wore work boots, dirty pants, a soiled blue shirt and shaded his eyes with a cap that, at some point must have been a bright, happy Caterpillar yellow, but over time and use had faded to the color of cornmeal and now was stained with splashes of black grease. I figured him to be a hard-drinking man who, with wrenches and welder, kept this hunk of pounding metal operating.

A lunch bucket was tied to the seat beside the cat skinner, probably something his wife had fixed him—the same lunch every workday for the past twenty or thirty years, never any surprises, just how he liked it. A small thermos of cold milk, half-dozen peanut butter cookies to snack on during the day, pair of jelly sandwiches, each in its own zip-lock bag and, for dessert, in a Tupperware container, a hunk of fruit pie with flaky crust and delicately crimped edges.

I rode on, losing sight of the ripping machine, but I was able to look back over my shoulder and judge its progress by watching the tops of trees yield before the blade. They wavered, bent and slammed to the ground as the dozer man tore at the earth like a glacier on the move, the soft soil yielding, curling, laid bare to the unflinching sun. Insects would come to feast on the uncovered leavings, and birds would follow to gobble up the insects. After the sun went down, the local deer herd would investigate. The buck, with bulbous branch antlers full of blood and coated with velvet, hanging back, refusing to step into the newly-created opening, but the curious does and fawns, wanting desperately to smell the earth and marvel at the changes, willingly exposing themselves to danger before trotting off, moving somewhere else, collecting ticks as they went along their way.

Even though I distanced myself from the sights and sounds of what was slated to become the *Resort at the Mountain,* I could not shake the image that this particular parcel of forest land was designated to become an aesthetic arrangement of houses surrounding an artificial meadow, bisected by yet another golf course with fake ponds and narrow ribbons of asphalt cart-paths. I was reminded of the prophetic words from *Tar and Cement*, that '60s song by Verdelle Smith, "*Many years later, tired at last, I headed for home to look for the past. I looked for the meadows, there wasn't a trace, six lanes of highway had taken their place. Where were the lilacs and all that they meant? Nothing but acres of tar and cement.*"

The sun was poised, ready to slide behind the razor-sharp edge of the Cascades. I cut my ride short, drove the back roads and killed some more time by stopping for dinner at the Tumalo Feed Company. The meat there is choice-cut. They take pride in cooking a steak the way the customer likes. After finishing the last bite, I had one more drink, stalling, wanting to make sure Travis was tucked in bed before I charged in on Sam to confront the inharmonious music that would surely be awaiting me.

Sam met me at the door, reached out, touched my arm and then pulled back like maybe she thought she had done something wrong. She wanted to know, "You need a drink?"

"Sure thing, Babe."

She ducked into the kitchen and I listened to the clanking of glass bottles as she pawed around in the liquor cabinet for the bottle of Black Velvet. I glanced at the vase of fresh-cut flowers neatly centered on the table and took notice of the floors, all clean and shiny. Everything was in its place, absolutely perfect. She returned with my drink and we gravitated to the sofa where she commented, "You were up and out of here awfully early."

I told her about spreading Bones' ashes on Big Nasty. And then I took the plunge, jumping in with both feet, outlining my Alaskan prospects, telling her about my conversation with Rosenbach.

"How did you find out about the job?"

"Moccasin telegraph. Friends talk to friends. Word gets around." I let it go at that because the thing about truth is a little pinch goes a long, long way.

Her fingers slid over my shoulder and entwined themselves in the hair on the nape of my neck. "I just hate to see you go away right now. We've been doing so well together, you and me." The muscles across my shoulders and up my neck gave a shudder.

"Yeah, it's been fine," I said. "But, Darlin', I do need to find a job." I allowed that to sink in and then hit her with, "Even a turtle has to stick his neck out if he's gonna get anywhere. Tell you what, I'll go to Alaska and if it looks promising, give me some time to get situated and then when the kids are out of school maybe you can all come for a visit. Hell, spend the summer."

Without intending to, I found myself saying that I hated like hell to leave, thanking her for allowing me to leave Charley on her pasture and concluded with, "If the situation up there has real promise and I tough it out, we'll have ourselves a pretty goddamn nice little nest egg." I left it at that. No promises. No nothing. Let her imagination kick in.

Chapter 5

Can't never tell much about a country until you get down in it and get some dust on your boots. (Barton Wilder)

Silver wings dipped and rose with the undulating air currents. I peered below me at inaccessible valleys wedged between long tendons of mountain ranges. We were flying over British Columbia, maybe even Alaska by now, and I knew there was some mighty tough country down there but from thirty thousand feet the land seemed as flat as a watered-down pancake. I was flying too high, and traveling too fast, to ever be able to feel the icy chill blow off a snow pack, experience the mist on my face from a high mountain waterfall, smell the fragrance of a single wild flower, or hear the forlorn cry of a loon drifting to me from across the brooding surface of an isolated lake.

For most travelers a trip to Alaska is little more than a meal and a round or two of drinks. I don't fly very often and for me it was a big deal—a long, bumpy, continuous dream with some incredible scenery thrown in to occupy my time. I suspected many of the far-flung reaches we were flying over had never known the footprint of man. That made the world I was accustomed to, the High Desert, seem incredibly small and irrelevant.

The stewardess—I know everyone calls them flight attendants, but I don't—was a cute gal but a little too short and plump for my taste. She asked if I'd like another beverage. "Yes please," I replied.

"Black Velvet, water back," she said with well-practiced competence.

I nodded. As far as I'm concerned there's only one way to fly—loaded to the gills. It ain't that I'm afraid to fly, it's just I hate giving up control of my own destiny like passengers are required to do. I have confidence in myself but it's a damn solid fact I can't ride a plane down, kiss the earth and expect to live to tell about it.

The stewardess returned and informed me, "This is the last one I can serve you. We'll be landing shortly." As if to punctuate her statement, the pilot cut the throttle and we started on the long glide into Anchorage International Airport.

Even with fortification I tensed as the landing gear snapped down and locked into place. I pushed back against the seat, bracing myself for touchdown and did not relax until we were taxiing toward the terminal. I felt I had tempted fate, and had won. I strolled across the tarmac with the full charge of the five-bucks-a-shot booze kicking in and found myself paying particularly close attention to the backside of an attractive gal wrapped snuggly in a red skirt. I jockeyed for position to make sure she was walking directly in front of me and thought how every skirt reminds a fellow of another gal, or if you've got it bad, the same gal. I chuckled because I'd had my fair share of short skirts and warm thighs. Sure as hell had.

I walked into a long corridor leading to the main lobby. Right off the bat I spied Cheyenne behind a row of glass panels. She was every bit the dazzling creature of my memory. Wrapped in a blue sweater, short tan skirt and knee-high leather boots, clothes undoubtedly bought for this particular occasion, she moved gracefully toward me. Her tawny hair bounced and flowed like a buttery waterfall in brilliant sunlight. And then she was running into my arms, hugging me, kissing me full on my lips. I made a foolhardy grab for my Stetson with one hand, encircled her with the other, pulled her off the ground and spun her in a pirouette the way leading men do in the movies.

After our hellos we made our way to the baggage claim area and stood waiting, giving each other gentle squeezes and exchanging sweet lies. I spotted my war bag, then my saddle and finally the box, sealed with silver Duct tape, holding my rifles and a few odds and ends. Cheyenne took the box while I grabbed my saddle by the gullet, wrestled it to my shoulder and picked up my war bag. We ambled toward a row of glass doors and, from the way people gawked, I had to figure a real buckaroo with a cowboy hat and a saddle slung over his shoulder western style, had never before set foot in the state of Alaska. I played it for all it was worth because, what the hell, I had the world by the short hairs.

Somebody called, "Hey, Roy, where's Trigger?"

I wasn't offended. The way I look at it—if a fellow like that New York clothes designer Ralph Lauren wants to be a cowboy so bad he has to cast himself as one in his print ads—then the real deal, like myself, ought to puff up and be proud. I painted a world-class grin across my face and kept right on walking.

On the taxi ride into Anchorage the tires hissed on slick, wet asphalt. Storm clouds spit rain on us as they scuttled across the sky but I wasn't paying much attention to what the weather was doing because Cheyenne's ripe young body was all over me. The gist of the conversation between us reaffirmed something a buckaroo once told me, *"It don't make a lick of sense to save the honey just for the honeymoon."*

I've never been a big promoter of public displays of affection and, as a rule, shy away from that sort of activity. Apparently Cheyenne was not of the same persuasion. She was brimming with pent up desire and it reached the point where I lost my normal ability to reason. The booze might have had something to do with it. Mostly it was the heat of her lips, her surging tongue and the way she ground her body against me.

Suddenly the back door was thrown open and the long legs and creamy softness of Cheyenne's inner thighs were exposed to view. The cabby got a free eyeful. He announced, "Captain Cook Hotel."

One of the bellboys came nosing around and I informed him I had the situation well in hand. Cheyenne again took the box wrapped in Duct tape and I grabbed the war bag and saddle and walked to the front desk. All I had to do was mention my name and the clerk snapped to attention. "Yes sir, Mr. Wilder. We are please you have chosen to stay with us at the Captain Cook. Mr. Rosenbach has taken care of everything." He handed me the card to open my door and gave precise directions on how to find the room.

Cheyenne and I took the elevator. At long last we were out of the public eye and I was a little unnerved because I thought this girl was going to jump my bones before we ever reached our floor. But we made it to the suite, a huge expanse of deep carpet and exotic wood with a magnificent view overlooking a part of the city and beyond to Cook Inlet. No sooner did I swing the door shut than Cheyenne began shucking her clothes. I allowed the force of gravity to pull the saddle off my shoulder and I set it lightly on the floor, placing the war bag beside it. I stood watching, mesmerized by the sight of Cheyenne undressing—as I had been that night at the ranch—marveling at all the wonders of her youthful body. When she was down to nothing but soft skin and warm promises she stripped back the covers and flung herself across the lavender sheet. She held her arms out to me as she impatiently, and adamantly, insisted, "Come here, Cowboy. Right now."

"I'm here," I said and began undressing, but apparently I was moving too slowly because Cheyenne sat up and began unbuttoning my shirt. Then, to my complete mortification, she swiped my cowboy hat and pitched it over her shoulder onto the wide bed.

There's one superstition a buckaroo holds sacred above all others—hat goes on the bed and you're in for one hell of a run of bad luck. Might as well forget romance. It ain't gonna be worth shit. I pulled away and swept up my hat as quickly as possible, depositing it, crown down, on a nearby chair.

"What's the matter?"

"Hat on the bed—bad luck. Real bad."

"You're kidding?"

"No, I'm not."

She gave a frustrated sigh, "Come on, Waddy," and tumbled backwards onto the bed, extending her arms and legs toward the four corners. She tempted me with graceful curves and sweeping lines, tight muscles and taut skin. I was trying to make myself believe the hat on the bed was a stupid notion: crazy myth, ridiculous fallacy, old wife's tale, hocus-pocus, mumbo-jumbo. Heat crept up my spine, neck and cheeks, revealing my embarrassment that a superstitious quirk in my personality had been revealed.

Cheyenne urged me toward a course of action. She leaped off the bed and, since my shirt was already unbuttoned, began tugging the sleeves down my arms. A wild combination of sensations and sounds aroused me: fingernails digging, teeth biting, lips nibbling, tongue slurping. Hat on the bed—silly superstition! I had my hands on Cheyenne's shoulders and was starting to apply pressure, toward the bed, when a sharp rapping of knuckles against wood interrupted me.

Jarred to my senses I groused, "For Christ fucking sake."

A jovial voice called from the far side of our door. "Room service."

"Didn't order no goddamn room service."

"Message to deliver," said the voice.

"Just leave it," I said.

"Can't. I have to give it to you personally. I also have a gift welcoming you to Alaska."

"Okay," I said, resigning myself to the intrusion. "Keep your britches on."

Cheyenne scampered under the sheet. I shrugged on my shirt and threw open the door, exposing a pimply-faced, string-bean-of-a-kid dressed in an ill-fitting maroon uniform with fancy gold chevrons. He nudged forward a cart containing a crystal bowl where a bottle of champagne swam on ice. For some odd reason, rather than block his path, I stepped aside and allowed him to wheel the cart into the room.

"Sir, may I open the champagne for you?" he asked.

At a loss for words, I nodded. He opened the bottle. It made a sharp pop when the cork came loose. He produced two glasses with narrow stems, poured them half full and with a flourish, handed me a note and just stood there. I took the hint, slipped him a couple bucks and he departed.

I read the note. "*Please join me immediately—for drinks and conversation upstairs in the Crow's Nest.*" It was signed in a nearly indiscernible scrawl but I could read enough of the letters to know it came from Phil Rosenbach. I don't know why but I gave a quick look at my watch and said to Cheyenne, "Guess I should have read this before I had him open the bottle. Oh well, better get dressed. Rosenbach's waiting."

"Let him wait."

She kicked off the covers and the sight of her once again enticed me but I told her, "Business before pleasure. Can't expect the man to sit and twiddle his thumbs while we play grab ass. We'll have time later, besides, I don't wanna rush a job that's gonna take the whole damn night to do right."

The Crow's Nest lounge, occupying the top floor of the Captain Cook Hotel, boasted a wine cellar with 10,000 bottles which, I suppose, would be a swell thing if a fellow drank wine. I've never been disposed toward that specific beverage. I hate the taste of grapes.

Floor to ceiling windows defined the borders of the exclusive lounge. One side of the room revealed Cook Inlet and the other a broad landscape of the Chugach Mountain Range. Between these two contrasting panoramas was a room of rich mahogany and gleaming chrome. I was still looking around, trying to get my bearings, when a gal flaunting a canyon of cleavage appeared at my side, requesting, "Sir, may I take your hat." It was more of a command than a request. I gave up my Stetson without so much as a whimper.

The crowd in the Crow's Nest appeared to be mostly young professional men dressed in suits and ties. I saw them stare at Cheyenne with their hungry eyes while continuing to sip wine or highballs. I could only guess what they were discussing—packaged ski weekends, recent features in *Playboy*, swapping lies about mountains they had climbed or secretaries they had poked. A handful of women were scattered around, classy broads judging from the sparkle of their jewelry and the cut of their clothes.

Cheyenne gave a cutesy wave and whispered, "There he is." She moved in the direction of a man sitting alone at a small oval table. He was wearing a white shirt and an expensive-looking business suit. He got to his feet and, when Cheyenne arrived, he gave her an awkward hug and a quick peck on her cheek.

I held back, wanting to size up the man as I walked in his direction. I guessed him to be maybe 35. He had a chubby face, as though he had never completely outgrown his baby fat. His hair, what wasn't in retreat, was pulled into a rebellious and pitiful little ponytail. A diamond sparkled on his left ear lobe. His shoes were too shiny, too pricey. The most colorful part of his attire was a paisley tie, a scroll of white, purple, black and hot pink. It was loosened at the knot. Looking at him it occurred to me that a few confused women might find such a man attractive. The appearance of money will sometimes do that.

Mr. Rosenbach set his black cigarette in an ashtray and, still standing, turned his full attention toward me, clasping my hand with both of his and pumping like he was trying to bring water up from a hundred feet below ground. His hands were soft, lacked so much as a hint of a callus, and had surely never been put to use pulling an engine, bucking a bale, or chopping a cord of firewood. He said, "Phil Rosenbach. It's awfully nice to meet you, Mr. Wilder. I trust your flight was uneventful and your accommodations adequate."

"No complaints," I said. "Call me Waddy."

If I had gone with my first impression of the man, and simply cut and run, I could have saved myself a lot of aggravation and grief in the long haul. But like the old saying goes, "*hindsight is better than foresight by a damn sight.*"

I'll give this to Rosenbach, he proved he had a wonderful gift of hiding his true intentions with an amiable demeanor. He was smooth as glass. Hell, if the man had five minutes to spare, I do believe he could have warmed the heart of the coldest whore. I think his power came from his reassuring voice and his eyes, eyes that begged to be trusted, faded green like a piece of good material left too long in the sun.

"I've met you before, somewhere," he said to me.

"I don't think so." I get that a lot. People say they've met me, or I remind them of someone. Usually I respond with a smart-ass remark, like, "Ever spent time in the drunk tank in Boise?" But on this occasion I bit my tongue, said nothing.

Rosenbach wagged a finger in my direction and continued to press, "It was somewhere."

I grew tired of his doggedness. "Well, I've been somewhere and I really don't remember seeing you there."

He pounded the back of his plush chair with an open hand, "That's a good one." He directed us, "Sit. Sit." He held the chair for Cheyenne, sliding it under her oval ass and scooting her to the table. He gave a nonchalant wave to the cocktail girl who immediately scurried to him. He called her by name, "Rita, I'll have another. The young lady would like Chivas Regal on the rocks." He turned toward me, "Name your poison."

"Double hooker—Black Velvet, water back," I said.

As it turned out, Mr. High-and-Mighty proved to be a gin martini, dry, with three olives on a plastic sword, drinker. He lifted his glass in a toast. "To America's pastime of extravagance and national consumption."

I thought his toast a little pompous and arrogant and offered a rebuttal. "And here's to space."

"Space?" He shook his head. "The space program?"

I raised my glass. "When God made man He made him out of string, had a little left over, so He made a little thing. When God made woman, He made her out of lace, didn't have enough, so He left a little—boys, here's to space."

I had used that toast in taverns and bunkhouses and it never failed to get a laugh but here, overlooking the city of Anchorage, it died an unnatural death. Rosenbach said nothing, simply stared at his martini. He must have been searching for a big idea because he suddenly opened his coat, fumbled at an inside pocket, produced a color photograph and handed it across the table to me. "I thought you would like to see ranch headquarters. It is a fabulous place with a ton of potential."

I looked at the photograph, obviously shot from an airplane because a strut and part of a wing were visible. What intrigued me was on the ground: a good set of corrals, barn, stock truck, pretty little log cabin, towering evergreens crowded close around an open meadow and, way off in the background could be seen the gentle sweep of the island.

"This it?" I asked.

"Chirikof Island. What do you think?"

I was impressed. "Not half-bad."

Cheyenne, looking over my shoulder, gave my arm a playful squeeze. She whispered, "Told you so."

"How many acres?" I wanted to know.

"Thirty-three thousand," he answered.

"Hope none of it's irrigated. Nothing I hate worse than pulling on a pair of rubber boots, jockeying plastic dams and packing a goddamn shovel over my shoulder."

He laughed. "All natural pasture."

"Does it have to be hayed?"

Again he laughed. "No haying. No feeding out. No fences. The cattle graze all twelve months of the year. And there is certainly no traffic, smog or overcrowding."

He knew what tripped my trigger. I asked, "How long have you owned this island?"

"I only recently purchased it," he said, and then began pounding out words like a Central Oregon real estate agent trying to hawk a rock patch to a rich Californian. "I'll be honest with you. The ranch has been neglected. I need someone to whip it into shape. There is an existing herd of cattle that date as far back as the Russian occupation. Without natural predators the herd has thrived, making it imperative that inferior animals be removed and new bulls be introduced to improve the bloodline. I'm in a position to spend whatever it takes to make this the best damn cattle ranch in the state of Alaska."

"It's a state?" I said, trying to be funny. "Since when?"

Rosenbach totally ignored my comment and, as if I hadn't been listening the first time, he doubled back and restated the various attributes of the ranch: the natural beauty of the land, the quaint isolation of island living, the high quality of the native grasses and the rare opportunity it would be for someone to take a rundown ranch and, using his money, make it a showplace. In a few months he claimed he planned to add several cowboys to the payroll and, if I took the job now, I'd be boss of the outfit. All the day-to-day decisions would be mine and if things were running smoothly he might come check his investment once or twice a year.

Rosenbach used his hands to frame his face, a face that seemed way too serious and sincere. He said, "Waddy, if you accept this position you gain monetarily, of course, but you also have to realize God never intended this beautiful and productive island pasture to be wasted. We need to work as a team to make this into an environmental utopia. It is our destiny."

I thought to myself, this man is so full of bullshit his green eyes are liable to turn brown. He must have read my reaction because he suddenly changed course, leaned forward, hands coming together as if beginning a prayer. "This will interest you. There are some dandy quarter horses on the island. Take your pick and he's yours."

I thought of Charley, stuck on Sam's five-acre parcel. "I've got a damn fine horse down home in Oregon."

"I'll have him shipped here," he offered, flashing a triumphant sneer and lighting another of those god-awful, black cigarettes. He shot a stream of stinky smoke straight up into the hazy air and asked, "Well, Waddy, are you on board?"

I stalled. "I'm thinking about it."

Rosenbach returned to his sales pitch. "Just so you know—Chirikof Island is part of a group of islands in the Gulf of Alaska, below the base of the Alaskan Peninsula. The Japanese current is its major influence and gives these islands a temperate climate. Nothing too severe as far as weather goes. Rainfall is twenty-four inches annually.

"Chirikof, considered the garden island, is covered by a blanket of volcanic ash deposited during eruptions of volcanoes on nearby Kodiak and Umnak islands. The depth of the ash varies from a few inches to more than 20 feet. During World War II the navy built several structures and operated a combination radio, radar and weather observation station on the island. We now use those buildings as ranch headquarters."

Apparently Rosenbach picked up on the fact he was sounding as boring as a college professor, or maybe he just wanted to wrap up the deal, because he directed a closing question at me, "Do we need to talk money?"

"I think the money's fine. I don't have a problem with the money." And I didn't. I tapped the photograph. "So, what's the deal with the log cabin?"

"Oh, the log cabin—well, that was added after the war, much later, back in the late 70s or early 80s. It has three bedrooms and a beautiful rock fireplace, and there is a wood stove, too."

Rosenbach leaned back and folded his arms across his chest. "A person can weigh every last detail of a business arrangement, but if he does he runs the risk of becoming neurotic. Me, I want my life bulging at the seams. In my dealings I sometimes may not be 100 percent sure, but if the opportunity seems right, I take the bull by the horns. Waddy, my good friend, I think you and I are a lot alike. We were put on this earth for a higher purpose—to say yes to great challenges."

I wasn't falling for his drama and said, "Tell me something, why do you want a ranch? I thought you were in the oil business."

"Diversification," he said. "That's the name of the game. Simply put, I don't want all my eggs in one basket."

He was using, for my benefit, so many corny country colloquialisms that I was afraid, if this went on another ten minutes, he might sound like the audio track from *Green Acres* or *Hee-Haw*. Flat out, I did not like this folksy, pompous, pony-tailed prick. Not his little earring, his smug attitude and not the superior way he leaned his weight on his elbows, the same as a thoroughbred horse owner will do while watching his horse race. But you don't have to like a man to work for him, especially when he's not standing over you with a whip, driving you in circles. I told myself I could probably handle having to deal with him once or twice a year. But something wasn't right. I operate under the theory that, if the deal seems too good to be true, it probably is.

I requested, "Go over the particulars one more time if you would."

He gave an exasperated sigh. "If you accept this job you receive food, a place to live and two grand a month to put in your pocket. Once a week the plane brings food and supplies and takes out an animal you have removed from the herd and butchered. Since the meat is disease-free, with no artificial growth hormones, the meat is about as organic as you can get. In today's marketplace it will bring top dollar."

That made sense. I figured an animal a week, sold by the pound to the health-food crowd, was going to go a long way toward covering my wages and expenses.

He reached into an inside coat pocket, produced a small telephone and handed it to me. "This is a satellite phone. It works anywhere on earth. I've already programmed the pilot's number. You call him with your list of supplies. He'll bring it out. You want ice cream? It will be packed on dry ice for you. Fresh vegetables. Fruit. Crab. Salmon. Absolutely no problem. Movies? We've got a Blockbuster, rent whatever movies you like, keep them a week, get more."

"There's a TV?"

"Of course. A 15,000-watt diesel generator provides plenty of power for television, lights and all the other creature comforts we have become so accustomed to in our modern lives. It's just like downtown."

I pussyfooted toward a commitment. "I'd sure as heck like to have a look-see."

"But I showed you the photograph."

"Pictures can lie," I countered.

He addressed Cheyenne. "Darling, why don't you accompany your friend to Chirikof. Come back at the end of the week with the supply pilot. I'll make it worth your while, take you on a shopping spree that will make your pretty head spin."

Cheyenne laid a hand on my leg. I noticed she was not wearing her wedding ring. I wondered if it was in her purse, or if she purposely had left it at home. Women are funny about things like that. She stroked my leg, leaned close and whispered, "Try it. If you like it, stay. If you don't, we can come out together." Her words were like a wind blowing across hot sand as she added, "A seven-day honeymoon."

My heart pounded my rib cage, and though I felt as reluctant as a fish nibbling a baited hook, I found myself saying, "Well, if I get there and like what I see, I might be willing to consider a six-month contract. At the end of that time, if we're both satisfied, we talk long term and incentive money."

The hook was set, the line snapped tight. Rosenbach rose to his feet, pushed his glasses up the bridge of his nose, reached for his wallet, opened it and peeled off three hundred-dollar bills. He laid them fanned out on the table. "You kids have a party. Live it up tonight, on me. My pilot will call in the morning and tell you where to pick up your food and supplies. Tomorrow is the only day he can fly, be ready."

He extended his hand to me, declared, "Waddy, it has indeed been a pleasure." He leaned over, gave Cheyenne a casual peck and told her, "See you when you get back." And then, after a quick stop to settle his tab, Rosenbach was gone.

Cheyenne, buoyant as a bride after the I-Dos, waved her hand requesting another round and while we waited she talked about how wonderful this little adventure was going to be. I spun the telephone Rosenbach had given me in aimless circles on the table top, only half listening as I puzzled over how I had accepted a job without ever having said I would take it.

Chapter 6

Life is a compromise of what your ego wants to do, what experience tells you to do, and what your nerves allow you to do. (Kelsey Wilder)

I'm a Leo. People who believe in that horoscope horseshit say I'm supposed to be neat, a little picky and typically have to have things my way. I've also been told, on more than one occasion, that I'm self-centered and try to dominate everything and everyone around me. But, that night at the Captain Cook, there were positively no complaints about my conduct, or performance.

Daylight broke and I lay in bed feeling sour-headed from the amount of alcohol I had consumed the night before, listening to Cheyenne hum to herself as she soaked in a small lake of hot water. I always figure a woman who is happy in the morning has been cared for the night before. I was scheming on a way to get her out of the whirlpool and back in the rack when the goddamn telephone rang.

I answered it on the seventh ring. A man's voice, laced with a liberal dose of Okie drawl, or Texas twang, said, "Howdy, this here is Jimmy Ray Johnson. I'm a pilot. Phil Rosenbach wants me to fly ya'll to Chirikof Island. We land on the beach, low tide, so we havta be outta here by no later than noon. Noon sharp. Be a car 'round in a half-hour to take ya'll shoppin'. Boy, best get a move on. Half-hour." And with that said the line went dead.

The car that picked us up was something like I've never seen. A silver Cadillac limo stretched long as Nebraska is wide, complete with driver, ice in a bucket, free booze and a pop-up TV. I fixed myself a drink and offered one to Cheyenne, but she declined, making busy with a list, writing down everything we might conceivably need for a week's stay on Chirikof Island. I drank and stared at her. Her hair was pulled straight back into a single braid that hung between her shoulder blades. She was wearing a fiery pink shirt and stonewashed Wranglers tucked into knee-high boots. I had bought the shirt and pants outfit for her with Rosenbach's money. I whispered in her ear, "Why don't I pull the curtain so we can make sweet music: my bow, your fiddle."

She laughed, pushed me away, said, "What are you, some sex-starved adolescent? Grow up and act your age."

I don't much care to be reprimanded, even in kidding. And what did she mean, act my age? Up 'til the moment she made that particular comment I thought she was oblivious to the fact I was old enough to be her father. I fired back, "How long is last night supposed to tide me over?"

She softened, tickled my ribs and gave me hope by purring, "Later."

We stopped to shop at the REI outdoor store on Northern Lights Boulevard. Cheyenne was still in charge and she spared no expense, buying sleeping bags that zipped together, a three-burner Coleman stove, a gas lantern, pots, pans, dishes, utensils—on down to outfitting me with work clothes, packer boots with a buckaroo heel, even T-shirts and skivvies.

She bought herself a variety of clothes, enough for a week's worth of fashion shows. When it came time to pay, all I had to do was sign my name. The bill went to Rosenbach. Simple.

Our next shopping spree was just down the street a few blocks at the Safeway store. We got essentials like two rolls of Copenhagen, beer, wine, whiskey, luncheon meat, bread, eggs, bacon, flour, sugar, pancake mix and a lot of canned goods. We included a few exotic treats: smoked oysters, stuffed olives, Brie cheese and crackers shaped like butterflies. Hell, when we got done shopping we could have opened a complete outdoor store and a fairly decent grocery.

The limo was so crammed with gear and supplies we were forced to sit up front with the driver. On the way to the airport I saw a gun shop and asked the driver to stop. I remembered I needed extra cartridges for both my .22 and my 30-30. Cheyenne, unbeknownst to me until I went to pay for it, slipped in a transistor radio and batteries. I tucked the receipt in my pocket. Rosenbach could pay me back later.

We arrived at the airport and Jimmy Ray was waiting for us. He was a short, fat, redheaded man with the ruddy complexion of a confirmed alcoholic. He immediately alienated himself by bitching, "Ya'll are fifteen minutes late." And when he saw the inside of the limo he whipped the Greek sailor cap off his head and angrily slapped it across his thigh. "Who in the hell do you think is gonna fly all this shit to the end of the earth? We ain't never gonna get off the ground."

The plane was a puddle jumper, faded from red to an unsightly pink and looked as though it must certainly have already flown its last mile. I was surprised, that after Rosenbach's spare-no-expense attitude, he would cut corners getting us to the island. From what people who had been to Alaska told me, I knew bush pilots were a peculiar breed and had to figure Jimmy Ray was careful enough to keep his equipment in tip-top shape. It was his life, as well as ours, that depended on it. I didn't feel like I was in any position to give the man hell.

After the plane was loaded I checked things out and since there was a second set of controls on the passenger's side—I didn't want to be tempted to take over the first time we hit turbulence—I allowed Cheyenne to have the seat next to Jimmy Ray. I crawled in back, creating myself a nesting spot among the gear and, trying to get as comfortable as possible, I promptly cracked a fifth of whiskey and took a swig.

After a lengthy run along the ground, with a couple of hippity-hops thrown in, we were airborne. Within a matter of minutes the engine noise became like the irritating whine of a mad insect. We flew through a layer of thick clouds and popped into brilliant sunshine on the topside. A range of mountains stood dead ahead and Jimmy Ray—not wasting gas with any nonsense like climbing over them—went through a cut between two imposing peaks. Tricky wind gusts threw us up, down and sideways.

We finally reached the coastal plain and soon after that the ocean. Jimmy Ray dropped down to hug the wave tops. Cheyenne turned in her seat and looked at me. Maybe I did look a little green around the gills because she hollered over the noise, "You all right?"

"I can't swim," I confessed.

The remainder of the trip was pretty much a blur, as the noise eventually deadened my hearing and the smell of burned gasoline and the bumpy ride made me sick to my stomach. But I toughed it out, kept right on sipping whiskey and figured sooner or later we'd either reach the island or run out of fuel and crash. The point came when I really didn't care which happened first.

Jimmy Ray cut the throttle and made a big lazy circle in the sky, the way a turkey vulture will do while he waits for his next meal to die. I tried to look out the window, but we were in fog as thick as pea soup. All of a sudden we hit a dead pocket and fell several hundred feet. When we finally caught solid air I bashed the window glass hard enough to raise a bump the size of a Buick on my forehead.

"Where's that goddamn island?" I barked.

Jimmy Ray poked a pudgy thumb downward. "There."

I looked through a hole in the fog and saw a quick impression of land. Jimmy Ray dumped the plane on its side and dove into the opening, free-falling toward a giant plume of surf breaking over the top of a rocky outcropping. I squinted, then slammed my eyes shut as my stomach fell away under the G-forces.

Jimmy Ray landed us as softly as if we had been dropped onto a pillow, on a narrow stretch of sandy beach. We came to a quick stop and the engine belched and died the way an old Power Wagon dies, with a sputter and a cough. At that particular moment my only desire was to get out of that plane, kiss the ground and give thanks I was still alive. When I looked around at my surroundings there wasn't much to see except for sand and gray fog clinging to everything in sight like great gobs of cotton candy. Above us, on a little bench, was the jagged outline of the roofs of a few buildings.

Jimmy Ray nodded in that direction and claimed, "That's home."

"I don't think so," I told him. "Where are the trees? You made a mistake. This ain't the right island."

"Phil said to put you down on Chirikof. As far as I know these are the only buildings on the island. Take a quick look while I turn the plane around. The last thing I want is to get socked in here."

Cheyenne and I climbed over driftwood that the stormy ocean had piled on the shore and followed a faint trail leading to the buildings. Cheyenne was frisky and playful, as if this was some sort of an adventure in pioneering. I was skeptical as hell and as we drew nearer my worst fears were confirmed. The little cluster of dilapidated shacks looked nothing at all like the photograph. The buildings were wrapped in oxidized tin and, in some places, the tin was torn loose exposing weathered wood, bleached white as bone.

I looked over the first shack we came to, saw that the lone window was pitted and nearly opaque. I twisted the metal door latch, pushed open the door. Judging from the interior, at some time in the distant past, this hovel had been used as living quarters. A wood stove dominated the center of a plain room furnished with a single chair leaking great handfuls of stuffing onto the floor, a set of bunk beds pushed against the far wall, and a table constructed from two-by-fours and a half-sheet of plywood. On top of the table, turned upside down, was an enamel washbasin flecked with gray where oxidized metal showed through. On the wall, a calendar that had quit working in October 1973, hung as limply as an afterthought. A string of yellow flypaper swayed from the ceiling and was encumbered with a horrid load of dead flies.

I was examining a collection of empty casings, which were arranged on the windowsill in neat rows like opposing soldiers on a battlefield, when I heard the airplane engine roll over and catch. The rpms built quickly. Without hesitation I moved through the low doorway and ran like a wanted man. My cowboy hat went flying as I scrambled over logs and debris, slid down the embankment, threw myself over the last pile of driftwood and ran out onto the beach. The engine noise had grown to a crescendo and then the plane emerged from the fog and I could clearly see Jimmy Ray at the controls, looking straight ahead, holding the throttle stick back between his legs. The spinning prop and screaming engine blasted past me, the tip of the wing passing a scant ten feet away from my outstretched hands. Fog quickly engulfed the plane, and helped to hide the diminishing rumble of Jimmy Ray's inglorious retreat.

Cheyenne found me sitting on the mound of boxes and gear that had been tossed onto the beach. She draped an arm around my shoulder. I wasn't sure if she was trying to console me or provide an excuse for Jimmy Ray's erratic behavior when she said, "He told us he didn't want to get stranded here."

I was holding the phone Rosenbach had given me and I shook it in front of her face, spitting words as though they were a vile declaration. "No signal. No goddamn signal. That bastard lied to us."

She took the phone from me. I guess she thought I might chuck the worthless piece of shit into the ocean. I sulked like a five-year-old.

On the way to the beach Cheyenne had recovered my cowboy hat and she set it on my head and wrapped her arms around my shoulders. "Let's not let this spoil things. We have a whole week to ourselves. Let's have some fun."

I was pissed at the whole goddamn world. She kissed my cheek, moved around and knelt in front of me, kissed my lips. I felt my anger begin to melt some around the edges. Maybe I was overreacting. I hadn't seen the island. We did have plenty of grub and a pretty good supply of alcohol. Come next Friday, when Jimmy Ray returned, I'd let him know I didn't appreciate getting dumped here. I'd catch a ride to the mainland and tell Rosenbach to take his job and shove it. I shouted, "You lying motherfucker!" My voice, muted by the crashing waves, the fog and the emptiness of my surroundings, sounded as dull and lifeless as a drugged man coming out of a coma.

I examined the buildings: a barn, a slaughterhouse with meat hooks and butchering tables still in place, as well as several other scabbed together sheds. It was apparent the shack we had first looked inside, sitting on a little bench above the beach, would be the easiest to adapt into living quarters. The interior was stuffy and dank, giving off a blend of offensive smells. I pried open the window and set a rock in front of the door to keep it from slamming shut. The wind, blowing in straight off the Bering Sea, helped suck the stink away.

I lugged what I figured was better than a half-ton of supplies from the beach to the shack and, when that was done, I broke down the cardboard boxes and tacked them to the walls, not only to provide insulation but also to add a more aesthetic look than the backside of two-by-four studs. The advertisements stamped on the cardboard gave me certainty in the knowledge we had cases of pork and beans, hominy, green peas, clam chowder, chili, beef stew, tuna fish, macaroni and cheese and Top Ramen noodles. Hell, we had enough grub to carry us a month, or more. After the work was done I did a little exploring, found a battered gun rack in the barn, brought it over, tacked it up in our little shack and put my rifles there.

Cheyenne occupied herself on inside work. She swept the wood floor clean with an old broom, threw out dead flies and mice shit and made shelves from boards and bricks, stacking the canned goods and other supplies in neat and orderly rows. I had to hand it to her, she made the place downright livable. At one point I told her I was dry as sand and she stopped what she was doing and popped open a bottle of beer for me. It was apparent she knew something about home decorating because as soon as I finished the beer she promptly turned the empty bottle into a vase with a handful of wild grasses she found growing near the shack.

I gathered dry wood from the pile of driftwood lining the beach and, with the sun riding low on the sea, I started a fire in the tin-sided stove. For a moment a thermal inversion held the smoke down, the fire smoldered and smoke oozed from openings in the stove. But the flue soon warmed, creating a draft that sucked air and smoke up the chimney. I lit the lantern and the Coleman stove. The lantern hissed and coffee boiled, going "blurp-blurp-blurp" in the shiny new aluminum coffee pot. The room was warm, light and cheery. It pleased me that the dismal shack had been transformed into a comfortable and cozy home. Just goes to show what a little work, and a woman's touch, can do.

I poured myself a cup of the coffee, added a shot of whiskey to sweeten it, and collapsed onto the big chair now covered with a bright-colored, four-bar Hudson's Bay blanket. I sipped my drink and watched Cheyenne go through the motions of fixing dinner. I told her, "I'm too comfortable. I don't want to have to get up. Could you crack open the door, please? It's hotter 'an hell in here."

She did, but it was still too hot. An inspiration hit me. I suggested, "Sweetheart, wouldn't you be more comfortable if you shucked your shirt?" And to my delight, she did just that. I watched intently as she stirred circles in a pan of gravy. Her flawless cha-chas bounced ever so seductively and every so often she casually flipped a handful of wayward blond hair over her shoulder, to get it out of her way.

Having finished the last swig of my coffee, I set the cup aside, rose from the chair and, as if seamlessly choreographed, silently and swiftly glided the short distance across the room and came up behind Cheyenne, biting her neck while simultaneously wrapping my arms around her. My prize was two perfect handfuls. She twitched and trembled under my touch. I dipped down and swung up in front of her, noticing faint blue veins on the underside of her breasts. I paused to lick each delicious nipple, sensing them harden, mashing them with my thumbs, enjoying the way they sprang back like brand new. We kissed. I pulled away to look at her and allowed the tips of my fingers to trace an affectionate line along the tantalizing skin stretched youthful and tight between her cheeks and jawbones. I gazed into her eyes and the tricky blue irises shimmered in happiness while the little creases at the corners of her mouth turned upward. She smiled as shyly as a schoolgirl smooched for the very first time.

"What are you looking at?"

"You," I said, keeping it simple,

If I had had a romantic bone in my body, this would have been the ideal opportunity to tell her that I loved her as much as I was capable of loving any woman. I would have told her she was beautiful, and desirable and a hundred other amorous things. Instead, I coarsely blathered, "Let's fuck."

She made one quick move, like a wrestler exploding from the down position, and was back stirring gravy. As a consolation she offered, "You're driving me crazy, but we're going to have dinner."

"Forget dinner." I made another grab for her but she countered my move and threatened me with the gravy spoon.

"If we don't eat now it'll go to waste. Set the table, please." She pointed toward a box. "Everything's in there."

I did as I was told, setting tin plates on the table and laying the silverware on top of folded paper towels. I opened two beers and for chairs pulled an empty nail keg and a box that had once held explosives to the table. I turned off the petcock that carried fuel to the lantern mantles and, to give a romantic atmosphere to the room, lit a candle.

Before Cheyenne served the food, much to my dismay, she slipped her shirt back on. Dinner included steak, mushrooms, mashed potatoes, gravy, green peas and a fresh salad with blue cheese dressing. After it was over I wiped my lips on the improvised napkin and told Cheyenne, who was busy clearing the table, "I feel like I've been dry-gulched. I might never let you go."

"Oh yes you will," she insisted.

I helped clear the table, relit the lantern and sat in the big chair sucking on a toothpick, drinking whiskey straight from the bottle and reading aloud bits and pieces of news from the *Anchorage Daily Times* we had brought along. When Cheyenne finished cleaning up, she served me a hunk of store-bought apple pie for dessert, ladling Cool Whip on top for good measure. She parked herself on the arm of my chair and I spooned dessert into her mouth. After we finished, she got rid of the empty plates, slid onto my lap and began unbuttoning my shirt. She smelled of dish soap. We fumbled with each other's clothes and tumbled off to bed in the bottom bunk. The little shack that had become our home was filled to overflowing with the hungry sounds of our lovemaking. Our appetite for each other consumed us. Horseshit, it gobbled us alive.

I awoke in the middle of the night. The candle had burned itself out. I got up, went to the door and stood in a gloomy world swallowed in fog. Along the horizon was a mysterious luminescent glow. I was not sure if it was caused by mist over the moon or if it was the sun slipping along just below the horizon. The sea boomed against the sandy shore and I could taste salt in the air and smell the odor of kelp and other curious ocean smells I could not identify.

An awareness of my confinement threatened to settle in around me and to counteract it I poured a tall glass of whiskey. After consuming the booze I went back to bed and lay there sensing, more than feeling, Cheyenne beside me. She moaned, rolled over and hitched herself up a few inches to face me. Her body gave off a palpable wave of radiation and I breathed in her musky aroma, touched her face to be sure where her lips were, and kissed her.

A simple definition of a kiss conveys it as merely the touching of lips but in this case it was much more complex than a simple definition. Our moist lips came together and set off a delirious explosion of probing tongues and primitive desires. To be sure, it was about sexual fulfillment but I also think it was about our need to hold and comfort each other, to be together and not be alone on a remote island in the Gulf of Alaska. I wouldn't hazard to guess how many times one, or both of us, awakened and, after a few stray kisses, kisses as soft and warm and welcome as raindrops in a July storm, that same cataclysmic cloudburst of passion was unleashed. To be honest—I lost count.

In the morning I expected the fog to continue as an unwelcome guest but when I awoke and went outside to take a piss, I discovered a light breeze had blown the fog away. The sky was a venomous blue and the sun a brilliant ball of quivering yellow. After drinking a beer to wash down a couple aspirin I worked on a maple bar and went through the process of starting a fire in the stove.

A few yards behind the shack a fresh-water spring bubbled from the ground and bled off to feed the ocean. I found a metal bucket in one of the sheds, dipped water and heated it on the wood stove while the Coleman stove did the work of percolating the coffee as well as heating a fry pan. When the pan was good and hot I tossed in sliced bacon that sizzled and provided grease to brown a package of hash brown potatoes.

Cheyenne was lying face down, sprawled across the narrow bunk with the sleeping bag pushed down to her bare waist. A tangle of blond hair sheathed her sleepy eyes and loose strands of hair tumbled off the side of the bed. When I went to wake her I parted the hair to kiss her and the tiny muscles in her lips twitched awake. She opened one eye, then the other, gave a quick start when she saw me, tried to shove me away, then grabbed me, pulled me down and kissed me so violently I thought she must have cut my lip.

Like a fighter pushing away the canvas before the count goes to ten, I struggled to an unsteady standing position. "Whoa, easy does it, Sweetheart. Water's hot if you want to wash up. Coffee's ready. Bacon's done. The hash browns will burn if I don't turn them. Eggs with the yolks cooked solid okay with you? That's the way I like mine. Want toast?"

"We don't have a toaster."

"Silly girl."

She slipped on one of my flannel work shirts, never buttoned it, and went about the business of washing her face, neck and underarms, then made a swath or two between her legs. By then the eggs were ticking on a sheen of grease, sending up the odor of wet feathers that comes from cooking too fast. I flipped bread on the lid of the stove, buttered it when it had browned, cut the pieces in two and spread the halves as borders around eggs, hash browns and bacon. To clean the pan I poured in a little water. The hot metal hissed and then placidly quit complaining.

I took my seat and dumped drops of Tabasco on my eggs and hash browns. Cheyenne was busy toweling off and told me to go ahead. Nothing I hate worse than cold eggs. I dug in, eating in quiet while remembering the many times I had enjoyed breakfasts in restaurants where the sounds of silverware clanking against plates and morning conversation coursed like a noisy river through the joint. Cheyenne finally joined me. Her bright smile made the tail end of my breakfast a special occasion. For a fleeting moment it seemed as though breakfast might be the only true continuity I had going for me.

As we worked on the second pot of coffee Cheyenne came fully awake and we talked about going out on a scouting expedition. Instead, we fell back onto the bed and got caught up in a little innocuous exploring of our own. It was not until midmorning that we ventured outside and then, for me, it was with a certain amount of trepidation and regret because I had come to realize the photograph High Pockets had shown me was clearly bogus. It sure as hell was not an accurate depiction of Chirikof Island. There was no good set of corrals, barn, stock truck, pretty little log cabin and towering evergreens crowding close around an open meadow. On Chirikof, there was not a single goddamn tree in sight, not anywhere.

I stood outside our shack and surveyed the dismal setting. Without question, Chirikof Island was the most desolate piece of real estate, and quite possibly the most inhospitable spot, on the entire face of the earth. The soil was ashen: a shallow dusting over a bed of solid rock and so nutritionally poor the tallest vegetation, tufts of tundra grass, reached no more than a scant six inches. What hit me hardest was the stark reality of sameness. Accentuating the featureless landscape was the monotony of the pounding waves as they rolled in a steady rhythm off the restless ocean and ran up onto our little beach.

Once I went on a salmon fishing excursion and, crossing the Columbia River bar, got seasick and puked for five hours straight. I hate the ocean.

Cheyenne came out and stood with me. I announced I was going to grab the binoculars, but actually I ducked inside for a fortifier. I popped the top on a bottle of beer and stood watching air rise, tiny bubbles floating independently and breaking the surface without fanfare. I indulged myself with the beer and bolstered it with a few drags off the whiskey bottle, hoping the alcohol would brace me against my bitter disappointments. When I rejoined Cheyenne I found she had hiked to the top of the small rise behind our community of shacks.

When I reached her I said, "When God made this island He was either having a real bad day or this is His idea of a practical joke."

"It's barren and ugly but, in its own way, it's beautiful, too."

"How can you say that?" I cried. When she did not respond, I tried to see it through her eyes. The booze made me reflective. Here were thirty-three thousand acres and none of it was cut by a fence or turned by a plow. That was good. Furthermore, it was not necessary to squint my eyes in an effort to block out a city of concrete cubes rising into a sickly sallow sky of industrial wastes and exhaust fumes. No bloated suburbs. No motels where maids used bath towels to wipe red lipstick from glasses they popped into *'steam sterilized'* wax bags. No Colonel Sanders, Burger King, McDonald's, Hot and Juicy, Orange Julius, 7-11, BP stations, pizza by the slice.

I took in the outcroppings of rock, the carpet of tundra grass and the uneven and uncomfortable hills that dropped off and ended at the rocky shoreline. Reaching in my pocket I fished out a tired dollar bill and snapped it open. "Buck for your thoughts."

Cheyenne surprised me with her irrational response. "We had a dog named Sugar. She bit the mailman so Daddy took her out in the country and gave her to a farmer. I found out later the farmer shot her for killing chickens."

I wadded up the dollar and tucked it in her shirt pocket while seizing the opportunity to cop a quick feel. I tried to figure what Cheyenne was driving at with her story but failed to make any sense of it. A single seabird hung on the breeze and lifted a hoarse cry that bounced across the wide pointlessness of the setting.

I wanted to look at this land and see potential and possibility. I tried to imagine the open flat and the sloping hillsides covered with meadow grass and speckled with contented Hereford cows and spry calves. But what I saw was the two of us standing there—tall pallid people with eyes reflecting the remoteness. We were like aliens who had landed on a strange, uninhabited planet named Chirikof.

I thought I would add to Cheyenne's psychosis. "Your story reminds me of the time this city fellar came to the ranch to hunt pheasants. He brought his bird dog along and wanted to know where was the best place to hunt. My Old Man told him, 'Mister, places to hunt are like pieces of ass, all are good, some just a little better. It's up to you where you decide to hunt.'"

Cheyenne shot me with a bland look. "So, like, what does that have to do with the price of potatoes in Idaho?"

I laughed because I think what we were doing was just talking and trying to fill up some of the emptiness surrounding us. I suggested, "We gonna explore this hell-hole, or not?" and led the way down the long incline that stretched for at least a half-mile before climbing into a series of low foothills.

Our walk across the shallow valley and up the long climb to the top of the next ridge was made more difficult by my high-heeled footwear. Cowboy boots may be the ticket for riding the open range but they're the shits if you're afoot.

Cheyenne had on a pair of Nikes and lorded them over me like I should be complimenting her on her terrific shopping abilities and incredible display of common sense.

There was one single event that happened on our walk that was worth writing home about—we found confirmation there actually were cattle on the island. On a well-worn trail we discovered tracks and a few piles of manure. This was an exciting discovery and proved that Rosenbach hadn't lied about everything.

As we started back on the return leg, a mean little wind began to saw at us, a wind that stirred around an oddball concoction of moisture off the ocean, island dust, transitory shadows and the hard-edged sparkle of the sun. That wind pulled in a major storm. Its full fury hit during the late afternoon: wind causing the grasses to lay as flat as sleek hair, wind howling, bellowing, roaring. Darkness settled in and the worst gusts shook our little shack like it was a stick in the mouth of a mad dog.

Cheyenne was scared. I tried to console her. "This shack's been here a long, long time. You know this ain't even close to the worst blow it's seen."

We hunkered together on the bottom bunk, enduring the inconvenience of wandering dust and sand that found its way inside through cracks in the walls, and the occasional belch of acrid smoke from the stove. We ducked under the cover of the sleeping bags and passed time by swapping stories from our childhood.

Cheyenne told me she was an only child, having grown up in Cincinnati, Ohio. Her mother was from there. Her father was born and raised in Wyoming. He was a successful businessman who owned a Ford/Mercury dealership in downtown Cincinnati. Her parents were married fifteen years, and were seemingly happy until the day her mother discovered her husband was having a fling with his secretary. The marriage was over. Cheyenne was 13. She said the ordeal, the divorce and its aftermath, was the most traumatic event in her life and that for a long time she had not been able to trust anyone.

"I had to adjust to having a part-time father," she said. "I saw him every other weekend and the odd holiday." Her father married his secretary but, since this woman had broken apart her family, Cheyenne could never accept her as her stepmother.

For my part of the conversation I stuck pretty much to describing the home place where I grew up, and the fact I come from pretty rugged stock. Mostly I talked about Grandpa Barton and ended it with the story about the day the doctor told him his time was near. Grandpa checked himself out of the hospital, took a taxi to Sisters, and sat there with his cronies in the back of the barbershop playing poker and sucking oxygen through a tube until he keeled over. He was dead before he hit the floor.

Cheyenne wanted me to tell her everything I knew about buckarooing. I laughed and told her that conversation would take a good long while because it had taken me a lifetime to accumulate everything I knew. But she was persistent.

"Where did cowboys originate?"

I suspected she was not so much concerned about what I said, it was just that she needed the sureness of my voice to distract her from the violence of the storm, the way the wind rose and sank, attacked and recoiled, punched at our little home until it was a real possibility it might knock down the walls. And so I talked, telling her the first men to chase cattle in the United States were vaqueros who drifted north from Mexico. They were low-paid horseback laborers who trailed longhorn cattle to railheads in Dodge City, Abilene, towns like that.

From that low-class beginning the cowboy grew to become a national hero in dime novels and later in the silent movies. I said the Hollywood cowboys had very little to do with the day-to-day life of a real buckaroo. The cowboy hero myth was dreamed up by a bunch of prissy screenwriters who insisted a western story must always incorporate a handsome leading man who saves the heroine and rights all of life's injustices.

My Old Man, from his days in the rodeo business, either knew or had heard stories about Hoot Gibson, William Hart, Tom Mix, Turk Greenough... the old-timey cowboys who went on to become movie stars. He shared their stories with me and I passed them on to Cheyenne. Eventually she began to softly snore. I lay there with her cradled in my arms and continued to talk, entertaining myself with tidbits I had gleaned from bunkhouse conversations—Jackson Sundown, the first Indian to ever win the Pendleton Round-Up, Johnny Miller leaping a horse over a Model T Ford filled with cowgirls, Bonnie McCarrol getting hung up on a bronc, breaking her neck and all but ending bronc riding for women because nobody wanted to see another pretty girl killed in the arena.

By morning the wind had lost most of its punch. I had itchy feet and rambling fever and wasn't about to spend any more of my time cooped up like a damn brood hen on a nest, not on account of a little wind. Having found tracks the day before made me antsy to look for the cattle. Any buckaroo worth his salt would want to find those cattle.

In preparation of facing the raw, cold wind, I tied a bandanna around my neck, slipped on three shirts and my waterproof Australian oilskin duster. I left my Stetson hanging on a nail rather than risk having it blow off my head. On the way out, I grabbed the binoculars and paused to blow Cheyenne a kiss, but she was wrapped in a Dacron cocoon and the kiss never reached its intended target.

I opened the door and the windy remnants of the storm whisked me away, pushing me over the lumpy land, along with the lean, gray ocean clouds. I put my head down and tipped a shoulder into the side wind. It yanked at my clothing, shot up my sleeves and jammed its cold fist down my collar. Wind, like splayed fingers, combed my hair. If the wind, having slacked off some, was still blowing this hard, just how strong had it been during the night when it really howled?

Refusing to listen to the rumble of the surf battering the rocky island, and ignoring the dank ocean smells, I played a little game and imagined myself in Nevada. I was in Spring Valley and convinced myself so completely that when I looked up, I was astonished not to see the benevolent peak of Mt. Wheeler. Instead, I saw a pair of horses trotting uphill. Immediately I dropped to the ground, pulled the binoculars from where they hung around my neck, and pointed them in the general direction of the horses.

Skylined, and staring hard in my direction, were two of the homeliest hunks of horseflesh I have ever laid eyes on. They were the absolute worst of a noble species—one looked to be a mutated Clydesdale and the other a miniature workhorse of some unrecognizable variety. They were sway-backed, shedding great gobs of loose hair and their manes and tails were long and terribly matted. The big horse lifted his ugly head and gamboled in a swing-footed gait over the hill. The smaller horse trotted hard to keep up. Just like that, they were gone.

When I arrived back at the shack Cheyenne was fixing lunch: heating a can of soup, layering butter and mayo on thick-sliced French bread and slapping on wedges of olive loaf, salami and cheese. She asked, “Do you like lettuce?”

I shrugged off my coat. “I don’t care, I’m just happy to be out of that infernal wind. Damn-it-to-hell.”

She pressed further, “Onions?”

“Sure.”

“Pickles?”

“Naw.”

“You don’t like pickles?”

“Dill are okay, but you got sweet.”

“Why didn’t you say so? I would have bought dill if I’d known that’s what you preferred.”

“No big deal. Don’t really matter.” I washed my hands in the pan of hot water on the stove, dried them on my pants and sat down on the wooden explosives box.

She set a bowl of soup and a sandwich in front of me. "Find anything interesting?"

"Found horses. Two of them."

"When can we go riding?"

"Don't hold your breath. If we did manage to catch them, I'm not sure we'd have much."

"What makes you say that?"

Around bites of my sandwich I told her, "They're a couple of jug-headed plugs, that's what's wrong with them. How in the hell can you work cattle with horses like that?"

She pursed her lips and blew air across a spoonful of soup. "Thinking about staying?"

"What the hell makes you say that?"

"You said the horses would be worthless for working cattle. If you aren't staying, why work the cattle?"

"Just the way I am. I'm here for a week. I have to do something. Even though Rosenbach is nothing but a scum-sucking con man who, I might add, got me out here under false pretense, I'll still give him a week's work for a week's pay."

"But he lied."

"Yeah, he lied. I can't forgive that. To me a liar is the lowest form of humanity. This sure as hell ain't the place in the picture. Been asking myself the same question over and over—why? Why did he do it?"

She tore off a corner of her sandwich with her perfect teeth. "What did you come up with?"

"Nothing."

She posed a question to me, "Would you have come if he had shown you a picture of this place?"

"Hell no!"

"That's your answer. You don't have to think about it any more. He must have thought if he could get you out here, even if it was by devious means, you might accept the challenge and stay."

After saying that she simply spooned soup in her mouth and said nothing more about it. I wasn't finished. I waited a few minutes and asked, "How did you happen to meet him, anyway?"

She laid the spoon on the plate next to the bowl. "My husband, Tom, that's his name, we stopped at a service station. Tom was wearing a cowboy hat. Phil was there and said he owned a ranch on Chirikof Island and was hunting for a man to run it. Said there was real potential for the right man. He asked Tom if he was a cowboy.

"Tom is most certainly not a cowboy. But I thought of you right away and when Tom got the job working on the North Slope I went back and told Phil about you. That's it."

"What was he doing at a service station?"

"He owns it."

"I thought you said he was in the oil business. Didn't think he owned a service station."

"He owns five."

"Service stations?"

"Yeah. What's wrong with that?"

"Nothing, I guess."

"You made it sound like there was." She returned to eating.

"You're the one who said he was in the oil business."

"He is."

"I thought he was a high roller, you know, figured he had his own oil field or a refinery, something like that. He lives pretty high on the hog for a goddamn gas jockey."

"Damn you, Waddy, why do you have to look down your nose at people?"

We sat in stony silence, both of us aware that the first ping of gravel had cracked our windshield of love. Going against my better judgment I went out of my way to make sure the crack split wide open. Or maybe I was trying to be funny. I don't know which. Taking a bite of my sandwich I muttered, half under my breath, "Yeah, I'll bet he did more than pump your gas."

She reacted way more aggressively than I could have imagined. She threw the last bite of her sandwich at me and snapped, “I don’t appreciate your insinuation. You’re a dickhead.”

I stared at Cheyenne and saw a tiny tear form at the corner of one eye, hang there and gently slide downward as if her cheek had been greased. I stripped off the bandanna from around my neck, handed it to her, told her, “Sorry, don’t know what got into me. Guess I’m mad about the way things turned out, pissed about the horses.”

“I was trying to help you.” She cried quietly into the bandanna. “That’s why I went back and told Phil about you.”

I kept my upper lip buttoned. When the tears did not abate in a reasonable amount of time, and with my soup getting cold, I went back to eating.

By afternoon, the incident had been forgotten. Anyway I forgot it. And when we went to bed I never detected any lingering hostility from Cheyenne. She was just as eager for sex as she always was and I obliged her.

We skipped breakfast but did have several cups of coffee. And then, while I drew broad stripes through the shaving foam on my face, Cheyenne pulled on layers of clothing. We finally stopped stalling and ventured outside. The unrelenting wind slapped our faces and pushed us up the little hill behind our shack. We dropped down into the shallow valley, to where I had seen the horses, and found a place somewhat out of the wind. We huddled together under a small canvas tarp I had had sense enough to bring along. Beneath us, I could feel the ocean throb against the land. Overhead the sky was steel gray, void of even a suggestion of Central Oregon blue. I found myself missing those mornings on the High Desert when the air vibrates with the yipping of coyotes and the harmony of songbirds. Here at the top of the world the sun rose early and stayed late. The only noises came from crashing surf, the caustic chastising of gulls and the utterly inaudible sounds of microscopic lichen munching rocks.

I lay there and thought big thoughts—about God and such things. According to the preachers, God created this world in his likeness. I formed a mental picture of God. He was an old man with a white beard, covered in a flowing white robe, standing on a cloud, pointing downward to this very spot and presto, an island was created. Don't read me wrong—I ain't born again and I don't put much stock in commandments, crucifixions, baptisms or, for that matter, preachers in general. I do believe in the Church of the High Blue Sky and always like my God best when I find Him outdoors. He seems too big to fit inside a building, even if it does have high ceilings and stained glass windows. Not for a minute do I believe God sent his only son down to earth to die for our sins, and somehow that unselfish act makes us eligible, if we lead exemplary lives, to go to heaven. I find religious rhetoric to be nothing but a pile of contradictions dreamed up by money-grubbing ministers out to pad their own pockets.

Here's what really gets me about religion. Say you have two rival schools playing a football game. Each team forms a huddle and says a prayer. I know it happens because I've been a part of it. Each team prays, hoping to bend God's ear and somehow win His favor. You tell me, how does God decide who wins the game? Does He base His decision on the school that has the fewest sinners, the best-looking cheerleaders, the linebacker with the most developed bicep? What are the criteria He uses? See how silly the whole thing is? Religion—it's for the birds.

An unseen jet, somewhere above in the clouds, rumbled away to the south. Every year it seems you have to look a little farther ahead of the sound to spot the plane. With my eyes closed, I followed the telltale white line that boiled from the silver plane and broke apart into twin contrails. A few miles back the jet stream would shred these man-made clouds into oblivion. Where were the people going? Mexico? Puerto Rico? Miami? I wanted to be in that plane.

Cheyenne woke me from my daydream. She was squeezing my right arm and in an electrified whisper she announced, "There they are!"

"What?"

"The horses!"

Sure enough, the horses were out there and I watched them through the binoculars. They were every bit as disappointing as they had been the day before. The wretched creatures slowly ambled along a trail, grazing on the tops of tundra grass.

Trails. Even though I was watching every movement of the horses my thoughts roamed far away to one particular trail in the Cascade Mountains near Mt. Jefferson. The trail I saw was worn deep by cattle, deer and elk. I was mounted on Charley and found myself watching his ears for any subtle warnings: Charley swinging wide around a boulder where a cougar once crouched and sprang onto the back of a fawn, Charley avoiding a flat lava rock where a timber rattler routinely sunned its cold blood, Charley skirting a huckleberry patch where black bears gathered to gorge themselves on berries.

Breaking into my memories, Cheyenne asked, "Can I see?" and held out a hand. I passed her the field glasses. She looked and said, "They aren't so bad. Can I have the little one? What should we name them?"

Do women have a loose wire? Do they really have to name every living creature they come in contact with, from calves to laying hens? I played along, sarcastically offered, "How about Mutt and Jeff?"

"Great," she grinned. "I'll take Mutt and you take Jeff. So, what are we waiting for? Let's catch 'em."

"Not so fast," I chuckled. "If we show ourselves they're gonna spook."

"What do we do?"

"Play it cool. Sit tight. Wait and see. Only way to catch a mustang is to get to know his habits. If we know where they go, and when they go there, we can lay a trap and outsmart them. Might be a snare, might be a makeshift corral with wings but if we manage to catch one it'll be as good as two because they're undoubtedly tight as twins. They'll stick together."

"How long will it take to catch them?"

"Might take a few days. Patience is the key."

"Days?"

"Can't rush something like this. No shortcuts. No room for error. Once spooked, they're gonna be gun shy. Might never be able to catch them."

"So we do nothing?"

"That's right. Watch and wait."

Time passed. She offered, "Want to play a game?"

"Like what?" Curiosity jolted my hormones awake because I thought she meant play-play.

"How about 'Favorites and Hates'?"

She ran four fingers and a thumb straight back through her pretty hair and shook out the ends. "I used to play it when I was a kid. It's fun. The way it works is I say something that is either a personal favorite or hate. Then you respond with something. It's real simple, but you learn a lot about a person, what they enjoy and what they don't. Okay, my favorite thing in the whole world is driving fast, in a convertible, top down. Just me, the car and the open road."

I didn't know what was expected of me. I've never played silly games and I never went to sleepovers the way city kids routinely did. She prompted me by asking, "What's your favorite thing?"

"Riding a good horse."

"Jeans are my favorite. I hate purses. I carry what I need in my pockets."

"I love skirts, chasing skirts." I smiled when I said it.

"And what do you hate?"

"Ahh, I guess I'd hate asking some gal to dance and have her turn me down."

"I don't believe that's ever happened, not to you." She gave me a playful jab.

"She'd have to be crazy," I assured her.

"Favorite sandwich—avocado, sprouts, tomato and Grey Poupon mustard."

"Hamburger and greasy fries. The greasier the better."

"Favorite drink?"

"Easy. Two favorites—whiskey and beer."

"Orange Julius. Name a flower you hate."

"Skunk weed."

"Peonies. Favorite smell—baking bread."

I was starting to catch on. "The smell of a horse when I pull the saddle after a day working cattle."

She began firing questions at me like rounds from a Gatling gun.

"Favorite author?"

"Don't have one."

"You have to."

"Okay, Louie L'Amour."

"Favorite pasta?"

"You mean like spaghetti?"

"Favorite pie?"

"Pumpkin with a spoon of home-made ice cream."

"Favorite expression?"

"I used to say, 'Fuck a duck, McCutchen,' but I don't say it much any more."

"Favorite cartoon?"

"Never did watch cartoons."

"Why not? They're fun."

"Grow up on a ranch and there ain't time for that sort of foolishness. You've been asking me all the questions, let me ask you one—what's your favorite position?"

"If you're talking about sleeping, it's horizontal. If you're talking about making love, it's me on top."

"Why's that, because you're the one in charge?"

"It hits me just right. I get off that way the best. You'd have to be a woman to know what I mean," she said and asked me what she must have thought was a question that could not have any possible sexual connotation. "Favorite season of the year?"

"Mating season."

"You're so funny," she said, rolling away from me and looking up the hill toward the horses.

I was feeling horny and was about to run my hands between her legs when she squirmed free and announced, "Got to go."

"Where you going?"

"Back to the house."

"Why?"

"Because." She was on her feet.

"Keep low," I admonished. "You don't want the horses to see you."

After she was gone I lay there alone, missing her. The sun was warm and I crawled out from under the tarp, propped it up in front of me to keep the wind away, and sunned myself like a lizard on a warm rock. I must have fallen asleep. While I slept the tide rose, seabirds crowded the sky, the storm broke apart and cotton candy clouds sailed away to the east.

I awoke from a wild dream of horses; screaming nocturnal shapes rising from the sea, teeth barred, manes flowing, front legs fiercely pawing the air. I rolled onto my stomach half-expecting the clodhoppers to be charging me. What I saw was almost as shocking.

The horses were standing within a hundred yards. Their heads were up, ears perked forward, nostrils quivering, intently watching Cheyenne. She moved toward them one deliberate step at a time. Fingers of wind ran through her long, blond hair making it billow behind her. With firm, purposeful movements she shook a metal bucket, offering it to the horses. The temptation was too great for the small horse. He trotted the short distance to Cheyenne and, as soon as he stuck his head in the bucket, she set it on the ground and allowed him to nibble the contents while she stroked his neck and used her free hand to slide off her belt and slip it around his neck.

When the horse finished his meal she led him downhill toward me. The big horse tagged along like a faithful old dog. Making sure not to make any sudden movements I stood, went to Cheyenne, took the end of the belt from her and quietly asked, "Where did you learn that little trick?"

She answered, "An old movie. It might have been *Flicka*."

"What's in the bucket?"

"Raisin Bran cereal."

I walked toward the barn, a low-slung building made from steel I-beams covered with a skin of heavy-gauged tin. A small corral was attached to the barn. I led the horses through the gate, closed it, went to the barn, flipped the latch and swung open the squeaky-hinged door. Inside there was a suggestion of smells that I could not readily identify, but they seemed to be from a combination of animals and aged medicine and liniments. I took a piece of quarter-inch Polly rope from my pile of tack, went outside, leaned against the building and began tying a halter.

A rope halter is an important piece of equipment. It allows a cowboy to have an advantage over a horse by giving the cowboy the upper hand. A halter is comfortable for a horse as long as the horse is behaving, but has some bite if a horse wants to fight it. Grandpa Barton was the one who showed me how to make a halter and, over the years, I've made so many I could make one blindfolded in my sleep. It's simple—involves a series of knots, mostly overhand knots, spaced correctly. A small horse, the closer the knots are. A bigger horse requires the knots to be farther apart. The first knot is the right ear knot, above that is the right nose, then left nose, throat latch and tie loop. I worked up one side of the rope and down the other. When the halter was finished I slipped it over Mutt's head, connecting a lead rope to the chin knot and fastening the lead rope to a post in the corral.

Jeff stood a few feet away and watched intently as I made another halter for him. Once he had been fitted and was tied off, Cheyenne and I took turns with my currycomb. We brushed loose enormous chunks of dead horsehair and broke apart the matted strands from the sorry animals' manes and tails.

At one point Cheyenne asked, "Do you think they might buck?"

"Probably try anyway."

"How long did you rodeo?"

"All my life. Professionally ten years."

"Ever get bucked off?"

"Lotta times."

"What was the best ride you ever had?"

"Every time I lasted to the horn was my best ride," I said. "But without question the best of the best was a bull named One Ought. His daddy was Double Ought, double-toughest bull in the world. Bucked three hundred times and never was rode.

"One Ought was a gray Brahma, big horns just like his daddy. But he wasn't no man-eater, wouldn't try and hook you from the blind side when you were on the ground. He did have one bad habit.

"See, there was a bull we used to call the Ballerina Bull. Come out, take two jumps, go up on one foot, fall over backwards, thrash around until he killed you. Well, One Ought had that same reputation as the Ballerina Bull. I saw him go over one time at the Stock Show in Union, Oregon. He made mincemeat out of Willie Woods, an Indian rider out of Sprague River.

"I drew One Ought, 4th of July, St. Paul rodeo, there in the Willamette Valley. Knew if I could shake and rattle I'd win. Damn sure needed the money. Got down on him, told myself come hell-or-high-water I was gonna ride. Took a suicide wrap. That's when you wrap yourself in so you don't come loose, not unless you pull the end of the rope and kick out.

"Well, it was a hell of a ride and I got the job done. Horn sounded. And then One Ought goes into his ballerina act. Comes up and over. Pins me. Bullfighter jumps in, unties my hand, pulls me free, or that bull would've eaten me.

"Walked off under my own steam but sure enough guarantee you I was busted up bad: shattered collar bone, six cracked ribs, 99 stitches." I rolled up my shirtsleeve to show her the scar that started at my elbow and ran down almost to my wrist. "See right here."

"I've noticed you've got a lot of scars," Cheyenne said.

"Yep, sure enough do. So anyway, when the doc tells me he stopped at 99 I tell him to go back to work and take one more stitch so I can brag it around I have a hundred. He wouldn't do it. Scored a 94 on that bull. Took home a little over nine-hundred bucks and that just about covered my doctor bill."

"How did you get that big scar on you leg?" Cheyenne asked.

We were taking turns with the currycomb and I had nothing better to do than tell war stories from my past. I guess she must have caught me in a talkative mood because there was just no shutting me up.

"That one came about at a podunk show in Jordon Valley, down in the southeastern corner of Oregon. Can't remember what year. I was riding bareback and drew a sweet little buckskin mare named Tinker Bell. She had a mean streak a mile wide and I knew it because she had been in my Old Man's string but he got rid of her on account of she was just too unpredictable. Tinker Bell knew the ropes, knew when the horn sounds to quit bucking. She did just that, started in running with me. The pickup man came up and I reached for him, but instead of keeping a steady course, so I could get off nice and easy like, he veered away and it jerked me over backwards. I hit the ground like a ton of bricks. My right spur hung up in the dirt and I heard my leg snap like it was a dry wishbone. Broke both big bones halfway between my knee and ankle.

"As if that wasn't bad enough the second pickup man ran right over the top of me and his horse stepped on my broken leg. I never lost consciousness or anything. I was awake for the whole damn thing.

"They hauled me out in an old army ambulance. The driver was so drunk we made it about a mile out of town and he ran into the ditch. A gal I knew, Kitty Sessler, a red-haired barrel racer who drove a baby blue El Camino, came along and loaded me in back. She drove sixty miles to Nampa and I ended up having a vet take a look at my leg 'cause we couldn't rustle up a doctor. He told me if I was an animal he'd shoot me.

"He packed ice around my leg, gave me a fifth of booze, and Kitty drove me on through to Boise. We got to the hospital and the bone specialist removed the ice and squeezed my leg where it was broken. If I could've swung and hit him I would've. Worst pain I ever felt."

I busied myself slipping my spurs over the heels of my boots. "Anyway, they had me on the operating table five hours trying to fit the pieces of the puzzle together. After that I was on crutches six months, couldn't sit a saddle for the best part of a year. I tried to make a comeback but really, that was more or less my last hurrah. Only had one ride since I retired and that was on a saddlebronc just before I came up here. Pulled an 86 at Sisters."

I made sure my spurs were tied down tight. I could feel adrenalin beginning to seep into my blood stream. No fear, just anticipation. I was going to ride the big horse, Jeff. I was not looking for anything special from such a jughead, but the fact of the matter is, anytime a buckaroo crawls on a fifteen-hundred pound animal, there is the potential for a wreck. If something did go wrong, like it had at Jordon Valley on a routine pickup, I'd be on my own with no doctor available to patch me together. I gave the dime-sized, blunt rowels that had once belonged to Bones a quick spin and listened to the metal jangle.

On a horse I'm not acquainted with, when I climb in the saddle, I don't try to be Mr. Nice Guy. It comes down to the fact you need to establish who's the boss and do it in a hell of a hurry. I never abuse an animal, but when I ride I want to have a horse's undivided attention, from the get-go. It might take a few words, or it might take a two-by-four. Depends on the horse. My motto is—use a firm hand and be consistent. That's the proven method to earn respect.

Animals can read humans. They know if you're out to hurt them or not. Animals trust me. This one time Freckles, a stock dog I had at the time, got into a porcupine. She had a mess of quills imbedded inside the gum-line, and I used my pocketknife and a thumbnail to pull the quills. It hurt her, hurt her for sure, but I pinched her foot and she forgot all about the hurting in her mouth. Sometimes a little trick like that will go a long way in a tough situation.

If I have to, and there's no way around it, I can put an animal down. I'd have trouble putting Charley down unless he was real sick and in pain. You have an animal for nine or ten years and you can't help but get attached.

To be perfectly honest, I understand animals a whole lot better than I ever could a person. I can't read people for shit. What is it that makes each of us tick? Why does one guy hold up a bank? Why does another become a rapist, Satan worshiper, child molester? Why does some fellow feel compelled to take a potshot at the President of the United States? No rhyme, no reason.

On the other hand animals are creatures of habit. Ninety-nine times out of a hundred I can predict what they'll do before they do it.

I approached Jeff, took my sweet time and allowed him to become used to me. I stroked, petted and touched him. I talked to him, encouraged him, flat out lied to him about what a magnificent horse he was, saying all this while I very gingerly laid the saddle blanket in place. Then I put my saddle on his back, and drew up the cinch a little at a time until it was tight as a cable on a high lead. Jeff never bothered to hump his back, look around, or even flick an ear. He acted positively bored, as if this was an event that happened every day, nothing out of the ordinary.

I led Jeff toward the beach figuring if he did fire I'd rather have him wear himself out in the heavy sand rather than risk him, or me, getting injured in a fall on hard pack. Separating the two horses proved to be a big mistake. They were lifelong friends and apparently had never been out of sight of one another. They put up such a fuss I went back and untied Mutt so he could follow.

Again I led Jeff down the pathway to the beach. When we reached the soft sand I double-checked to see that there was no play in the cinch.

Cheyenne called, "Honey, please be careful."

"Cake walk," I responded. "Easy-money."

I turned the stirrup out, reached for the saddle horn with my rein hand, took a quick step and vaulted onto the saddle. Without hesitation, I squirmed my butt down to grab a deep seat. Nothing. I bumped Jeff with my spurs. Still nothing. Again rowels flashed and this time I ground them against his ribs and could feel him hunker down. A sheen of sweat formed on my forehead, mouth went dry, eyes opened wide. All the vital signs were there. But Jeff only farted, crow-hopped a time or two and then, and only then, did he finally start bucking.

Time slowed and my world became crystal clear—horse twisting, going up, up, and each time he plunged down the reining rope stood straight in the air. It was a great feeling and I drank in the sunlight varnishing the hills, could taste salt on my lips and was aware of the ocean boiling, swirling, waves building, making long, smooth runs at the shore. For a few precious seconds I was in my element and having fun. And then the big clumsy Clydesdale lost his balance and went down on a shoulder and end-over-end. Luckily, I sensed there was gonna be a wreck before it happened and managed to jump clear. I hit the ground running, taking big ostrich steps, my feet barely keeping up with my forward momentum. I got stopped and turned back as quickly as I could. I managed to reach Jeff while his front legs were outstretched, before he could pull himself up. I knew if he stood he would be in control, but for a split second he was off balance and vulnerable. Using this knowledge to my advantage I drove my shoulder into the side of his head and shoved him to the ground. I lay sprawled on his head, pinning it down, while his wildly thrashing hooves kicked up a sandstorm.

> *Hold a horse down only long enough to let him know you're the boss. If you keep him down too long you risk destroying his spirit.* (Barton Wilder)

I stepped aside and allowed Jeff to stand. He was wild-eyed and scared, stood wide-legged, quivering all over, big chest heaving like a bellow pumping air. I talked to him, eased his doubts and, in a soothing tone reassured him, "Easy does it, Big Boy. It's over. You're too damn old and awkward to waltz no more." I stroked the bridge of his nose, moved to his side and loosened the cinch. He shook to raise his hair. Mutt came over and they tentatively touched noses. I left them there and went to retrieve my hat.

After waiting for Jeff to catch his breath I rode him up and down the beach before finally taking him to the barn where I pulled the saddle, rubbed him down with a gunny sack and rewarded him with a couple forks of hay. The hay was so old and dry I could not imagine it held much nutritional value. I guessed it had come from a former tenant and pondered who might have brought hay to the island. I figured it had to have been delivered by boat, maybe a boat with a square bow like the army used when they landed at Normandy Beach.

Cheyenne tried to ride Mutt exactly one time. She reined him and he threw his head, went where he damn well pleased. She kicked him in the ribs and he flat refused to go. Then he did go and she pulled back on the reins, hollered for him to whoa and he refused. He wouldn't do a goddamn thing. If I owned a horse like Mutt I'd take him out on the desert, shoot him and let the turkey vultures and magpies clean up the mess.

Cheyenne, with her hands on her hips, demanded, "Fix him."

"Hon," I told her, "he's too damn small for me. I can't ride a pony like that. My feet'd drag the ground." That was the last straw as far as Cheyenne was concerned. She never rode him again.

I was anxious to leave that desolate chunk of rock in the Gulf of Alaska and was counting down the hours until the arrival of the supply plane. Once back in Anchorage I knew what would stick in my mind was the swell romp I'd had with a fair-haired beauty. What I did not understand, and the one thing that continued to nag at me, was why Rosenbach, that worthless piece of coyote scat, had lied. It was probably exactly like Cheyenne figured—he tricked me to get me to the island, once I was here he reckoned I'd adapt, maybe even start liking the place. But his little game had backfired. I don't appreciate liars.

Still, since I was pulling wages, I decided to give Rosenbach a fair assessment of exactly what he had on the island and show him how he could make it a paying proposition. Let the next cowboy worry about implementing the plan.

I had Jeff saddled and ready to go on a scouting mission when Cheyenne called from the doorway, "Wait!" She came out drying her hands on a paper towel.

"I thought you were going to build me that privy."

I had made her a promise. But it seemed like a total waste of my time. "We're only going to be here two more days."

"I'm sick of squatting."

"Okey-dokey," I said, and led Jeff to the beach where I used my lariat, and Jeff's pulling power, to yard chunks of driftwood to the flat near the cabin. With nails I found in the old slaughterhouse, I set about constructing my lady a first-class shitter. I dug a hole and framed around it with driftwood. The back and sides were walled up to protect the occupant against the prevailing northwest winds. The roof was fabricated from a couple chunks of overlapping tin. The front was open and provided an uninterrupted view of our beach and the shoulder of the hill off to the east. For the seat I used a driftwood limb with a natural crotch, whittling down a smooth spot for a bare butt to rest. On a whim, and to add a touch of class, I used a meat saw to cut a narrow crescent moon from a weathered board. I was busy hanging it, using fishing line and a swivel so it twirled in the wind, when Cheyenne made a surprise visit.

"It's beautiful," she gushed.

"Try it out."

She skinned down, sat and announced, "Perfect." Then she laughed and with pants still around her knees she threw her arms around me. A short time later we were doing the nasty right there beside the privy.

I finally did manage to get in my ride. Of course, I had to kick Mutt loose from the makeshift corral and he tagged along like an ambiguous afterthought. I rode to the top of a long hill and from this vantage could see the lay of the land—the way the island was shaped like a boot with our shack located at the toe. In the opposite direction, the ground dropped and then rose into a series of brush-covered hills, leading to the highest peak, maybe a thousand feet above sea level. I headed in that direction. It doesn't take a genius to figure out the cattle would be holed up somewhere between the ocean and the summit.

While traveling, I came across plenty of sign: piles of manure and, in places, trails worn a foot deep into the spongy soil. Crossing a ridge and dropping into a long, narrow draw, I saw a red fox angling away from me, but what surprised me most was when a bull scrambled to his feet from behind some brush, ran a couple steps, wheeled, glared at me, snorted, lowered his head and charged off into the tangle of low-growing underbrush. It all happened so fast I was left with an image of hide, swishing tail and swinging scrotum. I couldn't identify the breed except to think—from the color, length of hair and confirmation—the majority of the bloodline had to come from Scottish Highlander.

I went after the bull but—this was really weird—a mystery fog came rolling uphill off the ocean and swallowed the day. One second the sun was swimming in a sky big and blue and the next I was engulfed in a thick fog and could not so much as see the hand on the end of my arm. It was spooky, being caught out there in that situation and having no idea where I might be. Hell, for all I knew, I could be inches away from a sheer drop-off. Guaranteed, my asshole did pucker, but I had enough sense to give Jeff his head and he found his way back, or I should say that Jeff and Mutt managed to make a beeline for the barn and the fork of hay I rewarded them with.

The barn, protected as it was from the elements, was a good place to hide out and I stayed there with the horses. I talked to them about the old days, back when I used to work rodeos with my Old Man. He bossed me and bossed the show but he couldn't boss the horses and bulls. A chute would swing open and all hell would break loose. No exaggeration, his stock was that rank.

It was a thrill to watch my Old Man work a rodeo. He started off each show the same exact way: riding a big black gelding—he had several over the years—to the center of the arena where he stood in the stirrups of his silver-mounted saddle and waved his black Stetson to the crowd. He wore brightly colored silk shirts with his pant legs tucked inside the top of stove-pipe boots. The Star Spangled Banner played and my Old Man, hat over his heart, never moved until the last fading refrain ended. Then he went into action, circling the arena at a dead gallop, racing through the open gate. A second later chute number one opened and the first bucking bronc was pawing the air. I don't rightly know how he managed it, my Old Man, but he could exit the arena on a dead run, turn around and be back inside riding pickup before the first cowboy needed him. All these years have passed and I'm still baffled how he managed to be in two places at once. But then there were a lot of things about my Old Man that confused me.

Rodeo is something that sets a man's blood to boil, becomes part of you, a way of life. Between working rodeos with my Old Man and going out on my own riding the professional circuit, I had a good long run at the game. No complaints, no regrets. I enjoyed it all: the action in the chutes and behind the chutes, the commotion of horses and bulls running down the alleyway, metal gates sliding shut, the nickering, the bawling, the kicking, the panic. Cowboys cussing. The smell of leather. Horse sweat. Rubbing liniment. Spitting tobacco in the dust. Easy money. Rodeo clowns bouncing jokes off the announcer. Hang your hat on the sameness of it. But I've never seen two rides exactly the same. The animals provide the uncertainty and there is always the danger of a cowboy getting hung up in the rigging, a saddlebronc falling, a bull hooking or stomping you.

The good thing about rodeoing has always been, if you buck off or pull a low score, there is always another opportunity for redemption, on down the road at the next show where the rough stock will buck hard and every barrel racer will have a nice, tight ass. Count on it.

Chapter 7

Kid, here's the best advice I can give you—Stay out of jail. Avoid hospitals. And try like hell not to get drafted into the army. (Kelsey Wilder)

The day the plane was scheduled to arrive broke cold and bleak, fog oozed from the ocean and an obnoxious wind stirred and swirled it into a rising bank of clouds that all but blocked the sun. I remembered times down home in Oregon, listening to the weather gal on TV explain about storms forming in the Gulf of Alaska and how these storms would travel the Pacific coast and hurl themselves against the Cascade Mountains. I had come to the conclusion, after having spent a week on this deserted rock, that Chirikof Island was probably the birthing ground for all the big storms that hit the left corner of the Lower 48.

I knew that even if a gutsy pilot, by some abstract miracle, did manage to launch his plane, he would never be able to find our tiny beach. And yet, I could not renounce the possibility that we might escape the island. As I went about the task of gathering my gear, these conflicting extremes caused my stomach to tie itself in anxious knots.

The miserable soup never did lift and, in the afternoon, Cheyenne and I began drinking booze and playing cards for match sticks with the forty-one-card deck I had found in a box in the barn. Then, just for giggles, we played strip poker. Cheyenne went down to panties and bra, lost again and that was it for the game. After making love, we fell asleep.

I awoke to a wonderful sensation—Cheyenne pressing the length of her naked body against my backside. I played like I was asleep, but she pressed so determinedly against me I thought she might push me off the narrow bunk. When I started to push back, she used her arms and legs to wrench me over onto my back and then she mounted me. I had the distinct impression, the way she went about her business of grinding against me, that I could have been any guy, or nothing but a hunk of hard wood, and it wouldn't have mattered one way or the other to her. She swung her hips back and forth and in a circular motion, growling and moaning while roughly kneading her breasts, something she had never done before in our lovemaking. Then she suddenly arched her back, grabbed hold of the wire springs on the upper bunk and exploded into shakes and spasms so violent I was afraid her tendons and muscles might rip loose from her bones. A moment later my own orgasm seemed a puny attempt at mimicking her earth-shattering crescendo.

I lay there on the bunk, with no idea why that particular tumble had been so markedly different from all the others we had shared, except that in those moments of sexual frenzy and rowdy ecstasy Cheyenne had become the aggressor. We never did talk about what happened, instead we got up, dressed and set a definite course for the remainder of the day—to purposely drink all the alcohol that remained. We polished off the whiskey and were down to a single beer, a half-gallon of red wine and several fingers of rum. By then we were pretty well lubricated.

Cheyenne surprised me with, "I wonder if Tom has something to do with this."

I said, "With what?"

"I was just thinking," she said and fell quiet.

"Am I supposed to guess?"

"What if Tom lost his job, or quit, or something? He might have come home, found me gone, put two and two together. Or maybe he came home and stopped by the station for gas and Rosenbach said something. I don't know. I'm just thinking."

"Does any of this have anything to do with anything?"

"Tom could have wanted to teach me a lesson. He might have paid Rosenbach to let us sit here for an extra day or two."

I felt my anger flare. "That's crazy talk. A man who catches his wife cheating doesn't react that way. More than likely he walks away. He sure as hell doesn't get sneaky, doesn't pay someone to teach his wife a lesson and leave her with some other guy. Get that shit out of your brain. Don't bring it up again."

My anger faded quickly and I attempted to explain, "Here's the scenario, plain and simple—no plane could fly today and land in this fog. The first day the fog lifts we're out of here."

I don't know how my words of reassurance hit Cheyenne, but I do know they failed to convince me. I had an inkling—a funny feeling I was trapped in this shack, on this island, away from everyone I knew. But on the other hand, I thought that perhaps, unaccustomed to spending so much time indoors, I was only suffering from a case of cabin fever. I got up and went to where our coats were hung on a row of nails.

"Where are you going?"

I shrugged on my duster and my hat. "Just out," I said, snapping my words way more than I had intended. To keep my hat from blowing away in the wind, I had fashioned a stampede string using a rawhide bootlace. I cinched the string down tight and opened the door. Immediately the cold drizzle and cussed wind bit at exposed skin on my face and neck and the back of my hands. As I made my way toward the makeshift barn I leaned into the nasty wind, flipped up my collar and watched a tiny river of moisture as it ran off the brim of my hat.

I found Mutt and Jeff huddled under the protective overhang of the roof and I joined them there, leaned against the tin wall, felt more isolated, alone and miserable than I had ever felt in my entire life. I actually wanted to cry. But of course, I never did.

It was dark when I finally started back for the shack. I saw through the window the cheery glow from a burning candle and Cheyenne curled in the chair near the fire, looking like a lazy house cat. Stepping inside, I removed my hat and coat, shook them out and hung them to dry. I went to Cheyenne, bent and kissed her. Her skin was warm and her breath smelled of rum and squirt. We had gone through the Coke in a hurry. Squirt was our only mixer. The bottle of rum sat on the table, a dead soldier.

I poured myself a cup of coffee and pulled the explosives box near the stove to steal some of the heat and be near Cheyenne. I leaned back, used her hip as my pillow and stared at the tiny cracks glowing orange against the blackness of the stove.

Cheyenne began talking. Her voice was strangely distant and seemed as if it were being piped into my world. Her words were slurred. She told about a friend of hers, a girl who had been killed in a car wreck, and said she was supposed to have gone with her friend that day but a feeling, a sixth sense, had stopped her. I could tell Cheyenne was upset and it was obvious she was having difficulty saying what she had to say. I don't know if there were tears, because I never looked back, but I thought to myself how strange it is that, when a man has a little too much to drink he wants to either fight or fuck. When a woman drinks too much, she usually broods and cries.

"None of it seems real any more," she said.

"What?" I wanted to know. But I really didn't want to know.

"My life," she said. Then she blind-sided me. "What do you know about me, really know?"

I didn't want to play her silly game, but I did. "You grew up back east."

"Ohio is hardly back east," she corrected.

To me anything past Boise is east coast. I tried to hide my indifference. "You lived in town."

"Cincinnati is bigger than a town. What else?"

I was getting nowhere fast. "You had a pretty normal childhood." I sensed she wanted me to keep talking but I didn't know what she wanted to hear. I went through the details she had shared with me, like flipping cards on a Rolodex: she was an only child, her folks divorced when she was in junior high, after graduation she had moved to California to become a movie actress. I asked, "What made you want to become an actress?"

"That's exactly what I've been sitting here asking myself." She paused for a long moment, as if collecting her thoughts, and then her words came in a rush. "People told me I was pretty. They said I should be a movie star, but I never wanted to become Julia Roberts or Nichole Kidman, never saw myself like that. If I'd stayed home, married some poor slob who owned a pizza parlor or a bowling alley, had a bunch of kids, I'd have been letting all of them down. I was their dream. They thought I belonged in the movies. If I couldn't make it in Hollywood, what hope did any of them have for success in their lives? That was what they were thinking, or what I thought they were thinking. That's why I moved to California."

"Isn't that a little egotistical on your part?"

She took a sip of her drink. "I guess so. I wanted everyone to like me. It was important that they like me. Basically, I've never thought I was all that good looking. My nose is crooked, my lips are lopsided and my feet are too big. Oh, I look all right, I'm not complaining, but I'm a long way from movie star perfect."

I've lived in line shacks, spent all winter feeding-out with other buckaroos and none of us ever had a problem with our self-image or how we related to each other. Introspection has never been a favorite hobby of mine, especially not with a gal. Say the wrong thing and she chops off your dick and hands it back to you.

All the women I've been with, if I'm with them long enough, have had a few drinks too many and fallen into a bottomless cesspool of self-loathing: "Does my butt look big?" or "Look at this. I'm getting wrinkles," or "Am I pretty?" or "Do you still love me?" As far as I'm concerned, all that contemplation, that self-examination of one's true feelings and private thoughts, is nothing but a stinking heap of donkey shit. It sure doesn't need to be shared. Hells bells, I got enough problems of my own.

I turned to face Cheyenne and tried my hand at sincerity. "Darlin', you're all peaches and cream." I rubbed her arm and my rough calluses were like coarse-grit sandpaper scratching the smooth surface of her skin. I felt the tickle of delicate blond hair on my fingertips and knew I should find a better way to buttress the fact that she was beautiful and desirable. But I didn't know how to go about it.

She went on, "Looks are only part of it."

I could tell she hadn't reached the bottom of the hill. Not yet.

"My real problem is, I'm one of those people who thinks she can do everything, be in control like the juggler who keeps all those balls in the air."

I said to myself, "Keep your damn trap buttoned, Waddy my boy."

Cheyenne cried softly into her hands. I got up, tore a hunk from a roll of paper towels and handed it to her. She wadded it and dabbed at her leaky eyes. I thought she needed a hug and made a feeble one-armed attempt, but she pushed me away with her forearm. The shack was silent except for the wind yowling around the stovepipe, the ping of sand against the windows and the occasional snap of the fire in the stove. Seconds dragged into minutes.

"If the plane doesn't come for a long time.... If I don't get off this island... Tom will think I left him."

I had never allowed that thought, the plane not returning for a long, long time, to enter my conscious thinking, but once the possibility we had been marooned on the island had been exposed, that possibility lay there festering. Maybe I wanted to get back at Cheyenne for saying those words, bringing them out in the open like that, I don't rightly know, but I do know every man who has ever taken up with a married woman has a natural curiosity about the husband: Why did she marry him? Why did she feel compelled to cheat on him? What qualities did he lack? Did she still love him? Those are the type of questions the other fellow always ponders. I started with something easy, asking Cheyenne, "So what's Tom like, anyway?"

Her answer was quick and snappy. "Nothing like you." Her tone suggested she might be building him up and putting me down. She sniffled. "Not very tall but not short either. Stocky. Black hair. Beard. Wears a gold nugget on a chain around his neck. Works hard. Plays hard. Likes to party. Handsome. He thinks he's God's gift to women."

She grew more reflective. "I'd never have picked him out of a crowd as my Mr. Right. We met at a bar in Santa Monica. He said it was love at first sight, that when he saw me he knew instantly I was the one he was going to marry.

"Let's see, what else. Well, he works with his hands—he's a welder. Lives and dies with the union. Hates politics, doesn't vote, has never set foot in a public library."

"Any hobbies?"

"His big love is hunting. When he's not hunting he talks hunting. That's why he wanted to come to Alaska, for the hunting. I can't explain it except I always fall for the take-charge type, the guy who seems larger than life. With Tom, from the very first, there was chemistry between us. We hit it off. We fell into bed and after that it was, 'Move in with me,' and I said 'Okay'. We lived together two weeks and he said, 'Let's drive to Vegas and get married,' and I said, 'Let's go'. I never intended it to go that far."

"Just a lark, huh?" I said.

"Always thought I'd have this big beautiful wedding, wear a flowing white gown, have lovely bridesmaids and flowers and friends and Daddy would be Daddy all over again and give me away. That was the way I saw it when I was a girl.

"The way it happened was, we got married in a chapel as small as this room. It was actually an addition built onto the minister's house. And during the ceremony, if you could call it that, I could hear his kids fighting in the room next to us. I was wearing a halter top and cut-off jeans, hadn't washed my hair in two days."

She ran out of gas and finally stopped talking. I took her to bed. She wanted me to just hold her. I wrapped my arms around her and held her in a tight embrace until we both fell asleep.

The next morning, stepping outside and walking to the spring for a bucket of water, I was greeted by a dazzling new day full of fresh promises and renewed hope. The demoralizing fog was gone. The air was dead calm and the sky looked 1950's blue with a clear coat of lacquer spray-painted over the top to assure it stayed that way. While I stretched and breathed in the crisp, clean air a whistle of wings sounded and a squadron of birds abruptly materialized, flew past me like a cluster of buckshot and playfully rolled and twisted in the sky. Their flickering wings reflected shimmers of sunlight and then they were gone. I smiled and felt damn lucky to be alive. I knew the key to my joy was in the knowledge that an airplane could most certainly fly on such a breathtakingly beautiful morning. I was confident Jimmy Ray would soon come buzzing from the eastern sky, turn that plane on a wingtip and alight sweet and easy on our lonely stretch of beach. I looked in that direction. The beach lay exposed and inviting.

Returning to the shack I was whistling a Kris Kristofferson tune, the one about Sunday morning coming down. I built up the fire and went about fixing a pot of coffee. Instead of waiting around for the water to boil I headed to the privy. I sat on the throne with my eyes closed and tried to recall every last detail from our departure the previous week. I concentrated so hard it seemed as though I actually could hear the airplane engine rev, smell the burned fuel, sense the vibrations and ripples of the aluminum skin as air raced over the wings and the little plane leaped into the sky. With those sensations so strong and convincing I just knew Jimmy Ray, at that very moment, was in the air and his magic carpet was winging its way to rescue us.

When I opened my eyes I saw the flat, blue-green sheen of the ocean. Sunrays speckled the sea with happy silver arrows that seemed aimed directly at me. A fresh breeze began to shake the air awake and my half-moon ornament spun in tight, jubilant circles.

Cheyenne was already up when I returned to the shack. She was wearing one of my shirts, open in front, and was washing herself with a washcloth she dipped in the pan of warm water on the stove.

"Top o' the morning," I said.

She groaned. "I've got a headache and a hangover. What makes you so cheerful?"

I turned my answer into a short poem. "I say, this very day, Jimmy Ray, is on his way."

She turned toward me with sudden curiosity. "What makes you say that?"

"Remember where we came out of the mountains and dropped to the ocean. That's where the plane is right now."

"How do you know?"

"Gut feeling. Better pull together anything you want to take. We'll be out of here in an hour, before noon for sure."

My enthusiasm was infectious. Cheyenne tossed the washrag in the water pan. "You really think so?"

"Before noon," I assured her. "Tide's still on its way out."

She came to me, stood on tiptoes, hugged and kissed me. I could taste soap on her lips. She threw her head back and emitted a husky, full-throated explosion of laughter. She said, "Sorry about last night. I was a little drunk."

"No need to apologize," I said. I went to the bed, stripped off the sleeping bags, took them outside and tossed them on the ground. I went back for Cheyenne. We made love. The warm sun kissed my shoulders and a cool wind spanked my bare ass.

After our session I went to the beach, found a sheltered spot in the pile of driftwood and sat there staring at the wide expanse of ocean. The tide changed. Noon came and went, and yet I stayed and strained my senses to hear the far away drone of an airplane engine. Nothing. I began to feel the same queasy sensation you get in the pit of your stomach on a carnival ride. The trouble was, Rosenbach operated this ride. We were at his mercy and for some insane reason he didn't have the decency to bring us home.

As I sat there hunched up in the lee of the wind, the most threatening thing to me was the solitude—the remoteness of the island encircled by the sea, the absoluteness of our isolation, the distressing sensation of desertion and loneliness, and my own depression and despair. I was defenseless against such an array of oppressive forces and slowly and steadily the sheer weight of solitude settled over me like the six solid sides of a coffin.

At home, when I was away from town and the boozy atmosphere of a bar, I welcomed solitude. I was happiest when

I was flush to my eyebrows in four seasons of solitude. Winter—white, pure, clean. Spring—a rebirth, short but glorious. Summer—green grass and plenty of it. Fall—a riot of colors. Yep, if you're a cowboy you welcome solitude as a good place to relax, a good place to think. I used to sit my horse on top of a ridge and watch the shadows march across the countryside. I was grateful for the sun's return and the way it restored the colors to the vast panorama. That's what I thought set me apart from most men: recognizing and appreciating the beauty of nature and welcoming all the little things that came my way. I found quiet soothed me. I counted solitude as a blessing. And, I scoffed at the average Joe who, after spending a few days hunting or hiking, came to scorn solitude. The aloneness got to them and they raced back to their existence of predictability in a crowd of like-minded folks. One thing's for sure—those city boys could never buy a lick of solitude in a downtown supermarket.

Now I was beginning to understand the anxiety of having too much solitude. A quiet fear crept over me as the malicious yellow sun crumpled into a pool of bloody red clouds. I wanted to strike out, hit something, kick, yell, scream! My thinking was sluggish. I saw myself stuck forever on this godforsaken island and the weight of solitude crushed me down like I was nothing but a paper sack full of hot air.

Taken independently, each day the airplane failed to arrive was a bitter enough pill to swallow, but an accumulation of days, days when the weather held and Jimmy Ray could have landed on our beach, but still did not, became such a cruel and bitter disappointment that it began to affect me mentally. Time passed, and it seemed as though I became an observer, standing on the outside looking in, watching my normally optimistic personality mutate into something sinister. I was easily irritated, quickly annoyed and suffered flashes of anger which were usually directed at Rosenbach.

If that dirty bastard suddenly appeared on the island I'm sure I would have choked the living breath out of him. He had abandoned us and I couldn't help but take that kinda personal.

And then the string of sunny days turned to shit—rain, fog, wind and more wind. The deterioration in weather served to amplify my madness. There was not a chance in hell of anyone from the outside reaching us. I developed an ache in my gut and was afraid I might soon suffer a bleeding ulcer caused by the stress I felt myself under.

Sometimes I sat for hours and dreamed about the way it was back home, in the high Cascades, where the last few snowdrifts still hugged the north side of the mountaintops. Meadow flowers were in full bloom: shooting stars, forget-me-nots, bachelor buttons, lupine, Indian paintbrush. Bees flitted from one flower to the next, grasses danced in soft breezes and birds sang in the pines. But on Chirikof there were no wildflowers and the grasses lacked any punch of color. I was surrounded by dormant shades of gray and the only sign of life were the damn seagulls that screamed at me and hung on the wind like starched shirts on a clothesline.

Once I was sitting above the beach on a rock watching one wave after another flicker with brightness and roll itself out flat onto the sandy shore, only to scurry back to the arms of the sea. I shouted into the wind. "Whiskey! Give me some goddamn whiskey!"

I had a tremendous craving for whiskey. Whiskey would round off the rough edges of my misery. Whiskey was the cowboy's television. Take a shot, lean back, be sedated. Christ Almighty, I did need a straight shot of sedation.

But there was no whiskey to be had on Chirikof Island. I talked to myself, said, "Well, buddy, at least you still got a can of chew." And that was true. I had been hoarding my Copenhagen, doling it out one small pinch at a time when I absolutely needed it the most, making it last as long as possible. I didn't even want to think about my life when I scraped those last few brown flakes from the bottom of the snuff can. I groaned, "Somebody just shoot me. Get it over with."

I had another obsession, this one vague and hard to define because it involved our abandonment and the possibility we might never be rescued. I needed something solid and sought security, safety and a place of refuge. Back when I was a kid on the ranch I had enjoyed those things, and now I reflected on images from the home place: the old family photo albums, the framed awards from the Cattleman's Association hanging on the wall, the braided rawhide lariats coiled and draped on the mounted deer horns, the topographical map with a line marking the ranch boundaries, the chunks of quartz mixed in among the lava rock that Great-Grandpa Alvie had mortared into the fireplace, the brands of local ranchers burned into the mantle, the drawer in my Old Man's roll-top desk where he stored water rights filings, brand inspections, registrations, breeding forms, veterinary records and current bills. These were concrete things that I believed, when I was a kid, would always be there.

Plain and simple I was homesick. The crazy part was I was craving something that no longer existed. What I had known as an absolute was now an illusion. Great-Grandpa Alvie, Grandpa Barton and my Old Man were dead, buried in the ground. The ranch had been divided, made small, sold to airline pilots who commuted to work at distant international airports, and claimed as second homes by doctors, stock brokers, executives, developers and bankers. Central Oregon had become a getaway, a destination resort where city slickers could spoil themselves with the ultimate outdoor vacation: or if the mood struck them they could shoot a deer, an elk or even a buffalo, slap down their Visa and pay for it on the next billing cycle.

In my four decades of living on the High Desert I had witnessed what some folks call progress. I remember Crooked River Bob twirling his cowboy hat on television to attract attention, and telling the workingman: *"God isn't making any more real estate. Better act fast, plunk down a cash payment to reserve your view lot in heaven. Pay by the month. Own a lovely parcel of sand and sage. Have it paid for when you retire. Spend those golden years in paradise."*

And when the investors did retire they invariably moved a singlewide trailer onto the property, drilled for water, never found any, and ended up with dry wells and cisterns, hauling water and shitting in outhouses. They lived like the homesteaders before them had lived, stretching their meager savings to the breaking point and waiting around to die.

After the small-time investors, the next wave to hit Central Oregon were the developers, fresh from California, with pockets so deep they stretched overseas. They built destination resorts and well-heeled visitors traveled north in swanky cars and never had to leave pavement: from freeways to interstates, roads to streets and into driveways. Developers invented upscale names—Black Butte Ranch, Sunriver, Eagle Crest, Deschutes River Ranch, Inn of the Seventh Mountain, Brasada Ranch, IronHorse—threw together a fancy lodge, slapped down asphalt runways, trails, golf courses, dug swimming pools, laid cable for television and telephones and computers and made sure the pampered vacationers never had to sidestep any of the amenities of a comfortable existence.

The richest of the rich, people frantic with land fever and the thought of possessing a chunk of ground in heaven, bought strategic locations around golf courses and built sprawling trophy houses protected by electronic gates and featuring spacious redwood decks, hot tubs and "country" views. These timbered castles, with gargantuan living rooms and decorative rock fireplaces, were situated so the Cascade Mountains were artfully framed into picture windows, and against which small songbirds frequently broke their tiny necks.

Recreational subdivisions were added for those seeking a modest second home. There were bike trails for those so inclined, and horseback rides for the daring. Guests were pampered according to what they could afford. All of Central Oregon became their playground: the mountain wilderness and the pristine streams and lakes. In winter they jetted around on snowmobiles or skied the groomed slopes of Bachelor Butte, now renamed Mt. Bachelor because some marketing genius thought that a mountain created a better image than a butte.

If any local Oregon boy ever planned on having a place of his own, flat-out, he couldn't afford to buy into the dream. Besides, there aren't rivers, lakes and forests enough for everyone. What the country had become was a recreational battle zone inhabited by an army dressed according to L.L.Bean, Cabela and Eddie Bauer. The invaders claim the favorite spots, are content to stand, or camp, or fish elbow-to-elbow. And if all this ain't bad enough we got ourselves a bunch of money grubbing, leftover hippies who bill themselves as non-profit charities. These bleeding heart liberal eco-freaks have shut down the woods, killed the logging industry and all but tied up the bulk of our natural resources in the name of environmental awareness. Nobody cares about the environment like a man who makes his living from it—logger, rancher, farmer, commercial fisherman. Each one makes damn sure he practices conservation because his paycheck, hell, his very way of life, depends on it.

Not that Central Oregon is the only place where this is happening. It's happening all across the western states: Arizona, Nevada, Colorado, Utah, Idaho, Wyoming and Montana. The rural areas are being set aside as a preserve for rich city folks. Heaven forbid if a man wants to try and wrestle a living from the land. They won't let him cut a tree, or run a cow on public land, or catch salmon in the ocean. Best for a man to just fall in line: run a string of saddle horses giving dudes rides into the legislated wilderness, run a fleet of rubber rafts down the Deschutes River for the splash-and-giggle crowd, be a fishing guide or a hunting guide or a tour bus operator. Catering to the tourist industry, that's what living in the rural west is fast becoming.

I sat there on my rock, the ocean laid out at my feet and tried to convince myself that Chirikof Island might well be the last frontier. I had often thought I'd been born a couple hundred years too late, that I should have been a mountain man trapping beaver, or a cowboy drifting herds of longhorns up the Texas panhandle to Kansas. I've always considered myself a throwback. Forget about pensions, social security, Medicare and all the other government handouts. The government can kiss my rosy red ass. I'm perfectly content living off the grid, without benefit of electricity, dipping water from a crick and living by my wits: fishing, trapping and hunting for subsistence. Claude Dalles, the cowboy turned trapper who killed two game wardens, might have had the right idea—that a man living out in the bush plays the game by his own rules and nobody ought to come messing around his camp.

I stopped bullshitting myself and admitted all my rhetoric was nothing but crap, that I was so hopelessly homesick I was starting to drive myself nuts. God, how I hated this forbidding island, its storm-washed beach, the black rocks that rimmed the ocean's edge, the rolling tundra and our sad collection of shacks. The ocean rose. The ocean fell. Rose. Fell. In time, and it wasn't going to be very long, I knew I would see this island like the convict who, with his practiced eye, knows every last crevice of his cell.

For some silly reason I thought about Ted Saunders. We were on the rodeo team together at Blue Mountain Community College. Ted was a bulldogger, but not very good at it. He saw the light, that professional rodeo was not in his future and became serious about his education, eventually becoming a history professor at Willamette University. I ran into him a few years back and he launched into a long-winded discourse about Northwest Indians and how they used to travel over the Rocky Mountains to trade with the Plains Indians. Right in the middle of a sentence he stopped, said, "Oh, by the way, I'm learning to play golf." And then he went right back to talking about Indians. Even now, that comment of his, about learning to play golf, sticks out in my mind like a big, fat sore thumb. It's strange how things like that sometimes hit you, what you remember, and when your mind feels compelled to play it back.

Impending nightfall finally drove me to the shack. Stepping through the doorway I was greeted with clothes. The air was close, warm and moist and held the sharp smell of soap, as well as a delicate trace of Cheyenne's perfume. Damp shirts, pants, shorts, panties and socks dangled from twine crisscrossing the room. I ducked under one of the strands and went to the calendar Cheyenne had drawn on the cardboard wall. She had penciled in a series of little boxes. I counted them. Twenty-two boxes had been X'ed.

The door opened and Cheyenne came into the room lugging a pail of water. She poured it into the big boiler on the stove and was too fast for me to help her. I flopped in the chair, said, "You've been busy."

"Yep." She said.

"Need more water?"

"No."

She lifted soapy clothes from another pail and placed them in the rinse water. She asked, "What have you been doing."

"Thinking," I told her.

She blew a puff of air and a weightless strand of hair flew up and immediately returned to lie across her face. She looked as though she was underwater, holding her breath and her hair was floating free. Holding out a stick to me she said, "In that case, it's time you did some work. Stir the clothes until all the soap comes out."

I got up from the chair and stirred the clothes for a while, but it was so damn hot in the shack I had to stop and remove my shirt. Cheyenne sat down. She said, "I'm sick of this." She motioned in a circle. "Clothes everywhere."

I tried to be funny. "An interior decorator from New York sees this, it could revolutionize the world. Think about it. What a great way for rich folks to show off their expensive duds." My wittiness went unappreciated. I added, "What a far cry from the night we spent at the Captain Cook."

No response. I tried again, "Damn fog and now it's raining. I wish it'd clear off."

"If I had a wish I wouldn't waste it. I'd wish I was anywhere but here." She began crying quietly into her hands. Lately it seemed her tears came easily and often.

All that night the rain continued, lightening flashed and sometimes the clouds thinned and the moon popped out, giving false hope, but then the clouds massed over and the rain came again with renewed vengeance. By morning runoff was filling every crease and splitting open the draws, sending roaring freshets to stain the sea a chocolate brown. And wind, there was always the wind driving the rain hard at the earth: wind grumbling and growling, crying, whimpering, screaming its fucking lungs out.

On the second day of the storm Cheyenne found the transistor radio she bought before we departed the mainland. She put in four AAA batteries, turned up the volume and twisted the tuning knob until, finally, a single station came in, fuzzy and far away but there were faint voices and Cheyenne sat on the floor, radio between her legs, with the look of a young girl on Christmas morning who discovers Santa has brought her exactly the present she wanted. The sight of her like that was cute, but pathetic, too.

If I had been near town I'd have swung by the flower shop, bought a dozen long-stemmed roses, written a ditty on the free card they provide: a card that said "With Love", and I would have added something sweet like, "My Darling, Even on a stormy day you make the sun shine in my heart. Love, Waddy."

Since flowers were out of the question, I did what I could for her, rigging up an antenna with a roll of wire I had found, stretching it from the outhouse to the shack. When I touched the bare wire to the little antenna on the portable radio, Spanish-speaking voices barked over the airwaves all the way from Old Mexico. It was a remarkably clear signal. The voices gave way to music and there were maracas and clickers and I could visualize pretty senioritas twirling in festive dresses.

The skip waned and for a while a station from Albuquerque came in, playing country tunes scratchy from wear or distance. I took Cheyenne by the hand and pulled her to me, just as any attentive buckaroo would do to the prettiest girl at the grange hall dance. We moved methodically to a song about a horse named Wildfire, sung by a fellow with a citified twang and Cheyenne laid her head on my chest, where my silk scarf was tucked inside my shirt. I wrapped my arms around her, my fingertips touching lightly in the hollow dish of her back. We moved together. Damp garments were hung here and there, as there always seemed to be, and we slid past them like they were other dancers on a crowded floor. She was my girl. Nothing else mattered or even existed outside of the realm of the two of us: embracing, swaying and dancing with a relaxed easiness.

The music changed to a cheating song about lost love and cowboy dreams. I spun Cheyenne in a tight circle and as the rhythm quickened so did our feet. I backhanded clothes out of the way and we became a blur of pale grace, hot breath and light sweat. If this had been a rodeo dance I'd have chosen this point to steal away with her into the night, get in my pickup truck, open a couple of beers and drive far enough out in the country for some privacy. My girl and I would spread a blanket on the ground and we'd drink beer, stare at the stars and make crazy love. I did the next best thing. I took Cheyenne to bed.

We had our fun and slept. I awoke to the sound of a human voice, a voice as haunting as the whistle of a steam locomotive approaching a crossing. A man's voice! He was right there in our little shack, giving the traffic report from San Francisco—two lanes on the Bay Bridge were blocked by an overturned tractor-trailer and it was bumper to bumper on 880 all the way to the Fremont exit.

Quite possibly Cheyenne and I were the only living souls in a radius of a thousand square miles, maybe even a hundred thousand square miles, and in San Francisco they were stacked up, riding bumpers, pumping brakes and whenever any little opening formed someone goosed the accelerator and leaped forward to fill the gap. It was hard to conceive of a traffic jam when you're hunkered down, riding out a storm in the Gulf of Alaska. What a wacky goddamn world!

I crawled out of bed, sat on the floor and fiddled with the radio. I dialed in a voice, guttural and harsh that I figured had to be Russian. We were a hell of a lot closer to Russia than we were to the Lower 48. After that station faltered I listened to a Southern Baptist preacher, all fire and brimstone, shout at me that my soul was doomed to everlasting damnation unless I sent him money. I wasn't listening to what he said as much as just enjoying the cadence of his words, or maybe it was simply the reassurance of another human's voice.

I must have dozed because when I awoke Cheyenne was standing over me, grabbing at the radio, trying to wrench it away from me. I really don't know if it accidentally went flying from her hands or if she purposely slammed it down. The effect was the same—plastic shattered against the floorboards, arced up and came tinkling down like a handful of loose coins carelessly tossed aside.

"You ran the batteries down," she screamed at me.

Wanting to be on equal footing with her I got to my feet and shouted, "You broke the son-of-a-bitch."

"Why didn't you just give me the goddamn radio?"

I can tell you this, I don't cotton to anybody getting in my face. If Cheyenne had been born male I'd have knocked her on her ass. But she was definitely female and fighting with a gal makes about as much sense as wearing down an opponent by beating your chin against his fist.

I found myself trapped in an impossible situation, forced to co-exist with a woman and contend with her emotional upheavals. I suspected she was suffering from more than menstrual mood swings. Normally, if a woman I'm with gets flighty, I'll just go away. In this instance, I'd likely have given a year's pay to be somewhere else, and to have a pickup truck at my disposal. I would disappear, drive to town, go honky-tonkin', stay gone all night, come straggling in the next day with a bad hangover and a limp dick and everything would have been fine and dandy in my world.

In reality, Cheyenne was only one of my problems. I was homesick, lonesome for Charley and desperate to be living my free roaming life. I was also spending a lot of time thinking about Sam and what we had going before I took off and left her high and dry. I kept catching myself glancing at my watch, and wondering what she might be doing at that moment. I'd think maybe she was on her way home from work, headed to the store, taking her kids swimming or maybe they had packed a picnic lunch and gone for a hike in the mountains. I had to admit I knew nothing. Hell, she might have found another man. What I did know—I was imprisoned on Chirikof, with another man's crazy wife. This was an entirely different gig than what I signed on for.

Chapter 8

Young gals do a lot of moaning and groaning. I prefer older women. They don't yell, tell or swell. (Jake Holt)

Over and over again I asked myself the same two questions: Why did Rosenbach send me out here? Why didn't he come get me? My mind concocted some extreme circumstances. For a while I believed he had been killed in a plane wreck along with Jimmy Ray, and then I thought he had fallen into a coma, had contracted cancer, had lost his mind and been sent to the loony bin, or arrested, abducted by aliens, hell, I'd believe damn near anything my imagination could conjure up.

What was painfully evident was the fact we were beginning to run low on grub. One evening Cheyenne opened a can of chili and I asked, "Have any cornbread? I plumb love chili with cornbread."

She snapped at me, "No! We haven't had any cornbread mix for weeks."

"Don't get your panties in a bunch," I said with a grin. "I was just kidding."

But she wasn't in a kidding mood. She ladled the chili into two bowls, plopped one down in front of me and sat down at the table with her bowl. She spooned a bite of beans and meat in her mouth and stated matter-of-factly, "Tom came home today. He must think I left him."

"Has it really been five weeks? He probably figures you're off visiting someone, a friend. All your stuff is still there. He knows you'll be back."

Cheyenne pulled one knee to her chest and hugged it. "I didn't tell anyone where I was going. Did you?"

"I told Sam." She looked at me questioningly. "You met ... well you didn't formally meet her." Again I grinned. "At the house that night. She was the one with the shotgun."

"Exactly what did you say to her?"

"That I was going to an island off the coast of Alaska to run a ranch for a fellow. Said if things worked out maybe I'd send for her and the kids when they got out of school."

The consequences of what I said hit me. I knew that, when Sam failed to hear from me, she would start calling the Coast Guard, the Mounties, or whoever the hell had jurisdiction. I tried to remember if I had mentioned the name of the island. I hoped I had.

My mind went silly and I asked myself, what would McGuyver do? Probably cut to commercial and come back with a hell of a plan involving a tube of toothpaste, black powder from a shotgun shell and a roll of electrical tape. He would blow his ass to wherever he wanted to go.

I began taking inventory of our meager stock of food, trying to calculate how much longer it would last if we rationed ourselves to the bare necessities. Cheyenne was sitting in the big chair, combing her blond tresses, as she did each morning and evening. She brushed until her arm ached and then changed hands and went on brushing. When she finished she faced me. She wanted to know, "What's the bad news?"

"I figure we've got enough food for a week, two if we stretch the hell out of things."

"And then?"

"I've got a gun. I'll kill a bull. That'll carry us a long time. We can dig clams, shoot waterfowl, steal sea gull eggs if we get hungry enough. We ain't gonna starve, Sweetie-pie. There's plenty to eat."

She never said a word in response, just went to the bunk bed, stripped off her clothes, pulled on one of my T-shirts and climbed in the sleeping bags. Damn, when she got down to pay dirt she was really something. I turned out the lantern and, in the afterglow, crossed the room, pulled off my clothes and hopped in bed. I was like a blind man feeling Cheyenne's breasts, measuring their roundness, firmness, rolling each nipple between my fingers and thumbs. My hands roamed south over her belly, but that was as far as they went. She placed her hands over mine, stopping me.

"Not tonight," she said. And then she rolled her back to me. That was the first time she had turned me down and what made it even worse was that I could still feel the heat of her body and picture the way she looked all naked and beautiful. Damn! I lay there wanting her and hearing every little sound—her measured breathing, the rattle of the fire and the moan of the wind. I couldn't quite put my finger on it, but there seemed to be a tense stillness inside our little shack, like the way the air feels just before a big electrical storm arrives. It hung there until I finally drifted off to sleep.

I was up before daylight, lit the lantern and looked all around for the box of shells I bought on the way to the airport, but I couldn't find them. I woke Cheyenne and questioned her.

"Didn't see them," she said groggily.

"Not even when you fished that radio out of the bottom of the box?"

"I told you, no, I didn't. Believe me." She rolled away and pulled a pillow over her head.

I looked and looked but the ammunition, sure as hell, wasn't on the island. That meant I only had one box of shells for my 30-30 and a carton of long rifles for my .22. I knew I was going to have to make every shot count.

Hours later, when I returned from hunting, I had blood from my hands all the way to my elbows. Cheyenne was sitting cross-legged on the chair, a towel draped across her shoulders, drying her hair in front of the stove. Her head was forward and her fingers blindly massaged her scalp. She gave me a dispassionate look from behind a veil of wet hair.

"I got one!" I crowed.

"One what?"

"A bull. I shot a bull. We've got meat."

"That's nice."

"I was expecting a little more—enthusiasm," I said. "I'd settle for 'Way to go, Honey'. But a 'That's nice,' just don't quite cut it, Babe."

I admit, I was a little agitated, but it didn't do me any good. I might as well have been talking to a black rock because she parted her hair with two fingers and just stared at me.

I muttered, "Jesus Christ," in Cheyenne's direction and went outside and walked to the old slaughterhouse. All the tools were still there and I used the hoist to raise the carcass of the two-year-old bull I had killed. I began skinning it and as I worked I thought about all the commotion that surrounds a person's death. The news of the tragedy spreads like somber waves rippling across a still pond. Family and friends are notified. An obituary is printed. Death certificates are copied and sent to insurance companies. The ripples of my death, if I were to die on Chirikof, would touch a lot of people: mother, aunts, uncles, cousins, friends, acquaintances, Sam, Travis, Joleen... even Charley would miss me.

But thinking such morose thoughts is about as good for a fellow as wandering around lost in the woods. I made a concerted effort to snap myself out of my doldrums and concentrate on the success of my day. The hunt had been spectacular. It began in the dark: slinging my saddle up and onto Jeff's high withers, leather creaking as I drew up the cinch, shoving the rifle in the scabbard. Overhead, the hunter Orion was busy stalking the Big Dipper and I said a prayer to Orion to guide me to an animal. I was feeling the pressure of having to put food on the table. If I failed… I didn't even want to consider failure. I worked to put myself in the proper frame of mind. Back when I chased the rodeo, and was down to my last dollar, I'd invariably draw the rankest bronc or the meanest bull. The only thing to do was cowboy up and make the ride. Most of the time, no matter how wild and woolly it got, I did just that.

Dawn came slowly. I found myself high enough on the hillside to look over the broad sweep of the island and beyond to the spiteful sea that curved in an arc and welded itself to the horizon. The sun rose and soon heat began to radiate up from the ground. Two bald ridges came together in a cluster of wind-tortured brush that grew bent away from the prevailing wind. We entered a tangle of low brush and followed a well-defined cow trail. Jeff suddenly flung his big head upward, smelled the wind and snorted. He shook his mane and danced like a racehorse will do when brought into the paddock.

It was then I spotted a pair of mangy cattle in a small clearing. They were lying down with their backs to me. Not wanting to chance shooting off Jeff, I slid to the ground, tied the lead rope securely to a shaft of brush and, on hands and knees, sneaked to within maybe 100 paces of the animals. I lay spread-eagle on the ground, deliberately brought the rifle butt tight against my shoulder and peered down the sights. One of the animals was an old cow and the other a young bull. I sighted on the bull, drew a breath, blew it out and without hesitation squeezed the trigger. The gun must have gotten bumped in transport because I missed, kicking up dirt beside the bull's head. He came to his feet but didn't run. My second shot was just over his back. He wheeled and took a step or two. I hit him with the third shot. His front shoulder caved in and he crashed heavily to the ground, spinning in circles like a crazy top. I hurried to him. He must have known his efforts were futile because he quieted and lay there with his bloodshot, hateful, unblinking eye fixed on me. Not liking to see an animal suffer I used my knife to cut his jugular and he died quick and easy.

It had been a good hunt. I was pleased and went to work hacking away the bloodshot meat from the carcass. The entrance wound, where the 150 grain jacketed slug had slammed into him, was the size of a red thumbtack, but the exit wound in the shoulder was a pudding of hair, shattered bone, clotted blood and chunks of white tendon.

The bull had a deep, brutish chest and gigantic hindquarters with well-defined, plaited muscles. If I had been built like that bull I could run thirty miles an hour and leap over tall buildings in a single bound. But according to the word of God I had been built in His likeness—too damn puny even for my own ego.

If the bull had lived, he would have been guided, no, consumed, by the urge to mate with any half-willing female. He would have gone hot and heavy for a few years before being replaced by a younger, stronger bull that would drive him from the herd. I had spent a good share of my existence consumed by that same raw urge to breed. How long before I would be driven from the herd? I laughed at myself.

My peripheral vision showed me a slight movement at the open door. Without turning my head I allowed my eyes to move in that direction. In the dim light I saw a tiny ball of red fur. It was an animal. I whacked off a thin slice of damaged meat and tossed it in that general direction. A fox pup emerged from the shadows, wrinkled its black nose and, keeping low to the ground, it crept forward, seized the meat in its mouth and dragged it back into the shadows. I waited a few minutes and then told the little pup, with a reassuring tone to my voice, "If you want more you'll have to come get it."

The fox pup had never before seen a human being and was more hungry and curious than scared. I kept tossing it meat, each time making it come closer until it was eating right out of my hand. The pup allowed me to hold it and I discovered it was a female. I told her, "Sweetheart, you and me are gonna be best buds."

Chapter 9

Livin' is like bustin' out a bronc. Damned solid fact you're gonna eat some dirt. Secret to success, you wanna get back up exactly one more time than you got throwed. (Kelsey Wilder)

I was having vivid dreams about food: mashed potatoes, white gravy, green peas, cottage cheese, tall glasses of ice-cold milk, buttered toast, French fries, barbecue chicken, T-bone steaks, fruit cocktail, thick chocolate shakes, hot fudge sundaes, banana splits, German chocolate cake, pumpkin pie with sweet, home-made ice cream....

In one dream I pulled a pistol and killed a man guarding a plate of celery filled with cream cheese. Another time I awoke with the taste of apple pie shrieking on the tip of my taste buds. Food dreams were understandable given the fact our diet had become, almost exclusively, red meat from the bull I had killed.

Most everywhere I've lived, back since I was a kid, I've had a smokehouse. I do like my jerky. Sometimes my smokehouse was nothing more than a hotplate set in an old refrigerator, but whenever I was going to be in one place for an extended period I spent the time and effort to build a smokehouse from two-by-fours and one-inch rough stock. It has been my experience that a slow burning fire, topped with green alder, gives jerky the best flavor.

The weather had turned warm and I knew the bull meat would soon spoil. I built a rather crude smokehouse from driftwood, covered with gobs of mud and grasses mixed together adobe style. The door was a piece of salvaged plywood. I cut the meat into thin strips, soaked it in boiled-down saltwater brine and threaded the strips onto fishing line with a needle. I hung the strands in my smokehouse, built a good bed of coals and laid chunks of green wood on top. Smoke seeped out the vent and made curlicues in the still air.

The fox pup, which I had taken to calling Pup, whined for meat. I told her to wait until the jerky was done. My admonishment must have hurt her feelings because she sulked, going to the side of the smokehouse out of the wind, curling in a ball and pretending to sleep. The sun rode low and seabirds crowded the cloudy sky, crying as the sun skidded toward the wine-red sea.

Cheyenne emerged from the shack, tugged the door closed behind her and angled away from me without a sidelong glance. She passed near where Jeff was tethered and napping on three legs and took the trail leading to the beach. From my vantage I could watch her, and did.

Since way back I have always figured every woman needs five basic things to survive: love, marriage, kids, home and security. Anytime I've gotten tangled up with a new gal I automatically assumed she needed those five things and that, above all, she wanted to have my baby. But Cheyenne was a different breed of cat. She was already married and as far as I knew not the least bit interested in long-lining me. She had come to the island figuring me for a good time. Anymore, it wasn't much of a good time.

We had reached a delicate stage in our relationship, a tentative thing, not easily defined and impossible to say the change had happened here, or here, or here. I suppose it was a cumulative thing. But it was apparent the knot connecting the two of us had frayed to the point where occasionally, even my mere presence, was likely to irritate some of her raw nerve endings. I never took it personally. I just assumed the fault rested with her hormones and cycles, her distress about being marooned, remorse, shame, guilt, cabin fever and island fever. I'm sure the lack-luster diet of red meat was also a contributing factor. In my opinion, the friction between us was more than likely anything and everything—but it was never about me.

Lately, it seemed as though Cheyenne blamed me for every little thing that went amiss. A case in point—we ran out of toilet paper and she complained, "You used it all up."

"Someone had to," I replied. "It was bound to happen."

I provided her a perfectly acceptable alternative, tundra grass. I even cut her a box of tundra grass and left it inside the privy. Did she thank me? Hell, no. In fact she actually admitted her true feelings—she thought if I had conducted myself as a proper gentleman I'd have been using tundra grass all along, and saving the toilet paper for her. How self-centered can one woman be?

She found fault with the amount of time I spent riding in the hills, the way I liked to whistle as I worked, and she bitched about nothing at all. An example of how tenuous and ridiculous her frame of mind had become: one time I was trying to console her about some damn thing and I made an innocent comment. I said, "I know how you feel."

She nearly bit my head off. "How could you? You're a man. You'll never know how a woman feels." Tough to argue the point, so I took the high road and just let it slide, like water rolling off a duck's back.

In good conscience, I could never put all the blame on Cheyenne's shoulders. I was to blame, too. I had gradually become thin-skinned and sometimes read more into a given situation than I should have. It was hard not to, especially when every day seemed to be a mirror image of the day before. Monotony will cause a fellow to hang onto the little things, build them up and make them more significant than they deserve to be in the first place.

I spent most of my time outdoors while Cheyenne sequestered herself inside the shack. I worried about her sanity. When I saw her walking toward the beach that evening I took it as a good sign. I wiped the salt brine off my hands, and onto my Levi's, and followed her. I judged this to be a perfect opportunity for us to talk. At the very least, meeting her somewhere besides the shack, would afford us a new arena in which to disagree.

In the growing darkness she walked to the far end of the beach and stood where the outgoing tide had left the sand damp and hard. Against the murkiness of the sunless sky, and the vastness of the hateful sea, the outline of her small figure seemed out of place and trivial.

I figured it best not to approach her directly and went to the waterline, where I squatted on my heels, took a handful of damp sand and clenched it until water ran out and the muscles in my forearm ached like an infected tooth. Cheyenne came to me, stood there and said nothing. I dropped the sand, brushed my hand off on my thigh, stood and told her, "Sometimes, life is like running down a steep hill. You have to slow down before the hill gets too steep, or else your legs can't keep up and you fall flat on you face."

Her head was up and she was staring at the thin pale line that marked the division between sea and sky. I looked at her face but it was too dark to read anything of importance. Sand birds flickered past like dry leaves spinning in a dust devil. I watched their shadowy forms wheel and settle together at the phosphorescent edge of a retreating wave.

Cheyenne turned away, walked down the tide line a few paces, bent over, picked up a small shell and plunked it into the sea. She came back and stood beside me. In a voice slightly louder than a whisper she said, "A zillion stars." She motioned toward the tiny bursts of twinkling lights emerging in the darkening sky. "What do you think, Waddy? Suppose there's a planet up there where something terrible is happening?"

To me the bodies of light in the heavens have always been like familiar strangers. I never considered they could be any different.

"Do you think there may be someone out there looking at us and wondering the same thing? That something terrible is happening on this planet."

I refused to say anything and take a chance on feeding her psychosis. She continued, "Do you think, when we die, they bury us and that's the end of it? Do you believe in reincarnation?"

I had to say something. "Hard to believe anyone would come back as a stink bug. You think we come back?"

"Yes."

"Why?"

"Because there are times when I remember specific things. They are familiar to me, and I know I haven't seen, or done them, not in this lifetime."

"I suppose we all have feelings like that," I reassured her, even though I didn't believe a word of what I was saying. I sensed she needed me, needed a man. I circled behind her and wrapped my arms around her shoulders. When I touched her she trembled.

She spoke to the night and to the stars. "I heard a comedian say the loneliest you can ever feel is when you come home at night and there aren't any messages on your answering machine. He didn't know shit about the way loneliness eats at you."

She wanted to know, "Waddy, when you felt lonely, back home, what did you do?"

"Drank away the heartaches. And if the whiskey wasn't working I'd look for one more honky-tonk angel and try to make it through the night." With my offhanded comment I was attempting to bring a little levity to the moment, but my words rang hollow and insincere and I was reminded of every country-western song I had ever heard.

I'm sure Cheyenne thought I was mocking her, but really, I wasn't. I just don't like it when the conversation becomes too damn serious.

I kissed Cheyenne's neck. Her skin was shockingly warm, incredibly soft and smelled good, too. I whispered, "God, I do love your perfume."

"Well," she sighed. "That's the last of it." A long moment passed, then she asked, "Do you ever think about dying?"

"No, not really. Do you?"

"Sometimes, more so lately. Do you believe in heaven?"

"This is kinda like the reincarnation question. I don't know, maybe. Yeah, probably so."

"Do you believe in hell?"

"Doubt it. Place that hot would cook you crisper than burnt bacon."

"How can you believe in heaven and not hell?"

"Just do."

The quietness and distance between us seemed to grow. It was as if all the days we had spent on Chirikof were nothing more than sharp nails sifting through a sack of grain. Eventually they would poke through the bottom, and destroy the sack. Yet I think we clung to the belief that we had each other, desperately wanting to believe such a lie.

"Let's take a bath," Cheyenne said. She took hold of my arm and led me up the trail back to the shack. Pup was waiting for us. She whined and I picked her up and carried her inside. Cheyenne lit a candle and I made a bed for Pup on the chair. She lay with her head resting on the blanket while I heated water over the stove, lots of water, and I broke out the metal washtub and used dishwashing detergent to make bubbles.

Pup was witness to our communal bath. Cheyenne and I took turns washing each other. We stood, because there wasn't room to sit. After I had toweled off Cheyenne I carried her to the bed and we made love like newlyweds.

As we lay together on the bottom bunk, submersing ourselves in the afterglow of our lovemaking, I made a vow to Cheyenne, promising, "I'm going to get us off this shit hole. Swear to Almighty God I will."

During the night Cheyenne rolled away from me. I reached for her, took her hand, squeezed it and received the tiniest bit of response, but it went away quickly and never came back.

Chapter 10

When them fellars landed on the moon they done messed up our world. Nothin' been the same since. Weather ain't been normal. Women got a mind of their own. Kids run wild in the streets. And me, I try to witch water, can't do it no more. Used to be the bark twisted right off in my hands, willow stick bob up and down like a woodpecker's head. Not no more. Center of the world done been changed. Sonofabitch. (Bones)

I knew it was up to me to pull a rabbit out of the hat and find a way to escape, or at least to alert the outside world to the fact there were desperate people in dire need of rescue. I decided to erect a flagpole on the rise near the shack and, when it was in place, I attached a white towel on which I painted "H-E-L-P."

I was standing there, proudly watching the flag flutter in the wind, when Cheyenne came out, looked up and commented, "So, we have surrendered?"

Her comment might have struck me as funny, some other time, some other place, and I fired a rebuttal in her direction. "At least I'm doing something. I'm trying."

She turned away, scooped Pup into her arms and carried her inside. I gritted my teeth and went on to my next project, laying out the universal sign of distress. I arranged a combination of rocks and driftwood and formed them into hundred-foot-tall letters. I knew it would take a miracle for a commercial pilot, passing high overhead, to look down and happen to see my "S.O.S." but sometimes long-shots do pay off.

One morning, sitting at the table drinking hot water and absently playing with wiry strands of my beard, I told Cheyenne, "God I wish I had some Copenhagen, just a pinch. I always enjoyed that first pinch of the morning, the way it sorta jump-started my heart, got me up and going. What a great way to kick off the day! I miss that more than anything."

She sat there, elbows planted on the tabletop, chin resting on the heels of her hands, staring. I looked at her. Her face was etched with the hard lines of despair and sadness. I told her, "I got a plan." And I did have a plan. "I'm gonna build a raft."

"Oh," was all she said, like somehow the concept of me building a raft to float us to safety was beyond her capacity to visualize. But I didn't let her lack of enthusiasm dampen my spirit of commitment. I went outside, rolled up my sleeves, and got to work searching the drift pile along the beach, selecting anything that would float. I used Jeff to drag the salvaged materials to a flat spot only reached by the highest high tide.

By afternoon I had retrieved nine fifty-five gallon drums, logs, board planking and partial sheets of plywood. I began lashing my odd assortment of materials together with nails, scraps of wire and rope. It took several days of hard work to construct the basic raft, and thinking it was necessary for us to be protected from the elements once we were sailing on the high sea, I scabbed together a lean-to shell on the deck.

I painted a sign on a board, "WADDY'S ARK," and had just hung it over the doorway when Pup wandered down to the beach and found me. We sat together on the deck. I petted her, stroking that sensitive spot under her chin and basking in the warm glow of my accomplishments. Throughout my life I've had some dandy cow dogs, some great cow dogs, and I will say Pup was right up there with the best of them. She was affectionate, athletic, fun, a good companion, but at times she could be a challenge: cunning, obnoxious and a little bit conceited. If she didn't get her way she whimpered and pouted. When she was pleased she squirmed and wiggled against me like a fat worm on a fishhook.

"You're a sweetheart," I told her. She licked my fingers and that made me laugh. I talked to her. "Do you want to go with us? Sail away? There's a whole world out there to explore. We hit the mainland and you might find yourself a handsome poodle, move to the suburbs and raise a litter of the cutest mongrels anyone ever laid eyes on. Yes, you might. But I better warn you about pickups, cars and trucks. Don't chase 'em. Take it from me—a tie is as good as a loss." I said all that and then for some stupid reason I used a high-pitched voice, a voice like a women uses when they play with babies, cooing, "My cute little doxy, woxy, moxy, fox."

"How do you plan to get this contraption in the water?"

Cheyenne had slipped up on me. I knew she had heard my brainless baby talk and I was embarrassed, embarrassed as hell, but I tried to carry on as if it had never happened. I explained I had everything figured out, that in the next few days there would be an extremely high tide and my raft would float free. I said, "Before then, we have to get everything squared away. I need to knock down another bull, jerk the meat and stow a supply of fresh water and survival gear on board."

I jumped to the ground, took hold of Cheyenne by the shoulders, told her, "Honey, take a deep breath. Ain't it great? That's the smell of freedom."

"We never talked about this."

"What? I said I was gonna do it. You watched me. What do you mean we never talked about it?"

"Did you ever ask what I thought?" Sensing my vulnerability she aimed below the belt and delivered a mean shot. "Anymore, when we make love, you never look me in my eyes."

"Hold on. I thought we were talking about the raft." I felt as uncomfortable as if I had slipped on a pair of new boots and found them to be way too small. Nothing made sense. A man can have a bad day, or a whole string of bad days and we bounce back and get over it. Women have this uncanny capacity to get so far down in the dumps it screws up their body chemistry and all their hormones and shit gets knocked out of whack. It's the same exact thing as when a horse gets spoiled on sugar. That's my theory on it anyway, and I figured that's what had happened to Cheyenne. She'd gone daffy in the head.

"What do you honestly think?" she said. "You think I go around collecting men like some girls collect candles, or shot glasses, or BCBG handbags? I'm not like that."

"What in the Sam Hill are you talking about?"

She brushed back her long hair with one hand, the same way she did that first night at the ranch, as she undressed for me. I had taken a great amount of pleasure in it then. Now I was afraid of what might be coming my way.

"The night I met you, the night I picked you up in that bar, I was trying to get back at Tom. We had come up from California. We were staying with Sheila, a good friend of mine who had moved to Sisters from L.A.—at least I thought we were good friends. We were having a party and Tom sent me after more beer. When I got back I walked in on them. They were on the couch. I wanted to even the score. That's why I fucked you."

"I just happened to be the lucky guy. The one you picked out of a crowd," I said. My body was as rigid as a fencepost.

Tired of supporting it, I leaned against the sureness of the raft and waited for the next volley. I didn't have to wait long.

"Face it—you're a lot older than me. You're not someone I would normally be interested in. But you're rugged and you're handsome and you looked like a man who could handle himself."

I asked just for the sake of curiosity, "Handle myself in bed with you, or in case Tom happened to come around?"

"Both," she said, and I thought she might leave it at that, walk away. She started to, but changed her mind and turned back. "I wanted to hurt Tom like he hurt me. He deserved it. But you know, I'm ashamed of what happened, and in the long run I've hurt myself way more than I ever could have hurt him."

Her top lip was trembling, but her blue eyes never wavered as she stared straight at me, through me. I had difficulty meeting her gaze. I looked down and noticed her left hand. She was wearing her wedding ring. I was trying to figure out the meaning of that, when she picked up the conversation. "My behavior was totally inappropriate for a married woman—cheating back doesn't make it right."

I caught myself nodding slowly to the rhythm of her words and, feeling a twinge of spitefulness, I remarked, "Revenge. Okay, I understand that. Regret, yeah, I can buy that, too. But if you felt that way why in hell did you call me, have me run up here and why did you hop in bed with me so willingly?"

"I had my reasons."

"What were they?"

"Okay, here's why—I was still mad at Tom. He screwed Sheila. You and I didn't finish what we started. The score wasn't even and besides, I thought we could have a harmless fling and nobody would be the wiser. You were like nobody I'd ever met. You were wild, unpredictable, fun. I wanted you. That's why."

"Answer this for me—you didn't have on your wedding ring when you met me at the airport. You must have felt guilt from the get-go, but that never stopped you. And now, out-of-the-blue, you've put it back on." I nodded to the diamond gleaming on her left hand. "Why?"

She started to answer, paused, and then the words came in a rush, words buttressed with absolute conviction, "All I know is that I don't want to sleep with you. I don't want to make love with you, ever again. I'm married. It's time for me to act like a married woman."

Her declaration hit me hard. I had the same sinking feeling a Canada goose must have when it gets blasted from the sky. Feathers no longer holding air. Wings folding. The muffled roar of the shot that had struck me rushed past and I was momentarily lost in the wind whistling around my ears, and the sensation of acceleration toward my certain fate. She was cutting me off. In parting, she added one last shot. "Another thing. You can't swim and I'm not getting on your raft. I don't want to get washed into the middle of the Pacific Ocean. The sea is too big, too powerful. Forget it. I'd rather die right here on dry land."

She started up the beach trail. I continued my tailspin. Ground zero was coming up fast. I suppose I should have felt lucky she walked away when she did. If she had stayed I might have felt compelled to try to talk my way back into her pants, using a jumbled string of run-on sentences, empty promises and, if need be, old-fashioned begging. I've never been any good at begging. But as I stood there, a serious state of bewilderment settled in behind my heart, and what hit me hardest was the certainty in knowing she was the only piece of ass around and I wasn't going to be getting any of it. Nobody, but nobody, was going to be breathing heavy and whispering sweet nothings and sugar zeroes in my ear.

Common sense shouted at me, telling me to keep my big trap shut, but I waved it off and bellowed at her retreating form, "Hey, Babe, I ain't no average Joe. Desire ain't the only horse in my cavy." I know, it was an incredibly juvenile thing for me to say, to yell at her. Hell, it didn't make any sense, not even to me.

I stood there wishing to hell I was back in Oregon—make it wintertime in Oregon, because when everything is chancy there is nothing quite as reassuring and peaceful as the perfection of wide-open country and a fresh coat of virgin snow to cover all of the little imperfections of life.

Chapter 11

Virgins and rich folks with overpriced horses place a high value on something that has very little actual value, except to the owner. (Kelsey Wilder)

The highest tide of the month touched the raft but did not set it free. It remained a beached symbol of my latest defeat. Its hulking form haunted me as I went about the day-to-day routine of survival: waiting for ducks to come close to shore so I could pop them in the head with my .22, digging clams, catching crabs, robbing bird nests, dragging in firewood.

Equally depressing was my living arrangement—here I was on an uninhabited island with a beautiful young gal who had become as frigid as a chunk of glacial ice. We slept in the same room but she occupied the bottom bunk. I was relegated to the top. For a rounder like me, the hands-off, no sex of any type, decree was a tough law to abide by, akin to telling Vincent Van Gogh he could no longer paint. If word got out of my banishment I'd be the laughing stock of every lounge and tavern in Central Oregon. I could hear the conversation. "Did you hear about Waddy? He's been livin' on a deserted island with this beautiful blond bombshell, gorgeous creature, hair down to her ass, and he isn't gettin' so much as a stinky finger. Poor son-of-a-bitch."

At first I tried to sidle up next to Cheyenne. I was charming, witty and a little flirty all at the same time. In retrospect I suppose my actions could have been construed as an obscure form of begging. And, like I said, I ain't never been all that good at begging. To her credit, Cheyenne was true to her word and never fell for my line of bullshit. Not even once. Yet in spite of the lack of any sort of encouragement, I continued to cling to the desperate hope that her resolve would weaken. But it never did.

Living with Cheyenne, and constantly being bombarded by her attractiveness—in every movement, gesture, the subtle rise and fall of her breasts as she slept, the swing of her hips when she was awake—made the appeal of her all the more tempting and tantalizing. Just being ordinary, without benefit of make-up, perfume or new clothes, she was still so good looking she would've made the Pope horny.

One morning, as I lay in my bunk listening to a fresh wind rattling the window glass and rain thudding against the roof, I could not force myself to get up and face yet another day. Pup was sleeping with me and I petted her and brooded. I wanted to be with Cheyenne, and make love to her. After a half-hour of utter frustration, I changed my thinking and began to quietly sing a Hoyt Axton tune, *"It's been raining in the mountains and the river's on the rise, we can't hardly make it to the other side. The devil deals in dying I can see it in his eyes, if you don't help the devil I'm sure that he will die...."*

Cheyenne's voice cut through my singing, "What makes you so happy?"

"Happy?" I said, rolling to the outside and lowering the top half of my body over the edge of the bunk. I said, "Must be 'cause I woke up with an absolute fox here in bed with me." I had been saving that gem for just such an occasion. She gave me a compulsory smile and I thought it was cute the way the unhappy little lines around her mouth turned into joyful lines. With this little bit of success bolstering me I tried to make a giant leap across the yawning chasm between us. "So, Darlin', just because you ran out of birth control pills, and cut me off, doesn't mean we can't do 'other' things."

The muscles in her face went slack and she shook her head side-to-side, almost apologetically. I took it as apologetically and reasoned her body was saying yes but her brain was saying no. I pulled myself back onto my bunk and lay flat on my back, starring at the ceiling and mumbling, "Well, it was just a suggestion." The bed beneath me wiggled slightly, whether from a laugh, or a sob, I couldn't tell.

When your existence boils down to basic survival, life becomes ridiculously simple. You do what you have to do to stay alive. But rarely is survival a full-time job. You find free time on your hands and that can be a problem because, if you don't have anything constructive to do, you spend that free time feeling sorry for yourself.

It became my routine to go to the outdoor privy first thing in the morning. One morning I took along a notebook and a pencil, planning to write a list of things I needed to accomplish, both a short-term and a long-term list. But instead, I spent my time composing a letter to Sam: describing the island, the shack and using a few choice names for Rosenbach. I compared survival to walking a tightrope over a canyon, saying there was no margin for error. Finally, I shifted gears and turned my ramblings into a love letter. I told Sam how much I missed her, missed being around her, talking with her, eating a meal with her, making love with her.

The wind came up and the temperature fell a few degrees. But I was warm and content sitting in the shitter. I found writing to Sam to be a liberating experience. It was almost as if we were together, carrying on a normal conversation.

Sam was a country gal. She had that going for her. Her father was a part-time ditch rider, turning irrigation water on and off for farmers. He also worked as a brand inspector, checking to make sure cattle brought to the feedlot were registered to the rightful owner. He was the salt of the earth. So was her mother, who had done what a decent woman ought to do—stay home, take care of the kids, milk the cow, bake bread, cook hot meals and always have chocolate cake for dessert. But she died. I suspect she worked herself into an early grave.

When a man is being tossed around on a stormy sea he naturally starts looking around for a safe harbor. And for me, Sam became that safe harbor. I knew that to make Sam happy all she needed was a good man, a good father for her children and a little room to swing her elbows.

I wrote, *"... there was something so sweet and tender in our first kiss. I'll never forget it. And when I told you, 'I want you,' it seemed so natural, being with you, our bodies melting together, there on the fresh straw in my horse trailer...."*

The first time Sam and I got together was a memorable event. It was back when I was on the circuit riding rough stock and she was competing in barrel racing. I believe it was Pocatello, Idaho but I could be wrong about that. Back then all the towns ran together. I do remember my rig was parked behind the stock corrals. I broke a bale of straw, scattered it on the floor in my stock trailer to make our bed and we spent the night right there.

I went on writing my letter. *"I just wanted you to know I was thinking about you. You've been very, very special to me for a long, long time. Ever since I've been abandoned on this rotten, stink-hole of an island I've dreamed of you, almost constantly. Tell Travis and Joleen hi for me. I miss you all."* And I signed it, *"Love, Waddy."*

Composing the letter, and daydreaming about Sam, made me realize that my feelings for her were way stronger than they ever were when we were together. I started laughing. What struck me as funny?—I had been sitting in that damn shitter for an hour, writing a love letter and if Sam saw me hunkered down out of the wind, a ring around my ass, she would bust a gut laughing.

I hitched up my pants, tucked the tablet down the front of my shirt and started for the barn. I planned to keep this letter, and any others I might write, hidden from prying eyes.

Cheyenne came out of our shack carrying a bucket. When she reached the spring she called out, "Come here!"

Pup had been with me and at the sound of Cheyenne's voice she darted between my legs, causing me to fall. All my years of rodeoing taught me to fall without breaking bones or tearing muscles. Trying to regain my balance I took several giant strides. When a wreck was inevitable I tucked my shoulder and rolled. As near as I could tell I did a full summersault with a slide thrown in at the end for good measure. I came up about ten paces shy of Cheyenne. She never offered a single compliment about my gymnastic ability, only pointed toward the spring and squealed, "Fish!"

Sure enough, the little pool was teeming with fish. They were the color of aluminum, all a uniform 16 inches or so and would go, I estimated, two pounds each. Most likely they were a run of sea-trout come to spawn. I hurried to the barn, grabbed the pitchfork and returned. My first scoop with the pitchfork yielded eight fish that flopped wildly on the ground. I kicked them away from the water as I instructed Cheyenne, "Kill 'em." She didn't know what to do and so I showed her how to hold a fish and pop it's skull over a rock. I told her, "It snaps their neck, kills them instantly. That way they don't suffer."

I have to give Cheyenne credit. While I scooped fish she killed them, never once protesting or complaining. I think she did it because the fish represented food and she was damn hungry. Otherwise, she wouldn't have touched a slimy fish, not with a ten-foot pole.

That day we had a fish fry to end all fish fries. We ate the pink, flavorful meat with our fingers, piling scraps on a plate in the middle of the table until there was a small mountain of skin and bones. After we had eaten our fill, Cheyenne dried her hands on a towel and from where I don't know, but she produced my tablet, the one I had used for my love letter to Sam.

"Lose this?"

I nodded. She handed it to me. Case closed. Nothing more was said. I don't know if she had read my letter but I suspected she must have. Anyway, it seemed to me that the temperature between us cooled a few more degrees. I think a woman falls for a man's animalistic nature and then when she gets slapped across the face with his romantic side she has a tendency to become confused and withdrawn. That's what I think. Of course it could have been that my letter had shown my softer side to another woman. But what do I know? I don't know jack.

During the run we took 568 fish, eating all we could and smoking the remainder. A few days later I went hunting and killed another bull. For the time being, we were up to our eyeballs in meat.

One night I had a dream that was so vivid I could have sworn I was at the cattle sale in Madras. I walked into the back of the auction yard, bundled up in a heavy Carhart jacket because the heater in my stock truck was on the lam. Sleet blew diagonally and the yardman leaned on his long prod and stared vacantly out across the pens of cattle. In my fingertips I could feel the squeaky grit of the Styrofoam cup I was holding, smell the staleness of the coffee, and taste its cool bitter, coppery flavor on my tongue. I tossed the cup in a fifty-five gallon drum used for garbage, passed the cute sales secretary seated at her desk typing out forms, and took a seat on the gray bleachers. Culled Holstein cows filled the ring while the auctioneer's voice, distorted and booming from worn-out speakers, chanted in sing-song, "Hey, hey, now what'll ya give me, who'll give me a dollar bill, one dollar bill, all right who'll give me six-bits, six-bits, six-bits, will you give me six-bits...." He was trying to sell cheap and fast and get on to the feeders that paid better. There were farmers in coveralls and black rubber chore boots, and expressionless buyers who indiscriminately flipped bid cards to show their number. When the sale was complete the cows disappeared down an alleyway. Another door opened and a man on horseback pushed more helpless cattle into the ring....

The dream began to unravel and I caught a curious odor, heavy and as sweet as a smoldering juniper log in a dying campfire. A campfire where cowboys were gathered around discussing how many cows a good range bull should be expected to cover. Very slowly I came to the hazy realization there were no cowpokes and there was no campfire. Smoke was beginning to tickle my subconscious.

One time, back in my rodeoing days, I came upon a wreck. It was a friend of mine who had swerved to miss a deer, caught a wheel in the gravel, tried to bring his rig back onto the blacktop but over-corrected. When I got there, his pickup was in the barrow pit, burning. He was standing in the middle of the road, holding a fifth by the skinny neck, and staring hard at his rig as though it somehow owed him an explanation.

You seldom see such a hot fire. Shirts hanging on the gun-rack flared and burst into flames. Tires expanded like black blisters and exploded, sending forth showers of sparks and shredded rubber. Inky smoke traipsed down the sky. We just stood there, taking turns pulling on the jug, watching his pickup burn.

Near me, low and throaty, an animal growled. My flesh crawled as I became aware of an odd sensation on my face, something warm, wiggly and wet was lapping at my mouth and nose. Sluggish seconds marched past as I struggled to make sense of it.

All in quick succession I realized Pup was licking my face, I heard a crackling noise, smelled smoke and opened my eyes to what I thought was a wave of sheet lightning. I hollered, "We're on fire!"

Looking back I have to marvel at how it all happened so fast and how everything fell into place and got done so quickly. I leaped out of bed, just had on jockey shorts, pulled on pants, grabbed Pup and tossed her out the door. Flames were visible on the ceiling where the stovepipe poked through the roof. Cheyenne came awake. There was enough light that I could read fear blinking neon-like on her face. She sprang from the sleeping bag without bothering to unzip it, wearing nothing more than a T-shirt and panties. I know this sounds ridiculous, but I noticed the way some loose hair puffed out and laid across her left shoulder. I felt a surge of tenderness come over me for that loose hair, wanting to comb the strand back into place. Something far more immoral than tenderness came over me when I saw the sleekness of her naked thighs.

"Grab the bucket! I'll get the ladder!" I yelled.

Outside, up on the roof, the searing orange of the fire was magnified by the blackness of the night. Cheyenne and I worked together as a team. She brought buckets of water from the spring and I carried them up the ladder and flung them on the fire. We worked hard to douse the flames and though the night was cool, when it was over and the fire was out, I stood clutching the ladder, not able to see much of anything, breath coming hard and fast, sweat rolling down my rib cage.

In an attempt to rid the interior of smoke, Cheyenne propped open the door to the shack, but it took time. We went inside, stayed low where the smoke was thinnest, stripped our sleeping bags off the bunks and hiked down the trail to the raft. With a few stray gallons of adrenalin still pumping through my veins and Cheyenne lying so very close in her sleeping bag, the sleeping bag that could have been zipped together with mine, sleep was out of the question. Overhead the stars shined like glittering spray from a wave breaking across a field of cobalt blue. All at once the northern lights began. Gold and green translucent curtains divided, flowed across the broad spectrum of glowing sky, and on stage were strange phantoms, translucent forms appearing, disappearing, and appearing again.

I looked at Cheyenne and a tiny silver earring she was wearing winked starlight at me. Her profile, although faintly lit, was perfectly chiseled. Her long, pale hair shimmered under the blush of heaven's light and her skin glowed whitish. I blurted, "You're so damn beautiful."

She rolled toward me, gave me a kiss on my cheek, the way a sister might give her big brother a kiss on the day he goes off to college. She started to say something, managed "You are...." and laid her head back down on the deck. My ego suspected the sentence she had failed to complete was "so loveable," or "so wonderful," or "my hero."

She gave an exaggerated sigh. A moment later she confessed, "For the first time in my life I think I understand why people commit suicide. Once you lose control of your life, and give up hope of ever regaining it, well, you might as well be dead."

I have never, would never, consider suicide. Don't get me wrong. If I came down with something terminal, not that life isn't, and it was gonna be a long drawn-out ordeal, I'd take a hard look at the cards and if I elected to fold, there would be no gun, no running head-on into a log truck, no pills. But I might consider taking a long walk on an especially cold night. I could do that. Just go to sleep and never wake up.

I lay there in that big night, Cheyenne so close and yet so far away, watching the metamorphosis of the heavens and listening to the ruthless surf hammer the sand. I thought about what I would have to do in the morning, to fix the roof, and all the little details of the fire came rushing back at me.

Just before I fell asleep my thoughts turned to Sam. I was sure, in the long haul, she was gonna be my girl. I needed someone like her, someone who could stand on her own two feet, live alone, or live with me. I have no use for a woman who wants to be my shadow. Sam had a wonderful sense of humor. She could keep me laughing when the whole world was crashing in around me. She could be tender in love or as feisty as a cornered bobcat. She would always be mine. She would share herself with me and, under no circumstances, would she ever withhold her love from me.

I thought about all those things and yet, I knew my faithfulness to Sam would fly out the window if the warm body next to me proved even half willing. Hell, I'd poke Cheyenne and feel about as much remorse as an old bull leaving his cows to walk the fence leading to a pasture of heifers.

Chapter 12

Life is good as long as you live it on your own terms. If you can't, you ain't livin' at all. (Barton Wilder)

It was the season of the fly, when the annoying insects realize the short summer of the Far North was fading and they would soon die. The flies on Chirikof, as big as B-52 bombers, cut dizzying slashes in the sunlight and attacked anything that represented a possible source of food. Meat had to be wrapped with cloth or netting. Still the troublesome flies found a way inside to lay rows of obnoxious eggs from which wiggly white maggots swiftly emerged. And flies pestered the horses, flying in their ears and congregating in black circles around their eyes. Flies were everywhere.

There were other indications of the change of seasons. Daylight hours conspicuously began to shrink. Tiny wild flowers burst forth and quickly died. What little grass there was turned brown and toppled over. Birds raised their young and flew away. Crab shells turned soft and the meat was mushy and tasteless. Weather made crazy swings, one day warm and pleasant and the next, foggy, windy and wintry.

I anticipated we might get lucky and have an extended Indian summer, but it wasn't something I was willing to bet the ranch on. Chances were, summer would fade into fall, and fall would slip into winter. Could we survive a winter on the island? I didn't even want to try and wrap my mind around such a weighty consideration.

A bully of a storm, huge and violent, rolled out of the Arctic, sending the flies into hiding and giving us ten solid days and nights of high winds and so much rain that, in places, it scoured the topsoil to bare bones.

More times than I care to admit I played the part of the fool, propping open the barn door and standing in the shadows watching the shack and urgently hoping to catch a glimpse of Cheyenne as she moved past the pitted window. I missed all we had had; especially our close friendship. Bullshit, I missed the sex. I was as horny as a tufted tit mouse in a sugar jar.

Me, I've been around the piss pot a time or two and know where the handle is. I purposely tried to limit the amount of time I spent near Cheyenne, giving her a wide berth rather than risk putting any additional strain on our fragile relationship. Most days I was either scaring up food or working on a series of vital projects that had the potential to make our life a little easier. I built a buck-stand that allowed me to saw driftwood into chunks, a covered box outside the door for firewood, a cover over the spring, a porch over the door and I yarded in a small mountain of firewood for future use.

Whenever I had free time, I went for rides. To an outsider these forays might give the appearance of a small-town parade with Mutt tagging along and Pup casting left and right, watching for any mouse foolish enough to expose itself, which she promptly caught and ate.

I returned from one of my excursions, pulled up at the crest of the hill and gazed down on our little cluster of buildings. The scene could have been a holiday greeting card—smoke issued from the chimney of our shack and for just a moment I had a warm, fuzzy feeling, knowing this was home and my woman was down there keeping that fire burning. But my sentiment was short-lived. Cheyenne was certainly not my woman, did not love me, had never loved me, and had gone out of her way to make that distinction perfectly clear.

Two days later I was out riding and an army of unruly clouds came marching at me. Fat raindrops raked the air and the habitual west wind suddenly switched direction and blew straight from the south, causing a flock of Canada geese, aiming their unerring arrow at warmer climes, to squawk loudly at the inconvenience of battling the strong head wind. It occurred to me those migrating birds owned something I might never know again—freedom to roam wherever will and wind took them. I was trapped and my life was wasting away. I asked myself why I didn't have the decency to just die and get it over with.

I rode near a sea cliff overlooking the crashing surf. Swells rolled in and the tops of the waves were wind-chopped. The ocean inhaled and water sucked down among the dark rocks, exposing stringy seaweed, gobs of soot-colored coral, orange starfish, crabs and an array of other wiggly creatures. The ocean exhaled and water surged in and up, making the seaweed flutter and bouncing driftwood on the tops of waves like ballerinas dancing on a stage of jagged glass. White spray rose high into the air and splattered against black rocks. The ocean growled and began once again to inhale.

Widening my point of view I saw sets of waves lined up across the mottled surface of the ocean, sweeping in and around and past the island. I remained there without moving, contemplating who and what I was: a tiny speck of nothingness clinging to a hunk of stone in the middle of the

North Pacific, an unsightly human blemish on the smooth skin of our spinning planet. The personal strengths I always relied so heavily upon—toughness and common sense—dissolved and were replaced by self-doubt and a paralyzing fear of what was to come. Dread ripped at my guts and I dug those gal-legged spurs into Jeff's ribs, propelling him into forward movement. We galloped into the teeth of the storm. Wind tore away my breath. Rain washed at my tears.

From the depths of this gloom the sun mysteriously exploded, falling in long symmetrical bars, splaying downward from a central vortex. The change to sunlight and brightness was so totally unexpected it would not have shocked me if God's booming voice had suddenly shouted to me from the clouds.

I pulled Jeff to an abrupt stop. We were in a basin surrounded on three sides by a rocky cliff. There was not a breath of wind and the air seemed close and supercharged with the sweetness of sun-warmed rocks and damp grass. I saw a girl I did not know standing beside an appaloosa horse. Primary colors flooded my vision. I had to shake my head in order to rid myself of the vision, hallucination, or whatever the hell it was. I realized that if I were to keep this up—seeing things that were not there—I'd soon be knocking on the door to the funny farm.

An eagle swept across the circular sky. Its shadow traversed the face of the rocky cliff in front of me. The island was full of shadows, illusions and ghosts. To ease the burning in my mind I rose on the balls of my feet, stood in the stirrups and shouted "Hey you!" Echoes ricocheted off the rocks, blatting back at me, "Hey you! Hey you! Hey you! Hey you!"

An unsteady silence followed and through the inside of my thighs I was vaguely aware of the swell and fall as Jeff sucked in and blew out air. I searched for a reasonable explanation. At length, I was able to piece together enough logic to explain away nearly all of the wacky happenings: it had been a combination of my being wet and cold, perhaps even suffering the early stages of hypothermia. Besides, I hadn't been sleeping much. Add this to my poor diet. Throw in worry, despair and loneliness. Under similar circumstances, I think most anyone would be able to find a tiny chink in their armor.

I said to the emptiness, "Just give me a dip, a tall boy, a heaping plate of ribs at Bronco Bob's and any halfway willing female. She doesn't even have to be all that good looking. That's it. That's all I want, all I need."

I foolishly thought that was as scary as things were going to get. A week later I suffered a relapse that could not be so easily explained. This time it occurred at night. A candle was burning and Cheyenne was sitting beside the stove, reiterating that we were never going to be rescued and that she felt like dying. I tried to tell her we needed to stay strong and positive, but when a woman gets down as far as Cheyenne appeared to be, there's not much a man can do to stem the tide of her melancholy. I gave up, deciding to put a little distance between us so as not to have her drag me down, too.

I stepped outside into the huge night where a crescent moon was casting an ashen light over the island. While I watched, the blue-black sky ruptured with color—iridescent green, orange and silver—shimmering and reflecting off the polar ice cap. An astonishing display of northern lights exploded so near me I could hear the sharp crackle of electricity. I walked up the hill and it seemed to me that it had always been this way, would always be this way. Me. Sea. Sky. We were three exotic metals fused together for eternity. And then it dawned on me I was overlooking the obvious. The forth element was this miserable chunk of rock I was standing on. It went straight down to the molten core of the world. I stamped one foot and an eerie hollowness reverberated through me. I flung myself on the ground and pressed my face into the carpet of damp, sour-scented tundra grass. My fingers savagely ripped at the thin layer of soil, nails scraping down to hardpan. And then, nearly as fast as madness had engulfed me, it swept past leaving me in a state of twisted confusion. I felt alone and bewildered, coldness crept clear through to my bones and my teeth began to chatter. The shakes took hold of me and I shivered so violently the only relief I could get was to pull up my legs and hug my knees to my chest. I rocked back and forth, crying like a baby.

It was at that point I experienced a revelation of sorts, coming to understand that my salvation was not to be predicated on some stranger appearing and rescuing me from this damn island. The image of Sam came to me. She held me in her arms, cradled me, soothed and comforted me. Sam, coming to me in that moment like she did, probably saved my life, anyway my sanity.

That night I slept in the barn, and in the morning I thought long and hard about my spell the night before. I had no choice but to admit I was not nearly as strong as I thought. In fact, I had become a plumb pitiful shell of the lover, fighter and wild horse rider my ego once told me I had been.

"My Dearest Sam,

"How I wish Travis and Joleen could grow up like I did—bucking bales, trapping and stretching muskrat hides, stacking firewood, using an outdoor privy, socializing at grange hall dances, competing at turkey shoots, eating raspberry jam on fresh homemade bread, sledding in the winter, racing fast horses, moving cattle, riding calves at barnyard rodeos...."

I was using a pencil, writing as fast as I could until I got sidetracked thinking about Joleen and wondering how, in this day and age, a girl was ever gonna survive the rocky road to womanhood. Girls are raised with dolls, cardboard kitchens and plastic serving sets. They play house and dream about a knight in shining armor who will come riding in on a white steed, kiss them to life and slay the fire-breathing dragon. And then a girl becomes a woman and embroils herself in a reckless search for *Mister Right*. She ends up settling for *Best Available Man* and has to hope he'll be a good provider, with sustained ambition and be a devoted and loving husband and father. Reality forces a woman to forget everything she learned as a girl. There are no knights in shining armor.

I laughed at myself. Modern girls were nothing at all like I had them pictured. They were not silly schoolgirls from my era. The sisterhood who preceded the current generation had burned their bras, triggered a sexual revolution, been liberated and motivated into careers of their own choosing. The current crop of pubescent girls enjoyed the benefit of social change while busily engaging themselves with MTV, cell phones and text messaging. They had Victoria's Secrets, the morning after pill, cyber-sex and an ex-president who claimed oral sex wasn't really sex at all. Who was I kidding? Only myself. My opinion about young women came from the Stone Age. I suddenly felt very, very old.

I do know women are complex creatures. Just when you think you have one kinda pegged she up and does something so outrageous you're left scratching your head and muttering to yourself in total amazement. That was exactly what happened to me the afternoon I returned from a ride, stepped through the doorway and found Cheyenne sitting cross-legged on the floor in the middle of the room, naked, scissors in hand. She was the hub and encircling her was a queer mosaic of golden hair. I shouted, "Woman! What the hell have you done?"

It was pretty goddamn obvious what she had done. She had hacked off her hair, off to the nubs. I rushed to her, wrestled the scissors from her hand and tossed them away. They skittered across the floor and banged against the far wall. My hands went to Cheyenne's head, either a symbolic gesture on my part, or simply an irrational act to protect what little hair remained. Her head was prickly. The cuts were ragged. Her golden tresses had been shorn until scalp showed through. God Almighty, I had loved her long, beautiful flowing mane of honey colored hair. And now it was gone.

She lifted her face to me. Tears stained her cheeks. Her nose was runny. She gulped air like a guppy in a fish bowl. Her pretty blue eyes, red-rimmed and misery-plagued seemed reluctant to focus on me. The tiny muscles in her face were as rigid as tent poles. But ever so slowly her hard edge began to dissolve. She slumped forward. I scooped her into my arms, carried her across the room and deposited her on the chair. Moving swiftly, I stripped my sleeping bag off the top bunk and tucked it around her to keep her from going any deeper into shock.

Water was heating on the stove. I poured a little into a cup, added the last of our precious honey, and spooned some of the energy-rich liquid into her mouth. Her lips were too pale, too dry.

"I had an abortion."

I immediately assumed she had given herself an abortion. I took a nervous glance to where she had been sitting, hunting for blood, and then down at her bare legs. There was no splash of red. I felt a wave of relief.

"I went to a clinic in Anaheim," she said. Her words were heartless, spoken in a detached monotone. "The nurse led me to a room. There was wood paneling. She had me lie on an examination table. There was butcher paper on it. Butcher paper."

I tried to spoon more of the honey-water into her mouth but she resisted. I said, "You don't have to tell me this."

"The doctor came in. He was bald and fat. He asked if I wanted an abortion. I said I did. He told me once he started I couldn't change my mind. I told him I knew that.

"He gave me an injection, asked if this was my first abortion, went on talking about things like we were meeting at a bus stop. Finally I told him, 'Shut the fuck up. Just get this thing over with.'"

I didn't know what the hell to do and used a towel to dry her cheeks and wipe snot from her upper lip. After that I just sat on the arm of the chair and tried to be a good listener.

"I remember looking up at this white light, the nurse draping a sheet around me, her patting my shoulder, telling me I wouldn't feel a thing. But I did. I did! One moment I had a baby in my body—safe, alive—and then the doctor was prying my legs apart, shoving a cold steel rod inside me."

I was frightened but I tried to reassure her. "You'll be all right. Everything will be fine."

She tried to speak but couldn't and tried again. "You should know this. I had a miscarriage today. I lost... your baby."

Not in a million years would I have dreamed Cheyenne had been pregnant. But suddenly it clicked—the emotional roller coaster she had been riding, the bouts of severe depression, the way she had pushed me away from her—it all made perfect sense.

A miscarriage. How was I supposed to feel about something like that? I didn't know. My baby. Was she sure? How far along had she been? Did any of that matter? I asked her, "What did you do with it?"

"With what?"

"The baby," I said.

She took a deep breath, exhaled. "I put it in a bag and threw it in the ocean. It was such a tiny thing."

After that we just sat for the longest time. I coaxed a few more spoonfuls of the honey-water down her and put her to bed. When I was sure she was asleep I went to the beach and walked back and forth along the waterline in the growing darkness. I don't know if I wanted to find the bag Cheyenne had discarded, or if I was hoping I never did. I can't rightly say. If I had found the bag with the little fetus inside I would have dug a hole and given it a proper burial. That's what I would have done.

When I came back from the beach I checked on Cheyenne. She was still sleeping. I went to the barn and talked to the horses, telling them about the goings on. I thought some about what it would have been like, if I had had a daughter. She would have been horse crazy, for sure. I would buy her the best barrel horse I could afford. She would be the queen of the roundup. And if I had had a son I would toss him up on the saddle and have him riding long before he learned to walk. We would work cattle together. He would rodeo. But there was no baby, and as far as I knew, Cheyenne's miscarriage was as close as I had ever come to fathering a child.

Darkness drew a curtain over the land. I went inside to be with Cheyenne. Mostly I listened to the outside noises as a fresh storm blew in. The wind shrieked, waves battered against sand and rocks. I wanted to cry but the tears never came. I just kept my grief bottled up inside.

Chapter 13

Sweetheart,

There are a lot of things I've done in my life that I'm not too terribly proud of but I've turned over a new leaf and I swear to God that, from now on out, I'm gonna be a one-woman man. I'll treat you like the lady you deserve to be treated like. I'll be a decent human being. When I come back, if I can't find work buckarooing, I'd even pull greenchain at the mill for you.

Love, Waddy

P.S. Can't wait to see you kids, bet you're growing up faster than spring calves on good pasture.

In the barn, under the diminishing pile of loose hay, I uncovered an old wooden trunk. Apparently it was a carpenter's tool chest, because inside I found a saw, hammer, T-square, various sizes of hand planes and several pounds of assorted nails. But what interested me was a map of Chirikof and a write-up about the island in an old issue of *Alaska Magazine*.

I read the article. It listed the location of Chirikof Island as 160 miles southwest of Kodiak Island and 2,500 miles due north of Hawaii. I looked south and tried to mentally transport myself to the sandy beaches where sweet morsels of feminine delight frolicked in swimsuits the size of postage stamps. This was just too much of a stretch for my imagination to comprehend. I went on reading. According to the story Vitus Bering, namesake of the Bering Sea, had discovered Chirikof back in 1741. He was a Danish naval officer commissioned by Russian tsar Peter the Great to explore the Far North.

A quote attributed to some fellow named Elliott, who visited Chirikof in 1886, stated, "Chirikof Island, that lonely, isolated, desolate spot was the point where the one-time Russian criminals who were guilty of murder, arson, and other capital offenses were shipped and left largely to their own devices for a livelihood. They were literally entombed on this islet... sometimes prisoners were buried alive, standing up, shackled in leg irons...."

I muttered, "Jesus," and a shiver ran the length of my spine. But I continued reading a detailed description of the various stock companies that had attempted ranching operations on the island after the Russians pulled out. The first was a San Francisco based outfit that supplied fresh beef to whaling vessels operating on the Bering Sea and Arctic waters. That operation had failed, as had subsequent operations, and each had failed miserably. In the words of one man, John Grounds, "Chirikof Island has been a challenge to its owners throughout its cattle history, leaving a trail of beached and broken ships, battered and lost planes, and missing men. The unfortunate...."

The article had been ripped apart in the middle of that sentence. I tried to imagine what other bad news I was missing. By simply signing on with Rosenbach I had become a part of the bleak history of Chirikof Island. If I died here I would be nothing more than the latest in a long list of distressing footnotes.

Pup came to me wanting a love. I petted her and told her, "For all I care that son-of-a-bitch Rosenbach can piss up a rope and go blind. He sends me here knowing it's never worked out for a ranch, and that it never will. I'll kick his ass 'til his nose bleeds."

I returned the article to the bottom of the chest and picked up the map. It held much more promise than the article and showed two places where civilization had touched Chirikof. One was our cluster of buildings on the southern shore. The other was at the extreme northern most point on the island, the only part I had not visited, where there was a small black square. According to the legend, this indicated a manmade structure. Near this symbol someone had written the words "Radio Tower," circled it, and drew an arrow to an X.

Seeing this as a possibility, I felt an infusion of hope and actually allowed myself to think there might be someone actually living at the site of the radio tower. My joy was short-lived. Rationally, I had to figure this was an unmanned radio tower. And yet from time to time it had to be maintained. If someone was coming out to check it, I'd make damn sure I was there when they came. But that didn't make sense. I couldn't be in two places at once. I told myself I could leave them a note, let them know where we were, that we had been abandoned and were in desperate need of rescue.

I kept the map, slammed the lid shut and vowed to explore the north side of the island in the morning. I should have done it weeks before but had never gotten around to it because it was a long ride and I'd been busy just trying to survive. Also, I felt a heavy responsibility to watch over Cheyenne, to keep an eye on her.

There was no need to share what I had found. No need to get Cheyenne's hopes up just in case nothing materialized. Her mental state was just too fragile to handle another setback. And yet, I reasoned that if by visiting the north side of the island it would somehow lead to our rescue, it certainly was worth the effort and the risk of leaving her alone.

That night I slept fitfully. At one point I thought about how we live in a world that is in a constant state of change: an old Indian woman dies and a hundred years of history dies with her, a sharpened chain saw bites into the backbone of a tree older than the United States, a highway cut dissects the strata of ten-million years. As I drifted into sleep, I dreamed about the north side of our island and saw a man wearing suspenders and pants snagged like a logger. His wife was a plain woman dressed in a red and black wool shirt and Levi's. They took us in, Cheyenne and me, and this woman fixed us such a wonderful meal that I awoke to the sound of my stomach growling.

When I got back to sleep I dreamed about a wall of water galloping down a rocky ravine, a flash flood. It carried me out to the open sea where I flailed about. Unable to go back to sleep, I got up, stoked the fire in the stove, threw a couple of handfuls of jerky in a daypack and filled a plastic bottle with water. Before leaving I checked on Cheyenne. She was sleeping, hugging Pup to her breasts as if the little fox was her lost baby. I bent and kissed Cheyenne's cheek. She came awake. Her eyes opened.

"Where are you going?"

"Up north, do a little exploring," I told her. "Keep the fire going. There's plenty of wood. I filled up the wood box for you. Whatever you do, just don't let the fire go out."

We were down to only a few matches. If we ever ran out of fire that was it. We might as well cash in our chips, because we were goners.

"When will you be back?"

"Soon as I can. Before dark I hope, but don't worry if I'm late. I'll get here when I get here."

"Give me a hug."

I moved Pup to the side and hugged Cheyenne. She hugged me back and when the hug ended, I returned Pup and she quickly snuggled back to where she had been. As I departed Cheyenne called, "Don't take any chances."

"Don't worry, I won't."

Riding along in the dark, using the dim light from a white moon that lay cocked over the heel of the Pacific, I sang cowboy songs. Old songs by legends of the industry: Bob Wills, Hank Snow, Sons of the Pioneers, Hank Williams. An occasional echo bounced a few words back at me. I kept singing because it was a damn solid fact my echoes weren't gonna sing to me.

When I grew tired of singing I imagined what it was like at home. This time of year the leaves of the cottonwoods and aspens would have turned brilliant yellow and the vine maple would be scarlet. Indian summer—warm days, cool nights, frost in the mornings. Fresh rain would bring the red-gilled, blue-backed steelhead into the Deschutes River to spawn. Deer and elk were migrating down, from the Ochoco Mountains and the High Cascades, to their wintering grounds. Ducks and geese would drop onto desert potholes to rest before continuing south. And after a few more storms the tamarack needles would lose their grip and stain the fresh snow with slender spikes of gold. Jesus, was I ever missing Oregon.

The sun came up like a pink rose unfolding one petal at a time. Overhead, mare's-tail clouds, whipped along by the jet stream, dragged in fluffy rain clouds. I turned up my collar, gathered the duster and buttoned it around me. Before long, oversized raindrops bashed against the crown of my hat and ran off the brim in one long, continuous stream. The wind gusted and I rubbed water from my eyes like some kid bawling on the playground. About then, Mutt, who had been tagging along, gave up and turned back toward the protection of the barn and the hay.

It finally stopped raining but the wind continued to blow. I glanced at my watch to see how many hours I had been traveling. The hands were frozen at 22 minutes past 7.

I tapped the crystal with a knuckle. Time refused to budge. Spinning cogs no longer fit together in precise synchronization. Skinny outstretched hands refuse to turn in constant circles. But really, what the hell did it matter that my watch was broken? Mother Nature was perfectly capable of handling it on Her own, rationing time by daylight and dark, seasons, lifetimes.

It stopped raining. The sky cleared some and a contrail shot across the sky. Like a slender thread stringing together odd-shaped beads, it pierced through puffy white clouds, leftovers from the fast moving storm. I never saw the steely glint of the airplane or heard the roar of its jet engines but all the same I accepted it was up there. This caused me to consider how often we are willing to acknowledge such abstract assumptions as jet airplanes and contrails. Go back one man's lifetime and there weren't any such things as jet airplanes. We take for granted a lot of other things; satellites curving across space, radio and television signals ricocheting around us, spaceships to Mars, men walking on the moon.

As Jeff climbed higher the country transformed itself from barren scab-flats to hillsides covered with brush as thick and course as a fur coat. We crossed a gully where erosion had worn the soil down to rock, the gray of a healed saddle sore. Coming up the far side a pair of cows flushed from a thicket and ran wild and bug-eyed. They made a semi-circle before stopping on a ridgeline to defiantly stare back at us. The cows called for their calves. The calves bawled for their mamas. Upon hearing the commotion, a bull emerged from the brush, stood a hundred yards out and shook his head side to side, bellowing a challenge and pawing dirt over his back. I told him, "I ain't interested in your harem or your kingdom. I'm just passing through."

I spotted the radio tower standing on the summit of a hill and tried to coax Jeff into a lope, but he bowed his neck and refused to share my enthusiasm. He proceeded at his customary pace, slow and steady. It seemed as if it would take forever to reach the stubby, metal-legged tower.

Adjacent to the tower was a small building wrapped in tin. I felt a tightness in my chest as I read the sign on the door, "Meteorological Project—University of Alaska". I jumped to the ground, tied Jeff to one of the guy wires and approached the door. To my amazement it was padlocked. I had to laugh—if this was not the height of governmental absurdity, to lock a door on an abandoned island. At least it was a cheap lock. After bashing it a few times with a rock it unlocked. I swung open the door and peered inside. It was dark but my eyes soon adjusted, and I saw the floor was crowded with a bank of batteries hooked in series, and the walls were choked with impersonal dials and writing instruments making slow lines on rolls of graph paper. The assortment of technological gadgets gave off a steady drone.

I was disappointed. Maybe I had hoped to see a telephone, or a couple college kids sitting behind a desk taking notes. I don't know. I groaned and muttered, "Fuck a duck, McCutchen!"

On the bright side, I could at least see that someone occasionally visited the site to restock paper and check batteries. I knew they would come again, most likely before winter set in with a vengeance. This was reassuring. I further reasoned someone was monitoring the instruments, probably by short-wave radio and the best way for me to attract attention was to kill the signal. I unhooked the lead wire and immediately the dials dropped to zero, the writing instruments froze in mid-stroke, and the hum of machinery died without fanfare.

I acted out the probable response my actions were having on some conscientious technician sitting in a cushy office in Anchorage. The technician would leap to his feet and exclaim, "Ding-dang-it! Chirikof has gone offline. All the instruments are down."

His discovery would set off a chain reaction: The technician notifying his supervisor, supervisor checking to see if there had been an earthquake or another natural disaster in the area. And then, assuming it was simply a battery failure or a mechanical problem he would send a flunky to Chirikof to check things out and fix the problem.

Before leaving I tore off a hunk of graft paper and used a pencil I found to write a note stating two people were marooned on the south side of the island and pleading for help. After closing the door and slipping the broken lock through the hasp, I eased Jeff off the hill toward a long sloping flat that ended at the sea. At the upper end of this flat stood the skeletal remains of a building. The wind had stripped away most of the tin and what remained of the roof leaned precariously to one side. As I came near, a cluster of pigeons poured out in a clatter of wings and ascended into the sky like a squadron of lost souls departing this world. Jeff snorted, sidestepped, and tried to hump his back, but I reined him around in a tight circle and he forgot about being startled.

After securing Jeff to a discarded 500-gallon propane tank, I began a cursory examination of the building. There was not much to see. Sand had come and gone as the wind pushed it around. There was a set of rusty bedsprings, parts of a chair and a three-legged table. The only thing of any real interest was a drab army footlocker with white lettering, badly weathered, but I managed to read, "Don Geer 2 AD SS". I unlatched the catch, lifted the lid, and was astonished to find a five-pound sack of Purina dry dog food, along with a small jar of Skippy's creamy-style, peanut butter. I fought the impulse to sit down and eat the entire contents of the jar of peanut butter. Cheyenne deserved her fair share. I took the jar, stuck it in my coat pocket and tied the small sack of dog food behind my saddle.

As I went to remount I looked down, at where Jeff was impatiently pawing the ground, and spotted something white. Using my shoulder to push Jeff aside, I got down on my hands and knees and began scooping away the sand. It quickly became evident I had found a human skull.

Finding the skull the way I did, digging it out with my hands, must have caused my mind to snap. I really don't know how to explain things except to say, when I pulled it free and held it up, the goddamn thing grinned at me. Grinned like we were long lost friends. One minute a fellow figures he's as sane as the next guy, and then the devil jumps up and pushes him over the brink and he falls into a canyon of out-and-out madness. I'm not necessarily saying that's what happened to me, but when I started to regain my senses, I was holding the skull up to my face, talking to the ghastly thing.

What I said was, "Marry me, Sam. Don't let me die alone." Swear to God, I saw Sam's face in the skull and I actually did say those words. Then I got a grip, tossed the skull back in the hole and hastily covered it over with sand. I continued to kneel there, panting, tears and sweat stinging my eyes. I don't know how much time passed because when I finally did look at my watch the hands were still stuck at 22 minutes past 7.

I did what any reasonable fellow would do under the circumstances—I tried to laugh it off, but my laughter came out sounding like a flat-head six cranking over on a January morning. It was more a growl than an actual laugh and I told myself, "Waddy, get your ass up off the ground. Next thing you know you'll be suckin' your thumb and slobbering like some crazy fool."

On the return leg to the south side of the island I was joyful, almost giddy, for a time. I anticipated sharing what I had found with Cheyenne and telling her how hopeful I was that my actions at the site of the meteorological project would result in our being rescued. But, as the day began to wane and the cold, wet wind picked up, my pleasant outlook could not sustain itself. I began to fret over my reaction to finding the skull. This led to a general downward spiral and my thoughts were consumed by how many dead things I had witnessed over the years.

I was used to seeing coyote carcasses draped over fences, decaying, held together by stringy tendons and tufts of hair. I had watched magpies walk the barbed wire tightrope, eating their fill of coyote and leaping into light-boned flight. I had dragged several hundred cows that died from disease or complications giving birth, to the bone-yard. Calves, too. And horses. I've skinned elk and deer. None of that bothered me in the least.

But the skull, seeing Sam, bothered the shit out of me. Why had my mind played such a malicious trick? And then it hit me. The answer was as simple as getting smacked up alongside the head with a two-by-four. I was in love with Sam. I told myself love did that to a fellow and made a promise to myself—if I ever did get home and had the occasion to see Sam in the flesh I was gonna drop to one knee and beg her to marry me. Hell, I'd even adopt her kids.

Sitting in the outhouse and watching the wind push my half-moon cutout in aimless circles, I speculated that the human skull I had found the day before was most probably a Russian prisoner. There was only one way to find out, but I sure as hell wasn't gonna return to the burial site to ascertain if the skeleton was standing upright and shackled with irons. If the skull wasn't Russian, it likely belonged to the last unlucky cowpoke who had been tricked into coming to this island ranch.

Stephen King wrote a book. I don't like reading Stephen King all that well, he's too damn scary, and I'd hate to have to live in his brain. But this one winter I was feeding out, had time on my hands and there wasn't a lot of reading material lying around, so I read this Stephen King book about a man who killed people. But he didn't kill them directly.

Instead, he set up a complicated scheme so they killed themselves. Maybe Rosenbach was like a character from a Stephen King book and this was all an elaborate plot for me to kill myself.

I had plenty of time to sit and contemplate bizarre conspiracies because, after returning from my trip to the north side of the island, I had shared the jar of peanut butter I found with Cheyenne, and then had indulged myself by eating dog food. I was hungry. It wasn't half bad. I had three bowls.

In the middle of the night I had been stricken with a severe case of Montezuma's Revenge and ever since, most of my time had been spent in the outhouse, waiting for the next bout of diarrhea to hit me.

On one of my many outhouse visits I composed a letter to Sam, writing that the reason I had come to Alaska was to make money and, hopefully, we could use it to make a down payment on a place of our own. I made promises; promising Sam she would be the only woman for me and promising to be a good father to Travis and Joleen. For some reason I added a P.S., stating I had never come to Alaska to horse on Cheyenne. That was a lie. I felt so bad about lying to Sam that I tore up the letter and threw it in the shit hole. When the next wave of diarrhea hit me I destroyed the evidence. I thought that was fitting and vowed to never lie to Sam. Not ever again.

From my seat on the throne I either heard a wave slapping wood or caught a spark of movement. I don't know which, but when I turned toward the sea there was a boat bobbing on the waves not more than a quarter-mile offshore. Two men were busy dumping crab pots off the stern. I ran like a penguin, pants around my knees, until I had sense enough to jerk them up and cinch my belt. I scrambled down the hill, raced onto the beach and splashed into the water with my boots on. I screamed for the boat to come back. I was a goddamn lunatic, stripping off my shirt and waving, shouting until I lost my voice. The crabbers kept working and never gave the slightest indication they had heard or had seen me.

I burst through the front door of the shack and in a hoarse, excited whisper told Cheyenne, "I saw a boat. It was only three or four hundred yards off shore." Her face went so ashen the tiny freckles on her cheeks showed as brown spots. She licked her lips, blinked several times, and overcome with emotion she simply flopped backward onto the chair. I was on my knees in front of her squeezing her hands, telling her, "They didn't see me but they were setting crab pots. They have to come back to pick them up. I'm gonna make a great big bonfire. We're gonna be rescued."

The remainder of that day, as well as the next, Cheyenne and I worked together to yard in driftwood to the flat above the shack. The afternoon of the second day Pup—she had been playing and hunting around the driftwood—started whining and yipping. She chased out a young bull calf. We had never seen cattle near our side of the island. I don't know how or why the calf was there, but figured it best not to look a gift horse in the mouth. This was a golden opportunity to acquire a supply of fresh meat without having to waste any of our precious bullets.

The calf went a couple hundred pounds and would have easily outrun my lumbering horse had not Pup, nipping at the calf's heels, turned it toward the ocean. The calf ran into the water, lunged into the powerful surf, tired quickly and turned toward shore. When it's feet hit land it raised up and I threw my loop, grabbed a quick dally, tied off and dragged the calf to shore. I got off. Made like a calf roper, going hand-over-hand down the rope until I reached the calf and drove it to the ground. I pulled my Leatherman free from its sheath, tugged the blade into the lock position, grabbed the calf's jaw and pulled the head up and back. With the neck exposed I used the knife to saw through the windpipe and the jugular.

To be sure it was a barbaric performance, but when you're facing starvation you react without contemplating subtleties.

For every Big Mac served to a customer, someone had to kill an animal. It was shot in the head with a stun gun, throat cut, gutted and the meat butchered. In the wilds you can't hire a hit man to do your dirty work.

When the throes of death had subsided I jumped to my feet and hollered, "Yahoo." I stripped off my wet shirt and tossed it aside. And then, covered in blood and sand, I hiked to where Cheyenne was standing and bragged, "Ain't too bad for a side-hill cowboy, now am I?"

She said, "You're such a good hand to have around I can't figure why you never got married."

I told her, "Guess I never met a whore who owned a liquor store." We both laughed. That was the first time we had laughed together in a long, long time.

A storm full of piss and vinegar hit the island broadside and rain poured from the clouds like a lake slopping over. Eventually, the wind blew the clouds away and the sun emerged, sending shivers of light to warm us. Then the wind miraculously died and the day turned warm and wonderful.

Cheyenne went with me to walk the beach to see if we could spot any boats. She watched the ocean. I watched her. She wore florescent yellow shorts and one of my white sleeveless T-shirts. No bra. I walked up close to her to tell her I was sure we were about to be rescued and noticed a rash creeping along the inside of her arms. Her skin was dry and flaky, cheeks hollow and squint lines had form around her incredible blue eyes. She had lost at least fifteen pounds. I told her, "You're beautiful."

She turned away. I distinctly remember the way her feet kicked up swirling patterns of white sand, the long strands of muscles in the back of her legs flexing, the rocking movement of the tan meat on her round shoulders, the perfect composition of the droplets of seawater she kicked from the waves. She was running and shouting, "There's a boat!

There's a boat! There's a boat!" She was pointing. I saw the same blue-and-white crab boat I had seen a few days earlier. It wallowed in the waves near shore.

This was the break we had been waiting for, praying for, and I sprinted toward the shack, grabbing the shovel on the way, dashing inside, scooping coals from the firebox and pouring them into a metal bucket. I carried the bucket to the top of the hill and dumped the coals on the kindling I had ready and waiting under a piece of black plastic. A puff of wind ignited the thin strips of wood with a whoosh. White smoke rose into the sky. I squeezed my eyes closed but still saw flames dance across my eyelids and felt heat spread across my face and chest.

Cheyenne was there with me. I tapped my heart with my fist and told her, "They have to see this!"

I knew it was only a matter of time before I would go home to my mud-splattered pickup truck, to Charley, to fields of stubble still golden and wisps of fog in the moonlight. I was going home to the mountains and the desert. And I was going home to Sam.

Cheyenne handed me the binoculars and when I had them focused I could read the name of the boat, the *Arctic Tern*. No deckhands were visible, but I didn't give up hope. I waited and prayed. Minutes dragged like an anchor being pulled through mud. My mind went numb.

One time I saw a mirage in Utah—there was a Greyhound bus where there wasn't a road within fifty miles. Another time, on the Alvord Desert, I looked out across the heat shimmering above the white sand and saw a guy water-skiing behind a boat.

God, I wished I'd see someone aboard the boat. I wished I had proof this wasn't a mirage. I opened my eyes and Cheyenne was staring at me. I did something really dumb. I acted like I was answering a telephone and spoke into my little finger: "Ring-a-ding. Hello there. This here's the rescue party 'board the good ship *Arctic Tern*. We'll be headin' your way ta pick ya'all up off that little island in 'bout 15 minutes. Sit tight, ya hear."

Cheyenne continued to stare at me. I guess she figured, at a crucial moment like this, humor should be in short supply. The only thing that might have made her loosen up was if the crab boat had run up on the beach to rescue us. Me, I needed a dose of levity to cut the incredible tension I was feeling.

The fire was roaring, throwing off so much heat we were forced to move away from it. The creosote-soaked planking I had arranged on top of the pyre was kicking up a roily cloud of black smoke. The crabbers had to see it. Just had to.

I watched and the little boat on that great big ocean moved steadily away from us. I sank to my knees and prayed into my hands the way a doomed man prays for his life.

"There's a man! And another! They're pointing at us," shouted Cheyenne, looking through the binoculars and waving her free arm.

"Let me see." I stole the binoculars from her, made a slight adjustment and saw a man dressed in a red and black wool shirt, with a blue watch cap pulled low on his forehead. He was waving. My heart thumped against my sternum. Relief, elation, joy and a thousand other emotions whizzed around and over and through me. Tears stung my eyes.

It had been two hours since the crew of the *Arctic Tern* signaled us. The sun was straining itself through clouds massed along the western front. The boat was still out there hauling in crab pots, re-baiting them and setting them out again. Tomorrow the tide would be right. Tomorrow a plane would come for us.

I was busy adding wood to the stove. Cheyenne was cleaning a pair of crabs I had collected from a pool at low tide. There came a distant sound that quickly grew in intensity until it was an avalanche of reverberations. I threw open the door and a huge red and white helicopter, bearing the insignia of the U.S. Coast Guard, was corkscrewing itself from the maroon sky and landing on the flat beside the shack. The wash kicked up sand and small rocks, forcing me to slam the door shut. I leaned against the door and turned to face Cheyenne. She seemed frozen with a crab in one hand.

The power of the spinning rotors lessened. I took a chance, opened the door and two men dressed in orange jumpsuits were standing there. One of the men shouted over the noise, "We got a call from a crab boat. They thought you might be trying to get their attention. Everything okay?"

"Hell no, it's not okay!" I responded. "We got abandoned here."

"Want us to lift you out?"

"Hell yes!"

"Get a move on."

The flyboys helped Cheyenne while I kissed Pup on the top of the head and turned her loose. I dashed to the barn, threw open the gate, pulled the halters off Mutt and Jeff and told them, "Get gone!" I grabbed my saddle and tack and ran to the helicopter, tossed them in, made a quick detour to the shack where I collected my rifles and personal gear. I raced back to the helicopter and jumped in. Cheyenne was already there, holding her bag of possessions on her lap.

We lifted off in a surge of power and pounding vibrations. Looking down I could see the glow of the signal fire and a long smudge of smoke traipsing down the sky. My dismal raft was there, and in the gathering twilight, I could see the dusty trail kicked from the hooves of the galloping horses.

On the way to the Coast Guard base on Kodiak Island the flyboys managed to patch me through to the operator. I had her dial Sam's number. It rang seven times and I was fixing to hang up when she came on the line. I shouted over the noise, wanting to know, "Why didn't you answer the phone?"

"Who is this?" she demanded.

"It's me. I just got rescued. I'm on my way in."

"Waddy?"

"You got it, Sweetheart. Who the hell else could it be?" I felt full of life. "Tell you what, I'm gonna be coming in to Anchorage from Kodiak Island in the morning. Catch the first flight you can. I'll meet you in Anchorage."

"Why didn't you call? Why didn't you write so I'd know where you were? I've been worried."

"I'll explain everything when I see you. Promise."

"I don't know if I can get anyone to baby sit on such short notice."

"Sure you can. I really want you there." I expected a quick response, but got nothing in return. My call was probably rocking her world. I told her, "I got something important to ask you. It'll change your life. That's all I'm gonna say. Be there tomorrow, okay?"

"I don't know where I'd get the money."

"Take it out of savings. Borrow it. I'll make it up to you, Darlin'. I swear. I've got money coming."

"I'll try."

"Don't try. Do it. Hey, Sugar, for some crazy reason I get a second chance at life and I swear to God I'm gonna make the most of it. You can count on me."

"Okay, I'll be there."

After the line went dead there were a hundred things I wished I'd said: telling her how she had helped to get me through this terrible ordeal, that she had given me the strength to persevere, that I loved her. And I supposed I should have inquired about the kids. But at a time like that you wing it, do the best you can, and don't look back.

Cheyenne tried to talk to her husband but there was no answer. She left a message. There wasn't much to it, just that she was coming home and would call him from Kodiak. I felt bad for her but there wasn't anything I could do.

The crew wanted to know all about our abandonment, and I was filling them in on the graphic details, when suddenly I remembered the notebook and love letters I had written to

Sam, some on the back of soup labels. I had left them behind. When I mentioned this to the pilot he turned toward me and asked, "Wanna go back?"

My response was lightning quick, "Hell no!"

When we were in sight of Kodiak Island I declared, "God, is it ever great to get back to the good ol' U. S. of A."

One of the Coast Guard men told me, "Chirikof is part of the United States."

"Bullshit," I told him. "It ain't a part of nowhere."

After landing at the Coast Guard base on Kodiak Island we were taken to the mess hall where the cook fixed us steak and eggs with hash brown potatoes. For dessert we had peach cobbler and real ice cream. Afterward Cheyenne, saying she wanted a hot shower and to sleep in a real bed with sheets and blankets, went off on her own. But I sat up into the wee hours, drinking and bullshitting the boys. They were a great bunch of guys. After they had heard my story they told me I should write a book about my experiences, said all I needed to get the ball rolling was a little publicity and offered to help me. They called a reporter they knew from the *Kodiak Daily Mirror*, the local newspaper, and he came right down and interviewed me. I gave him an earful and didn't pull any punches when it came to Rosenbach dumping us on Chirikof and leaving us for dead.

The only difficult part was how I could diplomatically answer questions about my relationship with Cheyenne. I guess one of the boys must have told the reporter Cheyenne was a looker because the reporter wanted to know all about her. He asked if we were married. I said, "She is, I'm not." And then I stretched the truth just a little by saying, "The reason she was there was because Rosenbach sent her out to get the headquarters set up. But of course the son-of-a-bitch lied about that, there wasn't no headquarters."

I went on to explain more about the shack we lived in, the horses we captured, the fox we made into a pet, finding the skull and the footlocker and my eating the dog food. He took a few photographs of me and concluded the interview with, "What are your plans? What are you going to do now?"

"That's easy," I told him, "Hell, I'm going to Disneyland."

The reporter promised his story would run in the morning edition and would go out over the AP wire. He suggested every newspaper in the country might pick it up and run it. I told him, "Have at 'er, partner."

In the morning my whiskey head was pounding but I got up, poured down several cups of coffee and took a look at the newspaper. My photograph was on the front page. I was holding a fifth of Black Velvet and looking all bleary-eyed and drunk. The headline screamed, "*ABANDONED COWBOY EATS DOG FOOD TO SURVIVE.*"

Cheyenne and I took a commercial flight from Kodiak and since the plane was not crowded they allowed me to carry on my saddle and personal gear, except for my rifles. I had to box them and check them through as baggage.

Cheyenne sat behind me, her choice, and when the stewardess came around I asked for a little hair of the dog that bit me. A couple of whiskeys later and I was revived up and feeling fine. When we landed at Anchorage I picked up my saddle and war bag and waited for Cheyenne but she told me to go ahead. I wasn't sure what the reception would be like inside and, not really wanting to say my goodbyes with Sam on my arm, I told Cheyenne, "Well, I guess this is it."

She offered nothing and not knowing what else to say I told her, "Hope you and Tom get back together, if that's what you want."

"That's what I want. Thanks for being so strong. Goodbye." She reached a hand to me, touched my face with the back of her fingers and promptly withdrew her hand.

I moved forward, away from her, squeezing down the narrow aisle between the rows of seats with my bulky saddle on my shoulder and carrying my war bag. I made my way off the plane and into the long corridor leading to the terminal. People were gathered near the gate. I spotted Rosenbach. He was dressed in a conservative brown suit, tan shirt and stripped tie. He stood out like a sore thumb and his appearance made me realize how rough I must look with my beard, holey jeans and my cowboy hat that had been reshaped by the rain and wind of Chirikof.

I walked straight to Rosenbach, rolled the saddle off my shoulder and laid it on the floor. I dropped the war bag. Rosenbach was perspiring. I could smell fear on him like a mean dog smells fear. He immediately went on the offensive.

"We need to talk. I can explain." He took a few quick puffs that passed for breathing and lowered his voice to just above a whisper. "I had some personal setbacks. My bookkeeper embezzled from me. And I was arrested for possession of cocaine. I couldn't afford to send a plane to get you."

"So you left us there?" I was so mad I could feel the muscles in my butt twitching. I tried gritting my teeth. My jawbone popped under the pressure. "You dirty, rotten son-of-a-bitch."

"I'll pay you every cent I owe you. Swear to God. Just give me time. Don't make a big stink, not here. We can work this out."

Bright lights engulfed us as a television crew pushed their way in close and a woman shoved a microphone in my face, saying, "According to reports, you were abandoned on an island in the Gulf of Alaska. Is that true?"

"Damn straight," I responded as I continued to glare at Rosenbach.

"Tell me about it. What was it like?"

I gestured toward Rosenbach. "Here's the S.O.B. who left us for dead. Why don't you ask him why he did it?"

The woman thrust the microphone toward Rosenbach. "Any comments?"

Rosenbach turned away from me and in a controlled and dignified voice he spoke into the microphone while flashing a weak smile for the camera. He lied, "This man I hired was a cheechako. He didn't know squat about the North. I gave him plenty of supplies for the duration of his stay. I have the receipts to prove it. On the advice of my attorney that's all I can say."

In my peripheral vision I saw Cheyenne. She was moving toward a stocky man wearing a leather coat and a ball cap. She stopped a few feet from him. He didn't welcome her into his arms but he didn't walk away either. I was waiting to see what happened next when the reporter wheeled back to me. "They say to keep from starving you ate dog food. What can you tell me about that? What is it like to almost starve?"

"Well, Honey, it ain't no picnic."

I guess Rosenbach figured I was preoccupied. He tried to sneak away but I reached out, grabbed him by the sleeve of his suit coat and spun him so he had no choice but to face the television camera. I said, "Everything this man just said is a lie. He told me he was arrested for drugs and he couldn't afford to rescue me. He didn't even bother to notify the Coast Guard. He just left me there to die."

Rosenbach said, "This is not the time nor the proper forum to discuss personal matters."

"I think it is a public matter." I turned toward the camera. "All you television viewers take a good look at this man. The next time you see him around town I want you to march right up to him and ask him when he's gonna pay that cowboy he abandoned on Chirikof. Make him number one on the list of Alaska's Most Wanted. Help guarantee justice is served."

At that moment I really wanted to uncork a roundhouse right, catch Rosenbach flush on his chin and send him sprawling. But kicking the shit out of him would have given me about as much satisfaction as hitting someone's grandma. He just wasn't worth the effort.

I turned away and as I did I spotted Sam standing alone, outside the circle of light, people and commotion. She was dressed in white pants, black boots and a frilly silver blouse with a buckskin vest. Her hair was full bodied and curly, like she had had it done special. She looked beautiful. I moved to her and when I drew near I instinctively threw my arms around her waist and pulled her against me. She seemed to melt in my embrace, and if paradise could be captured in a hug, then I held paradise in my arms.

I pulled back her hair and breathed in her ear, "Sam, I missed you so much."

Just then an Alaska Airlines stewardess, tall and lithe, with long brunette hair and a gray uniform skirt hiked up to reveal a set of perfectly proportioned legs, hurried past. I could hear the swish of her nylons rubbing together and caught the faint fragrance of her perfume. I was hugging Sam, but out of the corner of my eye, I was watching Miss Long Legs. I just couldn't help myself.

The End

Epilogue

As soon as I wrote the words *The End* I figured my story had been told and was finished. Although I did have sense enough to sweet-talk a gal I know, who teaches high school English, into reading my manuscript and fixing the spelling and typos. And when that was done I sent it off to a New York publisher. He was the brother of a friend, of a friend, of a friend of this woman I used to date.

Months went by and I had pretty much forgotten about sending my manuscript off. One day I got a call and this fellow launched into a big song and dance saying what a tough time he had had tracking me down and rambling on about how he was from the East Coast but positively did enjoy contemporary western stories.

I was not getting his drift at all and finally interrupted him. "Mister, I don't know who you are or what you want but let me just tell you, this has not been the best day of my life. My dog got into a porcupine, a head gate blew and I've got irrigation water running to hell and gone, I've got cattle to move, hay on the ground and I'm two men shy of having a full crew. So why don't you quit beating around the bush and just say what you have to say."

"I want to publish your book," he mumbled.

"Oh, well, that's great," I told him. But it turned out it wasn't so great because it was not a "we'll take it just as is" type proposition. He said he liked everything about my story and how I had written it, but claimed my ending wasn't really the ending at all and that readers would want to know what happened: Did Rosenbach do jail time and did I get any money out of him? What became of Cheyenne? Did Sam and I get married?

I really didn't want to write anything past my ending. I told the man, "Look Mister, I'm trying to run a ranch, and to be perfectly honest, I'm busier than a two-peckered billy goat."

The publisher mentioned an advance, ten thousand bucks, and that did get me interested, not that I plan on making a career as a writer or anything, but if this works out and they make a movie or something, I've got a shitpot of other stories I could tell. I mean, I do lead a pretty interesting life.

To put a big bright ribbon around my story and collect my ten grand, allow me to start with what has the most meaning to me—Charley. I've had plenty of chances to sell him, and for top dollar, but a horse of his caliber only comes along once or twice in a lifetime. He still works as well as he ever did, although here lately, I've noticed he has trouble going hard two days in a row. He's starting to get a little age on him but hell, so am I. Maybe we'll get turned out to pasture together.

One big change in my life—after my experience with Pup on the island—I decided I wanted a dog. I got me a butterscotch and white Australian Shepherd. I call him Andy. I don't know why, he just seemed like an Andy. He's learning to work cattle and I don't know what else to say except Andy is a perfect companion and a good friend who is always eager to see me.

Cheyenne. After we were rescued she went back to her husband and I guess they patched things up. I do know she went to a shrink. I got a call from her one afternoon. She said she was with her psychiatrist. I could hear him in the background prompting her to say something to the effect she had grown a lot, matured, and with professional help was getting in touch with herself. She thanked me for taking care of her while we were marooned on Chirikof and apologized for having had a nervous breakdown. I told her no apology was necessary. After that she went on a long involved discourse about how wrong it had been to cheat on her husband and how she was dealing with her issues of guilt and re-establishing her self image, things like that. I put the phone down and read an article about hoof rot in the latest issue of *Western Horseman*. When I picked up the phone again she was crying. That was enough for me. I hung up and I haven't heard from her since.

Rosenbach got off with a slap on the wrist. He was found guilty of drug possession and was sentenced to a four-month stretch in what I call a gentleman's jail, where there aren't bars or razor wire and an inmate has the opportunity to take college classes for credit and play tennis in the afternoons. While incarcerated, he corresponded with a young lady he met through a personal ad in *Ruralite Magazine*, a monthly publication put out by electric cooperatives and PUDs in the Northwest. When released, Rosenbach moved in with his pen pal and went to work helping her run her gift shop near Forks, Washington. They got married in June. I know all this because he had nerve enough to send me a wedding invitation, adding a little note in which he concluded by saying he wanted to let bygones be bygones. He never paid, not one red cent of what he owed me. When I tried to take him to small claims court, it turned out, in addition to the gift shop, he had branched out and was building software and operating an Internet company buying goods overseas and reselling them to the domestic market. Everything was in his wife's name. I couldn't get zilch.

The big question everyone who hears my story wants to know is whether Sam and I got married. That would make a perfect and predictable ending, if we had. And we came pretty damn close to tying the knot.

We spent our first night together at a Holiday Inn near the airport in Seattle. I was as traditional as a fellow could possibly be: taking her out to dinner at a fancy restaurant, getting down on one knee, giving her the gold ring I had picked up on Kodiak Island and asking her to marry me. It seemed like the right thing to do at the time. I really did mean it. But we never set a date.

While I was in Alaska, Sam's ex-husband weaseled his way back into the picture. He moved to Redmond, got a job, went through the court system and was awarded visitation rights with his kids. He took Travis camping and fishing and they played catch, flew kites and went to movies together. He ingratiated himself to Joleen by buying her clothes and make-up and splurged with a Hawaiian vacation at Christmas. Little by little, he resumed his role in the family he had abandoned. Whether he and Sam ever get back together is anyone's guess, but they are attempting to rekindle their romance. Sam told me so.

Not long after I arrived home, I caught a job fifty miles from Redmond running the TS Ranch for Bill Jordan. I don't suppose that helped knit together the fabric between Sam and me any tighter, but by then I was beginning to see the handwriting on the wall.

To be honest, the fact Sam and I split, didn't really break my heart. She's a great gal, but it's like I've said before, I'm not at all sure I'm the marrying type. Although, just the other night at the Desert Inn Bar I met this pretty gal, she's part Warm Springs Indian and a real looker. Anyway, we hit it off in a big way and....

Rick Steber, the author of more than thirty books and sales of more than a million copies, has received national acclaim for his writing. His numerous awards include the Western Writers of America Spur Award for Best Western Novel, Western Heritage Award, Benjamin Franklin Award, Mid-America Publishers Award, Oregon Library Association Award and Oregon Literary Arts Award. Two of his books have been optioned to movie production companies.

In addition to his writing, Rick is an engaging Western personality and has the unique ability to make his characters come alive as he tells a story. He has spoken at national and international conferences and visits schools where he talks to students about the importance of education, developing reading and writing skills, and impressing upon them the value of saving our history for future generations.

Rick has two sons, Seneca and Dusty, and lives near Prineville, Oregon. He writes in a cabin in the timbered foothills of the Ochoco Mountains.